IN$URANCE
TO
DIE FOR

IN$URANCE
TO
DIE FOR

A JOHN SMITH MYSTERY

CHARLOTTE STUART

LEVEL
BEST BOOKS

Author Photo Credit: Faye Johnson

First edition

ISBN: 978-1-68512-621-6

Cover art by Level Best Designs

This book was professionally typeset on Reedsy.
Find out more at reedsy.com

To Scott whose wicked sense of humor is an inspiration. And to his wife Faye and sisters Wendi and Cindi who have successfully navigated his teasing and jibes for many years.

Praise for In$urance to Die For

"A slapstick mystery with heart—you'll cheer on klutzy John Smith as he dodges crows, learns to cat parent, and chases down a killer."—Jennifer J. Chow, Lefty Award-nominated author of *Hot Pot Murder*

"While the whole story was written with an air of seriousness to the mystery, the crazy things John experienced daily gave this reader plenty to laugh at throughout the entire book. ... Readers are sure to enjoy this heart-pounding, while also amusingly funny, mystery.—Diana Coyle, Feathered Quill

"I could sum up In$urance to Die For by Charlotte Stuart in one word. Fun. ... I highly recommend this book to brighten up a dull day and put a smile on your face."—Lucinda E Clarke, Readers' Favorite

PRAISE FOR IN$URED TO THE HILT (A John Smith Mystery)

"Stuart brings fresh energy to the detective drama. The author's sense of quirky humor shines in just the right places, and that's a pleasant change of pace if you're looking for something unique in your sleuth stories... Fans of Agatha Christie mystery books will fall in love with the new style found in *In$ured to the Hilt*: A John Smith Mystery by Charlotte Stuart.—Tammy Ruggles, Reader Views

"I am eager to get my hands on more novels in the series, which I hope proves to be as exciting as this novel. Charlotte Stuart has planted the seeds for something entertaining, humorous, and well-paced."—Matt Pechey, Reedsy

"…balance of hard-boiled detective plotting versus the cozy, character-led drama and the subtle blend of wit and dry humor that ties the whole thing together."—K.C. Finn, Readers' Favorite

"…a lighthearted and spirited look at greed, murder and insurance fraud."—Sandy, The Reading Café

"Charlotte Stuart injects humor into Smith's wry observations of his situation and those around him. This is one of the hallmarks of a mystery that both titillates the imagination and leaves readers chuckling."—D. Donovan, Sr. Reviewer, Midwest Book Review

Chapter One: Crow Spite

The crow dive-bombed me. I screamed "scram, shoo, go away" and waved my arms like an out-of-control windmill. The malicious bird did its "caw-ca-caw" chuckle as it took another pass. At least I was wearing a baseball cap so it couldn't pull out more hair. The chunk it took a couple days ago made me look like I was getting bald from the side of my head.

The blasted bird jabbed my cap as I opened the door of my yellow 2001 Saturn and quickly jumped inside. Then I slammed the door and made a face at my attacker as it flew off. "Damn dinosaur throwback," I said to no one in particular. Before I'd seen the chart at the museum about how birds have evolved from carnivorous dinosaurs, I hadn't thought much about crow ancestry. Now, each time I raced from my houseboat to my car or vice versa, I felt like an extra in a Jurassic Park sequel.

Maybe I needed to start wearing a disguise when outside in the houseboat community where I lived. At least until those damn crows forgot how I'd destroyed the nest they built in the tree next to my parking spot. Bird poop can ruin paint, so I had to do something. It wasn't until I poked the nest with a broom handle and the whole thing came tumbling down, spilling broken olive-green eggshells across the parking platform, that I regretted my action. But then it was too late. And now it wasn't safe for me on the path to my mailbox or to and from my car.

I backed out of my narrow parking space, turned on the radio, and started singing along with Beyoncé while tapping the beat on my steering wheel with both hands: "I'm in the mood..." Tap, tap, "missing." Tap, tap, "prescription."

I started keeping time with the music with my right foot, the Saturn jerking along, a syncopated dance step for Firestone tires. There wasn't much traffic for once, and I was in a good mood, if not *the* mood. Not that I was entirely sure what the song was all about.

When I reached the freeway, Beyoncé quit singing, and I quit tapping, although I still occasionally warbled a phrase to blot out the news that had come on at the top of the hour. I was on my way to a work assignment as a claims adjuster for Universal Heartland Liability and Casualty Assurance Company of America, Incorporated—*"The Company with a* ❤*."*

Being a claims adjuster isn't as exciting as you might think; I spend a lot of time on paperwork. So, getting out of the office to visit a client almost feels like a mini vacation, a road trip in my sunshine-bright car.

Today, I was headed out of the busy city across two bridges and an island on the other side of the lake. It would only take about forty minutes to get there, but time spent out of the office was like playing hooky. That was the one good thing about laws against driving and talking on the phone or texting—my employer didn't expect me to work en route. Nor was I obligated to answer if they tried to get in touch; it was understood that if I was in my car, they needed to leave a message. There was nothing to do but enjoy.

Well, admittedly, it wasn't one hundred percent pleasure. There were gigantic trucks whose wall-like presence made me feel like I was driving with blinders on, gas fumes seeping in through the vents, stop-and-go traffic that made me curse my manual transmission, rocks leaping out of nowhere to attack my windshield, and large potholes that could swallow a tire in one gulp. In some ways, it was like being behind the wheel of an online driving simulation game where you never knew what to expect. Still, it beat sitting behind a desk, staring at a mountain of paperwork.

In the year I'd been at Universal I'd focused mostly on car accident claims, a lot of fender benders, some justified by weird explanations that didn't require much investigation.

"No one should put a chicken coop that close to a busy road." "It was foggy, or I

never would have missed the turn and ended up driving into his house." "I'd turned off my hearing aid to avoid listening to my wife talk about her relatives, so I didn't hear the aid car." "I wasn't actually drinking, unless you call having a couple of glasses of wine drinking." "I'm sure I would have noticed if I'd fallen asleep at the wheel." "They must have just put up that telephone pole."

I'd also handled some theft of personal property claims. According to my boss, they were the reason I was being given the opportunity to take on jewelry and painting appraisals and losses. The person who normally did that work had left the company. The opportunity to take over his assignments surprised and pleased me. It was a cozy niche with job security. Of course, I didn't know much about jewelry or paintings—well, actually, I knew next to nothing about either. Except for my class ring and watch, I didn't own any jewelry. And I was fairly certain nothing painted on velvet counted as insurable art. But then I hadn't known much about cars either when I joined the company. Even if they wanted me to take some classes, I wouldn't mind. Trinkets and pictures—that didn't sound too complicated.

Someone gave me the finger as I cut in front of a lime-green Audi to reach my exit. A truck had blocked the original sign, so I admit my move may have been less than legal. Still, it was tempting to give him back the finger. But when you drive a yolk-yellow car you have to be careful not to insult anyone. Just in case you end up at the same destination.

Soon after leaving the freeway, I entered the land of construction look-alikes. The kind of neighborhood where every house has an extra-wide driveway with at least two cars parked in front of a double-car garage. Yards carefully landscaped. Everything in its place. A fine example of housing for middle and upper-middle-class professionals. Of course, people in low-rent housing developments probably didn't get paintings appraised by their insurance company. And the really wealthy undoubtedly had special coverage for their expensive art. We might be the "company with a heart," but our heart didn't cover anything over about thirty thousand dollars. We insured cars for a lot more than that. What did that say about art?

The client's house was on a cul-de-sac in a row of cul-de-sacs. I missed it the first time around the circle, confused by the lack of landmarks and by the hard-to-read ornate house numbers. The second time, I got better at reading the numbers, like learning a foreign language.

Before getting out of the car, I checked out my hair in the tiny mirror on the back of the visor. I was always surprised that even to me, I look forgettable. Bland. The kind of appearance that would frustrate an eyewitness to a crime trying to come up with some defining characteristic. The mirror told me that my mud brown hair was appropriately smooth, there was no spinach in my teeth, and my nose hairs were under control. I was ready to meet my clients.

A blue Tesla pulled up behind Bee, the name my mother had given my car when she owned it. At the same time I got out, the woman in the Tesla literally bolted from her vehicle, almost as if "passenger ejection" was one of the car's functions. She was thin, professional-looking, and not my type. I like my women well-rounded, with enough flesh showing to preview what might be available if I managed to score. Not that I did very often. But there's always hope. This woman was zipped up tight in a grey pants suit with a red turtleneck poking out from the top of her jacket. Her blond hair framed a narrow face, her piercing eyes assessing me as she held out a hand. "I'm Carla Bridges," she said in a voice that demanded I tell her my name in return.

"John Smith," I said as I shook her hand, trying to squeeze back as firmly as she did. Our company manual warned against both the limp and the too-macho handshake. We were supposed to deliver a moderately firm grip and disengage within 3 seconds. One, two, three—disengage. It was too late—she'd already dropped my hand.

"Shall we go inside?" Carla said, her tone suggesting that it was time to make things happen. My mini-vacation was over.

Connie Winslow opened the door before I could use the antique Fat Boy door knocker. My hand was still in mid-air as Carla introduced us. Mrs. Winslow invited us in and shut and locked the door behind us. We were immediately met by the dark, hulking presence of a hall coat tree already partly filled with what I assumed were decorative pieces of clothing and a bench that could rival some sofas. Next to it was a copper umbrella stand with two umbrellas sporting carved wood handles. On the other side of the hall was a humongous mirror in a swirly metal frame that screamed *extravagant purchase*.

Although, in my opinion, the frame looked a bit like a soup can lid after my mother opened the can with one of those kitchen tools where you stabbed the blade into the top and then sawed up and down all the way around the rim.

Introductions over, we were led into the dining room, where two paintings had been placed side by side on a large, clear glass table. It crossed my mind how uncomfortable eating at that table would be. What if you dropped a crumb in your lap or needed to scratch?

Carla immediately went over to examine the paintings. Mrs. Winslow was explaining their provenance, but I wasn't paying a lot of attention. I was still looking around, wondering what it would be like to live in a house like this one. Did she have to dust all of the art objects herself? And what was the twisted piece of bronze on the table in the corner supposed to be?

I didn't really need to study the paintings. Carla had been the appraiser of choice for the company for over four years, and if she said the paintings were authentic and came up with a number within our parameters, then I'd recommend insuring them. It was that simple. I was already thinking about where I could stop for lunch on the way back before returning to the office.

Suddenly, Carla turned to me and said, "What do you think, John?

That I would like a hamburger and fries for lunch. Fortunately, I didn't say that out loud and managed to direct my eyes to the two paintings. One looked like something a chimpanzee could have done with a brush, a paint palette of primary colors, and a couple of hairy fingers. Bright splotches and smears of paint were randomly distributed across the canvas. The other looked like motel room art to me, a cow standing next to a tree with a river in the background. "You're the expert," I said, trying to sound like I had an opinion, but I bowed to her wise counsel.

Carla didn't press and quickly gave an overview of the assessment to Mrs. Winslow, followed by a preliminary estimate of the value of each painting. Nothing outrageous, but high enough to compensate the hotel owner and buy a bushel of peanuts for the monkey. "But," she added, "as I mentioned on the phone, I'll need to take them back to my office for a few tests. I'll return them the day after tomorrow." She turned to me again. "Would you like to meet me here for the final report?"

"Absolutely." I hadn't realized I would get a second field trip out of this assignment. What a bonus. This was definitely a specialty to pursue. I silently thanked Mr. Van Droop for giving me this opportunity.

Carla went out to the car to get some cases to transport the pictures in, leaving me to make small talk with Mrs. Winslow. I'm not good at small talk, but I gave it a try.

"Interesting table," I said. "Is it difficult to keep clean? I mean, my beer mugs always seem to come out of the dishwasher with spots."

She looked at me as if I was some strange creature that had just crawled out from under a rock on the beach, but politely said, "Our cleaning woman is very good."

Of course, she was.

Carla fortunately returned promptly with her cases, packed up the pictures, and we said our goodbyes. I wanted to carry at least one or both of the cases—it was the manly thing to do—but Carla wouldn't relinquish them. "I'm used to this," she said. Her tone implied she didn't trust anyone but herself to keep them safe. That was fine with me; I try to avoid assuming too much responsibility.

"Same time the day after tomorrow, then," I said as she got into her car.

"Yes. Same time the day after tomorrow."

It was a good thing I didn't find her attractive because her tone and lack of eye contact suggested she felt the same about me. Oh well. I'd have a leisurely drive back, stop for a good lunch, and then face an afternoon of paperwork under the lyncean eye of Emma, our office manager. Maybe I could sneak out early. Mother had suggested I stop by a pet store to see if they had any recommendations on how to deal with my crow problem. It hadn't occurred to me that a pet store would offer advice about dealing with wild animals. But Mother seemed to think they would. I hoped she was right; I was tired of trying to do a combover on the side of my head.

Chapter Two: Sniff This

I admit that I spent a lot of money at the pet store. But it felt justified. War is costly.

The next morning, I prepared for battle. Chin up, shoulders back, I headed out brandishing my red and black high-pressure water blaster, ready to take on the local crow population. When they came at me in formation, I let them have it. But instead of deterring my crow enemies, they seemed to think it was spa time. Get your shower and attack the home wrecker—for them, it was a twofer. For me, a huge disappointment.

When I finally made it to the parking area at the top of the steps, I dropped the water blaster and sprinted for my car, swearing under my breath. Once inside, I immediately noticed the splattering of crow poo across the hood. Poor Bee. I would have to put her through a car wash before the acidic white smears ate through her paint. I sincerely hoped my other purchases worked better than the water blaster. The staff I'd dealt with at the pet store hadn't actually guaranteed success, but given the amount I'd spent, I was assuming that some or all of the items they'd sold me would work. Watch out, crows, I'm going to win this war yet.

After putting in a tedious morning on a fender bender claim, I went online to see if anyone else recommended using a water cannon to deter crows. Maybe there was some trick to making it work. And sure enough, one person said it was only effective if you used a mixture of water and vinegar. That sounded worth a try.

On the way home I stopped and bought a large plastic jug of white vinegar. If it didn't work on the crows, I could make pickles or clean my floors.

The following morning, I once again prepared for battle. I filled the blaster's tank with one part vinegar and two parts water. Supposedly, you could hit targets from thirty-two feet away with the blaster, but I intended to let them get a little closer than that so I would be sure not to miss. Armed and ready, I headed out.

When not a single crow approached on the way to my car, I was disappointed. All that effort for nothing. I put the blaster in the trunk so it would be handy when I returned home.

Carla's Tesla was out front at the Winslows', but she wasn't in it. She must have arrived early and gone in ahead of me. I knocked on the front door, and Mrs. Winslow answered, smiling. "Come in," she said. "Carla and I have been chatting in the kitchen." Chatting and drinking coffee, apparently. There were two coffee cups on a marble-topped bar. Carla was seated on a fancy leather stool with curved iron legs in a row of similar stools.

"Oh, you're here," she said to me with an "it's about time" tone. I glanced at my watch to make certain I wasn't late. "Well, I think we're about done," Carla added, sliding off the stool. I assumed that meant I wouldn't be getting any coffee. It was just as well. I find it hard to feel comfortable perched on a bar stool. One time I even caught the heel of my shoe on a cross brace and ended up on the floor.

She handed me a file. "I went over this with Connie. You can call if you have any questions."

Mrs. Winslow, "Connie" to Carla, was all smiles. "This looks good to me," she said.

"I'll need to check it over before making the final decision." That was the truth, but I came off sounding like an officious paper pusher rather than the person in charge. Both women frowned, two sets of downturned mouths relating displeasure. "But I'm confident this will do the trick," I added quickly. No use fighting the formidable Carla's expert recommendation.

Carla and "Connie" chatted like two old friends as they walked over to the sink with their coffee cups.

Looking around, I saw that the two pictures were again on the glass table in the dining room. There was a young girl bending over them, her nose almost touching the cow in the idyllic country scene, her long brown hair tucked behind her ears. When she noticed me standing there, she waved me over. "This one smells funny," she said as I approached. She stepped back, leaving a space for me to get close to the painting. "Take a sniff."

"Ah, no thanks, I'll take your word for it." Body odor and fertilized farmland smelled "funny," so that wasn't an invitation I wanted to accept.

Carla and Connie were still deep in conversation, but now they were slowly walking toward the front door. "I'm John Smith, your parents' claims adjuster." I didn't hand her a card; it would be a few years before she would be looking for insurance on her own.

"Hi. I'm Savannah." She smiled, then glanced back at the pictures.

"Well, Savannah, do you like these paintings?" I asked because I couldn't think of anything else to say.

She looked at me as though I'd lost my mind. "I'd rather have 'A Girl Like Me' poster, signed by Rihanna."

"Who wouldn't?" I said, then quickly added, "But these are worth a lot more." I glanced over my shoulder to make sure Carla hadn't overheard my comment.

"It isn't about the money." Two tiny lines appeared on Savannah's forehead as she thought about my comment. "I mean, who wants to look at a cow standing next to a tree?"

She had me there.

"And I still think you ought to smell it." She waved me toward the painting. I was about to cave and give it a sniff when Carla came up behind me and grabbed my arm. "Time to go," she said. She smiled a little too sweetly at Savannah.

"Nice meeting you, Savannah," I said as I let Carla guide me toward the door. "Connie wants us gone," Carla whispered in my ear. "She's meeting someone for lunch."

Connie was waiting for us at the door. We said our goodbyes, and I heard the door click shut firmly behind us as we stepped outside.

Carla suddenly seemed to relax. "Ugly, weren't they?" she said as we walked toward our respective cars.

9

"Not my cuppa," I admitted.

"Mine neither. But nicely done."

"And definitely original?"

"No doubt about it."

"Savannah seems to think that the cow picture smells funny," I said.

"Funny?"

"I didn't smell it, so I don't know what she meant."

We'd reached Carla's car. She nodded in the direction of Bee. "Your car is very yellow," she said.

"It's a 2001 classic," I said proudly.

"I guess it's all a matter of taste." She shrugged. As she got in her car, she gave me a weak smile and a half-wave goodbye.

I was about two feet away from Bee when I noticed the drone hovering overhead. How long had it been there? Was it following me? Was I on camera? I looked around but didn't see who was flying it. It seemed like more and more people played with drones these days. At least it wasn't a crow shadowing me.

Back at the office, Emma greeted me by pointedly glancing at the clock across from her desk. She takes her office manager job seriously, part prison guard and part Miss Manners. I wish my tiny office was a little further away from her desk, but I liked the fact that I had a door, even if my space was between a closet and an alcove that housed some hard copies of closed files that had not been transferred to a digital format and probably never would be. The rest of the employees on the floor were in cubicles with chest-high partitions—if you were short, that is. For almost everyone passing by, those on the outside could see everything on the inside. There was little to no privacy.

In the cubicles, any eating of chips or picking your nose was definitely verboten. Whereas I was free to do what I pleased, as long as I wasn't caught by a surprise visit from Emma. I used to be able to lock my door, but I'd lost the key and was too embarrassed to ask for a replacement. I kept hoping it would show up, although of late it has crossed my mind that maybe Emma was responsible for its disappearance.

Once back at my desk, it didn't take long to fill out the form and approve the insurance coverage for the Winslows' two pictures. Carla had given me all the language and information I needed. I was the rubber stamp, committing my company to something about which I knew next to nothing. On the other hand, I wasn't worried. Most personal property claims were made because of damage caused by fire or some natural disaster. If the Winslows suffered a typical loss, there would probably be very little left of the paintings, so no one would be questioning their authenticity at that point. Carla's assessment would automatically be the basis for reimbursement. Case closed. Client satisfied. My reputation intact.

That evening when I got home, I noticed that our houseboat community sign was listing slightly, as if it had crested a wave and was about to descend into its trough. "THE HAVEN" was printed in block letters that looked like they had been stenciled on, centered above a picture of stick figures holding hands. Mother thinks the stick figures are there to suggest we are a close-knit community. In my opinion, the landlord didn't want to pay a professional sign maker and, therefore, let his young son design and paint it. Even the wood it was painted on looked like scrap material. In addition to the sign's vertical challenge, there were streaks of white defacing one of the stick figures. Perhaps the crows thought the figure represented me.

I pulled into my parking spot and looked around. There were no crows in sight. I sat there for a minute, wondering if they were lying in wait, ready to attack the instant my defenses were down. Or was it possible they had surrendered and moved on?

Suddenly, there was tapping on the passenger side window. At first, I didn't see her, but then I noticed the eyes just above the bottom of the window. For an eight-year-old, she wasn't very tall. Or else she was crouching down for some reason only understood by an eight-year-old mind. Of course, she was the one who had told me she was eight. Maybe she'd exaggerated to impress me. She looked sweet enough, but she could have been the inspiration for the little girl in the movie classic *The Bad Seed*. I suspected she was responsible

11

for putting dead fish, gum, and goopy popsicle sticks in my mailbox. I'd tried complaining, but the landlord and her father were tight, and both claimed it was someone else who had it in for me.

I rolled down the window and asked, "What do you want?" It wasn't a very gracious question, but we did not have the kind of relationship where you pretended to be nice.

"Your mother's here," she said.

"What?" Since she didn't drive, Mother seldom came by on her own. But she did have a bus pass and had recently learned how to call an Uber. As a good son, I've warned her to be careful about Uber drivers, although instead, they probably needed to be warned about her. She carries pepper spray disguised as a miniature flashlight and took a YWCA self-defense class for seniors. She's no Vera Stanhope, but still not someone you would want to cross.

"Thank you," I said to the little girl's retreating figure. She was wearing a red bandana, like the mutant ninja turtle Raphael. I pushed the button to roll the window back up, but nothing happened. Had she done something to my window? I got out and went around to open the door to see what was wrong. It looked fine. But the window refused to roll up. I jiggled it. Still nothing. I slammed the door shut and tried again. Still nothing. Well, if Mother was truly waiting for me, I'd better get going. I could figure this out later.

I cautiously made my way down the stairs, anticipating an air attack at any moment. When I made it back to my houseboat without incident, I was amazed. I started humming "Today's the day the teddy bears have their picnic." There had to be some reason the crows weren't around. Nor was my mother. Or the little demon girl. But my door was unlocked.

"Mother," I yelled when I went inside. "I've told you not to pick my locks."

There they were, the two of them, my mother and the bad seed, sitting together on my couch with a plate of cookies between them.

"Johnnie," Mother said. "You're late."

"Late for what?"

"For taking your mother out to dinner."

"Oh." That didn't sound so bad.

"And for opening your birthday present."

"But it isn't my birthday." Surely my mother, of all people, ought to know when I was born.

She got up and grabbed a box from behind the couch. It looked unwieldy, like something was sliding around inside. "Sit down," she ordered. Always the obedient son, I sat. "Here, open it." Mother carefully placed the box on my lap. It was a plain cardboard box with a ribbon around it. And it was moving around on my knees as if something inside was about to explode. Or maybe it was filled with Mexican jumping beans that would suddenly turn into moths when I opened the box. I had wanted Mexican jumping beans when I was about nine; not so much now.

"Go on, open it," the little girl said, my mother nodding agreement.

Warily, I untied the bow, and even more warily, I slowly removed the lid.

A black streak of fur burst forth, leaping onto my shoulder, grabbing me with tiny, sharp claws, and wailing like a wolf howling at the moon. Before jumping off onto the floor, it swiped my ear with what felt like tiny razor blades. Blood dripped from what was left of my ear onto the couch.

"It's a kitty," the little girl said gleefully. She raced after it as it ran around the room like a crazed thing, either seeking to escape or looking for a place to pee.

"Happy Birthday," my mother said, smiling broadly. Her gray curls bounced with happiness.

"Why?" I asked. "I've never wanted a cat."

"This one is special." We watched as the girl struggled to catch up with the black streak.

"Okay, I'll bite. What's special about it?"

My mother has smooth skin with jowls just starting to form on both sides of her face above her chin. For just an instant, I saw them sag ever so slightly before she got all perky again. A new "tell"? That could be useful.

"And I want the truth," I warned.

"I really do think you could use some companionship. But…"

"But…the truth?"

"Oh, you're bleeding." She took a Kleenex out of her pocket and handed it to me. "Alright. My neighbor couldn't handle him and took him to a shelter...and they called her to take him back."

The cat was still bouncing off the walls with the young girl in pursuit, like racquetball without racquets.

"I think I can see why." I pinched my ear with the Kleenex.

"She was going to have him put down."

"Then why don't *you* keep him?"

"The condo association frowns on having pets."

"I seem to remember your neighbor has a poodle."

"Well, *this* particular cat has been, ah, banned."

"How does a cat get 'banned' from a condo?"

"Okay, I admit it. My neighbor let it outside, and it scratched a child."

Everything had suddenly become very quiet. We looked over and saw the girl cradling the black kitten in her arms, stroking it gently. Both the kitten and the girl seemed content.

"What's your name?" I asked. How was it possible that I didn't know her name after several years of being plagued by her?

"Valerie," she said.

"Do they call you Val?" I asked.

"No, my name is Valerie," she said firmly. "And this is …this is Wild Thing."

"You know the cat's name?" I asked, glancing at my mother for confirmation.

"He was only with my neighbor for a couple of days. She hadn't named him yet."

We both turned to Valerie. She was making baby-talk sounds to Wild Thing, and he was starting to purr, a loud, bumpy hum that echoed off the walls.

"Would you like to have Wild Thing for a pet?" I asked Valerie. "For your very own?" Mother scowled, but she didn't protest.

"Oh, yes. Please."

"He's yours." Happy Birthday, I muttered to myself.

She didn't wait for a signed contract but rushed out the door and vanished into the night with Wild Thing.

"Problem solved," I said. "Let's go have dinner."

Dinner was pleasant. Mother didn't seem particularly displeased by my decision to give Wild Thing to Valerie. She chatted happily about her book club, the people at her condo, and local politics. She didn't once mention that I needed to get married and give her grandchildren. We shared a dessert and lingered over our decaf.

Feeling mellow after dropping Mother off at her condo, I tried to whistle some cowboy song I couldn't remember the words to. I had to give up when the expulsion of air started to make me light-headed; I've never been much good at whistling. Still, with the night air rushing in from the window that refused to roll up, filled with Italian carbohydrates, and pleased to be rid of Wild Thing, life was good. Then I got to my home and found a box on the front porch.

Chapter Three: Missions Mostly Accomplished

My first thought was that kids from the neighborhood were playing some sort of trick on me. Probably in collusion with Valerie. No doubt the box contained snakes or dead rats or something incredibly smelly. I was tempted to leave it there and deal with it in the morning. Then I heard angry mewing coming from inside. "Oh no," I said out loud. I would have preferred snakes.

Before I could make up my mind about what to do, I heard someone coming rapidly up behind me. I whirled about, wishing not for the first time that I was a black belt. Even a lowly green would do. I've always liked the color green.

When I saw that it was Valerie's father, I let my guard down. Too soon, apparently. I suddenly realized he looked mad, really mad. There were angry creases around his eyes and lips, and he sounded even madder than he looked when he yelled: "We don't want your damn cat. Do I make myself clear?"

"He isn't really *my* cat," I said. "Besides, he's just a kitten. And Valerie said she wanted him."

"You don't give a pet to a child without checking with their parents. That's common sense. Got it?"

"Got it." It did seem like a reasonable rule.

His face relaxed slightly. He turned to leave, then paused to say, "And keep that thing away from my dog." With that warning, he hurried off. They have an aggressive German Shepherd, a hairy brute that scares the bejesus out of me, although I've never complained. Men are supposed to like big macho dogs.

Reluctantly, I picked up the box. "So, Wild Thing, what did you do to make Glen Arnold so mad?" Or was his name Arnold Glen? I could never keep it straight.

In some ways, I felt sympathy for the poor, unwanted critter. Everyone he came in contact with rejected him, except for Valerie. They had obviously bonded, and now he had been ripped from her loving arms and put back in a cardboard box. Poor kitty.

My "poor kitty" attitude lasted until I got him inside and started to remove the lid. A clawed paw reached up through the narrow opening and swatted me. "Okay, okay. If you don't want to end up in the lake, you'd better behave." I pushed the lid down and left the box on the floor while I got out two dishes, filled one with water and the other with some leftover chicken, and put them in the spare room that doubled as an office and catch-all space. Then I shoved the box inside the door, reached in, flipped off the lid, and quickly withdrew, firmly closing the door behind me. When I didn't hear anything happening, I was tempted to peek inside to see what was going on, but it was late, and I'd had enough drama for one day.

Friday morning, I was feeling chipper. I didn't have plans for the weekend, but even if all I did was sleep in, lounge around, and eat chips and dip while watching reruns of Law and Order, it was still time off to look forward to.

I was halfway through my get-ready-for-work routine when I remembered my house guest. As quietly as I could, I opened the door to the spare room a crack. A black nose immediately tried to push its way through the tiny opening. "No," I said, closing the door. A yowl accompanied by a scratching sound made me worry about what had gone on in there during the night. At the very least, I would obviously have to do some repairs to my door. Maybe I could hire a pest control person to remove Wild Thing. He was definitely a pest.

As I stepped off my front porch on my way to work, I saw flashes of black overhead. The crows had returned from wherever they had gone. Since I'd left the blaster filled with water and vinegar in the trunk of my car, I went back inside and got the noisemaker I'd purchased. It supposedly broadcasted crow distress signals. That was to warn them to stay away. I wasn't sure what normally caused them distress, but I hoped they accepted the warning without asking too many questions.

Back outside, I tested the tool by pushing a red button, and a cacophony of weird cawing filled the air. It sounded like a group of old cowboys who had spent too many years smoking Marlboros and yelling at cattle.

Initially, it seemed to work. The crows stayed away until I was a few feet from my car. Then, one large crow with slick feathers and a menacing beak ignored the distress calls and came at me. I pointed the gadget at the crow as it descended. "Take that," I yelled. He swooped past me, cawing twice. In crow language, I think he was saying, "No, *you* take *that*."

When I was safely inside my car, I thought the drama was over, but a crow came and sat on the rim of the open window and swore at me. At least that's what I think it was doing. I swore back, put my car in reverse and whipped out of the parking space, relieved when the crow flew off instead of slipping inside and putting on a seat belt.

As soon as I got to the office, I called a mobile repair service to have my window repaired, hoping my insurance would cover it. Maybe I should ask Glen to pay the repair cost; after all, it was his daughter who'd jinxed it.

After my exciting morning trip to the office, work seemed tame. Eighty percent of my job involves reviewing claims, assessing their legitimacy, and assigning settlement amounts. Occasionally, I do simple investigations on my own. For anything complicated, I have to run it past my boss. I managed to get through several lengthy files before lunch. Afterwards, I made a few business-related calls, then took a deep breath and rang Mother to give her my carefully composed speech about Wild Thing. I got her voice message and hung up. To talk to a machine, I needed extra rehearsal. I knew that each word could come back to haunt me. After practicing what I wanted to say about Wild Thing's fate a few more times, I called again, prepared to leave a message. Instead, she answered in person.

"Valerie's father gave him back," I told her. "And before you say anything, no, I won't be keeping him. I'm going to drop him off at the animal shelter. After hours, so they can't refuse to take him."

"He'll be put down," she said sadly.

"You don't know that."

"Won't you at least try to make friends? You saw how he was with Valerie."

"I'll think about it," I said before hanging up. But it was a lie, and my mother knew it. Tonight, as soon as it was dark, Wild Thing was going for a ride. The only question was how I was going to get him back in the box. Maybe I needed to get some protective clothing, a face shield and a hard hat. And whatever restraint equipment they used when dealing with wild animals.

After work, I had both my water blaster and my crow distress call maker ready as I stepped out of my car, but there were no crows around. Sometimes, they toyed with me like that. I think they're familiar with Pavlov's work on intermittent reinforcement.

Valerie was waiting for me on my front porch. "I want to see Wild Thing," she said, her voice small and surprisingly gentle. She was wearing pink pants and a pink T-shirt with multi-colored flowers on it, all sugar and spice. Even though I knew the truth, I succumbed to the vulnerable image she projected.

"Would you like to feed him?" I asked. I didn't mention that it could be his "last meal."

"Could I, please?" When she said "please," my heart melted, like an ice cream bar in the sun.

I opened the door to the spare room, and Wild Thing charged toward us like a raging bull, pausing when he saw Valerie. She called out "Wild Thing" and raced to meet him. He leapt into her outstretched arms and rubbed his head against her chest while she made singsong cooing noises. While they fawned over each other, I filled his water bowl and got out some pastrami I'd been saving for a sandwich.

Valerie and I watched while Wild Thing inhaled his food. Then we all went into the living room. Wild Thing hissed at me before leaping into Valerie's lap. He obviously had no idea how much I'd been looking forward to that pastrami sandwich. Or, maybe he did.

"Sorry your dad won't let you keep him."

"But I can visit him, can't I?"

I hated to break it to her, but I had to. "Wild Thing isn't happy living with me, so I'm going to find him another home."

"You mean you're taking him to the farm? Like my dad did with the puppy he didn't like?"

"The farm?" My father had taken my favorite dog to 'the farm' when I was young. I'd been brokenhearted.

"I'm not stupid," she said. "I know what that means."

I hadn't realized the possibilities until that moment. "No," I said. "My father wouldn't have lied to me."

She gave me a wise child look. I was devastated. All this time, thinking Butch had spent his final years running free across green fields among the cows and sheep, living the good life until he finally died peacefully in his sleep.

"You're not doing that to Wild Thing, promise?"

"I promise." I could hardly tell her the truth, could I?

"Cross your heart and hope to die?"

I started to cross my heart.

"And no crossed fingers behind your back."

I hated lying to a child, even a manipulative child like Valerie. Guilt started to gnaw at me. Her own father had taken her puppy to "the farm." And now I was going to do the same thing with a kitten she obviously had feelings for. Given what I now suspected had happened to Butch, how could I do that to her?

As if he sensed his life was hanging by a thread, Wild Thing seemed to settle in after Valerie left. Keeping his distance, but not attacking me or my furniture. And when I checked it out, I found that he hadn't done much damage to the spare room. A few items knocked off my desk, some chewed papers, a rip in a blanket I used as a spare. Wild Thing had also used it, but as a potty. Well, it wasn't as if I'd made arrangements for his bathroom needs. Okay, I would give it another day. But if he stayed, I'd have to either let him out occasionally or get a litter box. If I was lucky, maybe he'd run away on a bathroom break. Valerie couldn't blame me for that, could she? Then there was cat food, maybe a toy, and a couple of catnip mice to amuse him between visits from Valerie. Meanwhile, he could have the blanket he'd ripped to pee on for one more night.

Instead of lazing around all day Saturday, I made another trip to the pet store, this time for Wild Thing. With the assistance of a clerk who seemed excited by the thought that I had a new kitten, I learned how easy it is to spend money on a pet. First, I bought a "calming, fleece-covered bed" that created a "safe place where your pet can relax." I wasn't sure which of us needed calming more, but the cat did need a place to sleep. Then I purchased a litter box and litter, cat food and treats, food bowl, water bowl, and, at the clerk's insistence, a combination climbing tree and scratching post. "He will love being high enough to see his surroundings," she assured me. "Cats love to hang out on these."

I also picked up a refillable catnip squirrel that was kinda cute, a toy the clerk assured me would soon become my pet's favorite. And a cat collar with a bell attached. If he was going to be prowling around my home when he wasn't hanging out on his tree, I wanted to hear him coming.

The last item I purchased was a cat carrier. Not the deluxe version with the "cozy faux lambskin liner" and a zippered ventilation flap like a sun roof on a car, but your basic plastic box with a handle on top. My hope was that I would eventually be using the carrier to transport him to his "forever home," wherever that might be.

That weekend, an uneasy peace settled over my houseboat home. I actually gave Valerie a key to my place so she could come by each day to play with Wild Thing. In return, I warned her that the first dead fish to show up in my mailbox and the deal was off. For once, she looked chastened. I added that if she broke her promise, I'd be changing the locks and taking Wild Thing to the farm. It felt good to have leverage.

I was on a roll. Kitten dealt with. Check. Bad seed dealt with. Check. Mother appeased. Check.

There was only one cloud on the horizon. Wild Thing refused to wear the bell collar I'd bought for him. Valerie hadn't liked the idea in the first place. "He's not a stupid cow," she'd complained. Still, when I'd pulled "the farm" card, she'd put the collar on him. However, he immediately went on strike, refusing to leave his bed. He wouldn't eat or drink anything. By Sunday evening, I gave in and let her remove it in spite of the fact that I was suspicious that somehow the two of them had conspired to make me acquiesce.

My next mission was to win my war with the crows. Unfortunately, too many neighbors had complained about my distressed crow calls for me to continue to employ that method. Besides, it didn't seem to be working all that well. Nor did the vinegar-water mixture in the blaster prove effective. The crows seemed to think it was salad dressing and got angry because it didn't come with greens. However, I still had a few more tricks to try.

Sunday afternoon I put up wind chimes next to my car. Several sources had indicated crows didn't like wind chimes. Who does?! They are more annoying than "hold" music while you're waiting to talk to a representative on the phone. When a client had complained to me about Universal's hold music, I'd learned that the reason it sounded so bad had something to do with "industry standard compression and EQ coupled with lossy codecs." I have no idea what that means, but it told me that there was nothing I personally could do to improve the situation. Anyway, I put up the chimes and hoped the crows hated it.

Meanwhile, I decided to try out one more weapon: a black umbrella saturated with aromatic bird repellant. Like many gourmet foods, there were unrecognizable ingredients in it. And it smelled not just *funny,* but *terrible.* Which was, I guess, the point.

Monday morning, I found a crow sitting on the wind chimes, swaying back and forth, apparently trying to use the Chinese tonal scale to create his own composition. It made me hungry for chow mein. At least he didn't attack my umbrella. Because it smelled so bad, I left it next to my parking spot rather than taking it with me.

During the week that followed, the umbrella seemed to solve the crow problem. And I became immune to the odor. I did, however, notice that Emma's nose started wrinkling each time I passed by her desk.

Wednesday evening, Mother called to tell me that she needed a ride to a funeral service on Sunday. I wasn't thrilled, but it seemed like something a good son should do. There was a reception immediately following the burial. I hoped there would be something good to eat.

"I do have one question," I said before tapping the "off" symbol. "It's about Butch."

"Butch—you mean that scraggly dog you had when you were young?"

"That's the one."

"The one you were supposed to feed and take care of and didn't?"

"That's not how I remember it."

"Well, that's the way it was."

"Is that why you and Dad took him to 'the farm'?"

"He needed more space."

"'The farm' is a euphemism for 'euthanasia,' isn't it?"

She didn't respond immediately. "My, such big words."

"Is that a *yes*?"

There was another pause. "Why are you bringing that up now?"

"I think you know."

"But this situation is different. Wild Thing is just a kitten; she will improve with age. And Valerie loves her."

"The jury is still out. But you need to know that Butch's fate will be considered when the judge is making the final decision about Wild Thing's fate." In truth, I didn't like the idea of being a judge making a life-and-death decision. But Wild Thing was on probation with at least two strikes against him. Strike three, and the kitten was going on a trip where the cows never roamed.

At the end of the day on Friday, Emma came to my office to let me know that if I was wearing cologne, I should switch brands. When I assured her that I wasn't wearing cologne or aftershave, she suggested I take my suits to the cleaners. I couldn't bring myself to tell her about my crow problem, so I blamed the odor on some remodeling they were doing on my houseboat. "I'll look into it," I promised.

Even though the umbrella seemed to be doing the trick, maybe it was time to move on to the motion sensor water spray. Although I hated to give up on something that was actually working.

Chapter Four: Drone Guy

As it turned out, my mother didn't know either the deceased or the parents of the deceased. But she was friends with one of her condo neighbors who did. And since neither woman had a car, I was their chauffeur.

The service was held at a small funeral home on a hill overlooking the cemetery, its lush grass carpet dotted with colorful flowers next to well-kept graves with impressive headstones. My mother's friend was the mirror image of her—grey curls, motherly smile, a bit jowly, not too tall, tending toward plump. Either could have been cast as a modern Miss Marple. However, the friend was slightly round-shouldered, whereas Mother stood upright like she was balancing a stack of books on her head, so it was easy to tell them apart.

The two women left me behind as soon as we went inside. I wandered over to a picture board to see who had died. He was younger than I'd anticipated, still in his twenties if the pictures were current. A thin, geeky-looking guy. There were photos of him at various ages. Some with his parents, playing video games, standing next to a Nissan Leaf, holding up a new computer at a birthday party, posing for selfies with friends. There were also pictures of him with his drone collection, like a hunter showing off his taxidermy trophies.

It's hard to capture someone's life in pictures on a single picture board, but I did feel I had a sense of the person after seeing snapshots of him frozen in time. Although they were all happy scenes. He must have had at least a few sad moments in his life. But those were seldom shared on picture boards at funerals.

When the service was about to start, I joined my mother and her friend seated mid-way to the front, but off to the side. The wood pew benches were uncomfortable, unforgiving for bony bottoms and poor posture. My mother was constantly reminding me to stand up or sit up straighter. In spite of being in the midst of a large group of people and sitting on a hard surface, I felt myself nodding off during the minister's talk of life and death and the promise of life after death. He had a soothing voice, like listening to ocean waves or raindrops and flowing water. If my mother's elbow hadn't jabbed me in the ribs from time to time, I might have enjoyed a refreshing nap. Once, after a particularly sharp poke, I jerked upright and noticed several people glaring at me. What was that all about?

At one point, sounds of sobbing penetrated my brain fog. My mother's friend was losing it. But she wasn't the only one. The man behind the podium must have said something to produce not only crying, but a pandemic of nose-blowing, coughing, and sniveling. Even my mother was dabbing at her eyes. I was the only survivor.

Finally, it was time to go to the graveside. Since I hadn't known the deceased, I decided not to follow the crowd being herded down the hill to where the casket was waiting. I told Mother I'd meet them back at the car and instead roamed around the cemetery reading tombstones.

I've never liked graveyards, but I was tired of sitting, and there wasn't any place else to walk. I was reading names and dates and thinking about my own mortality when I came across a tombstone that caught my eye. "Kate's Fudge" was engraved at the top. Next came the recipe. It ended with "She will be missed." If her fudge was that good, maybe I should try it. I searched my pockets and found a scrap of paper, barely big enough to write out the whole recipe. I didn't know what the "soft boil stage" was, and I don't have a "marble slab" to process the mixture on, but I thought I could punt. Maybe they'd have some fudge at the reception.

"You should have come," Mother said when we met back at the car. "It was a nice eulogy."

I was tempted to tell her about the fudge recipe but got distracted by the address she gave me to punch into my GPS for the reception. It looked familiar, but I couldn't quite place it. As we got near, it all came together. The reception was at the house next to the Winslows', the clients with the two paintings Carla had appraised. Maybe the young man who had died owned the drone hovering over Bee the day I was there. The coincidence shouted, "small world." Still, as Agatha Christie said, "One coincidence is just a coincidence." It takes three to act as proof.

"What was the deceased's name again?" I asked.

"Lonnie," my mother's friend said. "A very talented young man."

"How did you know him?" I asked.

"I used to live in the neighborhood, before moving to the condo." Did that make it "two" coincidences? What had Agatha said about "two" coincidences?

"How did Lonnie die?" I asked. Because of his age, I thought she might say "drugs" or "car accident." Or even "colorectal cancer"—I'd read it was happening more frequently to young people of late. And no one knows why. It was one more thing to worry about, along with tsunamis, tornadoes, earthquakes, asteroids, and new spider species. Not to mention vengeful crows and crazy cats.

"He fell off a cliff while playing with one of his drones," she said. "They wear some kind of special goggles when flying them. It's apparently great for piloting the machine but makes it hard to see the immediate area."

"Was he with someone?"

"He should have been. His parents were apparently always warning him to be careful."

"So tragic," my mother said. "Kids should listen to their parents."

I let the last comment pass. I was still trying to come up with the rest of the Christie quotation.

At the reception, I would have preferred to stay in the background, but as we entered, we were funneled into the reception line, and I had to introduce myself to Margaret and Rex Weller, Lonnie's parents. I mumbled something about being sorry for their loss, thankful they didn't ask how I knew their son. Then, I left my mother and her friend to their own devices while I went in search of food. It was an impressive spread. I had just filled my plate with a variety of delectable tidbits when someone said, "John, is that you?" I turned to see Savannah holding a full plate of food.

"Savannah, I should have realized you would be here. How are you?"

She popped what looked like a bacon-wrapped scallop into her mouth and replied with her mouth full. "Sad." At least, I think that's what she said.

"You knew Lonnie?" The minute the words were out of my mouth, I realized it was a stupid thing to say. Of course, she did; they were neighbors. I stuffed a crostini with mushrooms into my mouth and started chewing to cover my embarrassment. I felt a few drops of sauce dribble down my chin. I should have taken it in two bites. I was looking around for a napkin when Savannah handed me one.

"Here," she said. "Ignore what dropped on the floor."

"Thanks." I avoided looking down as I wiped my chin, hoping I wouldn't step in it. "Sad," I agreed. "I hope he didn't suffer."

"I can't imagine he didn't have at least a few seconds to realize what was happening."

"I take it he fell a long way."

"From a cliff overlooking the water to rocks below. He loved that place for launching his drones."

"You know the place where he died?"

"Yeah, I went with him a couple of times. He was so into drones. I'm not surprised he lost track of where he was and got too close to the edge."

I wondered whether there was an investigation into cause of death but didn't have an opportunity to ask. My mother and her friend joined us with plates of food, oohing and aahing over the variety and quality. I get my love of food from my mother, although she criticizes me for the amount of junk food I eat. And for eating too fast. And for not adequately chewing before swallowing. And for occasionally dribbling food on my shirt. You know, mother stuff. Age doesn't matter; she's still my mother.

When I got home, there were several crows perched in the tree next to my parking space, obviously waiting for me, perhaps enjoying a wind chime concert. The smelly umbrella was still there next to my parking spot, but I knew I would have to be quick to get to it before they could attack. Since Emma's complaints, I'd done some reading about the smell. The scent was Methyl Anthranilate, an ingredient found in the seeds of Concord grapes and used as an additive in bubble gum, candy, soda, and some perfumes. The aroma wasn't supposed to be offensive to humans, but very unpleasant to birds. Maybe Emma had some avian dinosaur blood in her veins.

I took a deep breath, leapt out of the car and lunged at the umbrella, popping it up seconds before they descended. It was like having a personal missile defense system. It may have been my imagination, but I thought I heard them wheezing as they flew off.

My landlord was trimming some bushes in front of his house as I went by. Wearing overalls, like a farmer. It's the only home on land at The Haven, nestled on a narrow strip below the parking platforms and stretching out to the water. The path to the houseboats follows the shoreline in front of their house. They have little privacy, but an unobstructed view. "What's with the umbrella?" he asked.

I slowed down to reply. "It keeps the crows away."

"It stinks, you know."

"So I've been told." I was about to move on when he took a few steps toward me and said,

"You know your cat attacked Glen's dog. He had to take it to the vet. I think you should reimburse him."

"Really? It's a German Shepherd. Wild Thing is a kitten. I'm sure my cat was just protecting himself." Did I really just defend *my* cat? The demon that I was unable to tame with claws to rival Edward Scissorhands. If I started thinking of him as "mine," I would never be able to make that trip to the farm.

The next morning at work, my mind kept going back to Lonnie and how he died. I knew people fell to their deaths on hikes and that freak accidents happened all the time. But there was something niggling at my brain, preventing me from concentrating on the files in front of me. Finally, I gave in to my niggles and called my childhood buddy, Sergeant Bruno

McGinty. As kids we did everything together, more because of proximity than a true melding of minds. Now, I was a nondescript claims adjuster with a manipulative mother and a malicious cat. While he was a brawny hunk who wielded power through size and position. But we were bonded in childhood memories. And he'd spent so much time at my house when we were growing up that my mother was like a second mother to him.

"John," he said, "To what do I owe this dubious pleasure?"

"Why do you say it like that?"

"Because you only call when you want something."

"That isn't true. Sometimes, it's to invite you to a poker game."

"Are you inviting me to a poker game?"

"No, sorry. I want something."

"I thought so."

"But it isn't much. Just some information. About an accident—the kid who fell off a cliff while flying a drone."

"Oh, yeah, I heard about that. Really too bad."

"Any chance it wasn't an accident?"

Bruno didn't respond immediately. After a few seconds, he said, "Are you asking for a reason?"

"Just curious. He lived next door to a client of mine. It's a long story, but I ended up going to his funeral."

"Well, I can't tell you much. The officers called to the scene followed protocol and determined it was an accident."

"What does that mean—they followed protocol?"

"Just what it sounds like. They examined the scene of the incident, checked for signs of a struggle, anything unusual. And they tried to locate possible witnesses."

"Well, was there anything even slightly suspicious?"

"John, leave it to the police. But *no* to your question; there was nothing even slightly suspicious."

"Then why did you hesitate when I asked whether it was an accident?"

"It's nothing."

"Convince me."

"John...unless you tell me why you're asking about his death, this conversation is over."

"Fair enough. How about we talk over a drink after work?"

"Only if you're buying."

After I hung up and gave it some thought, I wasn't sure why I'd called Bruno in the first place. I knew he couldn't tell me anything, even if it had been a suspicious death. And I didn't have any real reason to suspect it was anything but an accident. Still, I was glad I'd called him. It would be nice to get together. It had been a while. And maybe I *should* host a poker night. I hadn't done that in a while, either.

Chapter Five: Gemstones & Beer Buddies

That afternoon, another appraisal case landed on my desk. Actually, the file was unceremoniously flopped down on my desk by Emma. Even though she hadn't slammed it down, it felt like an aggressive act. There is something intimidating about a woman with a husky voice who wears her hair in a bun, a bun secured with a silver pin that could easily double as a weapon.

"For me?" I said, trying to lighten the mood.

"Yes, and I can tell that you didn't take my advice." She wrinkled her short nose in disgust.

"It's made from grapes," I said.

"What is?"

I didn't want to admit that it had nothing to do with any remodel like I'd originally claimed, but I'd let slip the part about grapes and now owed her some explanation, if perhaps not the whole truth. "It wasn't the remodel, after all," I said—a truth about a small lie. "You see, there are some birds nesting in a tree next to my parking space." A kernel of truth and a tiny lie—knocking down the nest had been the first salvo. But I didn't want to admit to destroying habitat. "I'm using an aromatic repellent to keep them away." A true fact. "To prevent them from ruining the paint on my car." Another true fact. Although what had begun as a simple act of protection had morphed into a battle of epic proportions.

"Well, I think it will keep more than birds away," she said as she swirled about and left. If she'd been wearing a cape, it would have been an even more dramatic exit. Unfortunately, she hadn't given me time for a clever comeback, not that I had one ready to fire. More often than not, I was like Charlie Brown, thinking of the perfect retort a day late.

I opened the new file. The client wanted to insure some jewelry. The appraiser was Carla again. It was too bad she was better suited to pose for an exercise equipment ad rather than the swimsuit edition of *Sports Illustrated*. Still, she seemed competent, and it was probably better to keep work relationships professional anyway. Especially given my track record with women.

"Carla," I said when she answered my call. "We need to set up a time to meet with the Jacobsons about the jewelry they want to insure."

"Sorry, John. I made plans several weeks ago for the first visit. As you know, Universal gives me access to detailed pictures and information about appraisal requests before they start the official process. That gives me a chance to say whether I'm interested in taking on the assignment and do some preliminary research. This one must have gotten lost in the handoff from your predecessor. Sorry."

"When is the meeting?"

"This afternoon. In just over an hour, in fact. You are, of course, welcome to tag along."

I bit my tongue to keep from being too blunt about the fact that I was *supposed* to be there, and not as a tagalong. "I can't approve the appraisal if I don't see the jewelry," I replied somewhat stiffly. Although no one, including myself, would label me as an ambitious employee, if I was to continue partnering with Carla, I needed to be a player. Corporate America wasn't known for being lenient with employees who couldn't pull their weight. Her highhanded response left me no alternative: "Then I'll see you in an hour," I said. Rolling over was not only easier than making a big deal out of a slight stab to the old male ego, it got me out of the office.

On the way, I thought about what Carla had said about non-company appraisers having access to the company's art and jewelry requests before Emma handed off the file to an adjuster, in this case, to me. It seemed like a strange way to go about it, but if that was the way it was done, I would adjust. Obviously, I needed to take it slow until I learned the ropes.

The client's house was on Queen Anne hill, not a long drive, but frequently interrupted by stoplights and heavy traffic. In spite of that, I was early and decided to stop at a popular bakery to pick up some goodies for later. When I pulled up in front of the Jacobsons' Victorian house, I paused to admire its spectacular view of the city with glimpses of water and mountains. Then I noticed that Carla was already there, sitting in her car. Had she been waiting for me to arrive? Maybe I had misjudged her. She got out as soon as I turned off my engine.

"Sorry," she said, not sounding at all sorry. "I was going to call you later today and save you a trip. I'm a bit iffy about these three pieces. If they ended up looking like something you wanted to insure, I figured you could come with me when I returned them."

"That was thoughtful," I said, not at all sure it had been. "But I like to be involved from the start. In case the client has questions about coverage." And as an excuse for a mini road trip.

"Well, here we are." She took the lead up the steps to the front porch, practically floating from one step to the other. No doubt she ate right and exercised daily. Whereas the goodies waiting for me in my car already made walking up the steep steps an effort.

I glanced back at the incredible view from the porch while Carla pressed the doorbell. An organ medley of notes echoed from somewhere inside the house. "Weird," I said at the same time Carla said, "Nice."

When they answered the door, my first thought was that Griff and Paula Jacobson looked more like a couple who should have a doorbell that played a guitar and tambourine duet rather than organ music. Both had on bell-bottom jeans. She was wearing a gauzy floral blouse that hung down over one shoulder, exposing her smooth skin. He had on a gold and black striped collarless pullover shirt. It was like being a time traveler and not knowing for sure what year you'd ended up going back to.

"Come in. You must be Carla." They smiled at her and looked questioningly at me.

"John Smith," I said. "I'm the claims adjuster with Universal Heartland Liability and Casualty Assurance Company of America, Incorporated..." I had to take a breath before adding, *"The Company with a Heart."* I took out a card and handed it to them. The corner was bent slightly, putting a crease across the middle of the tiny heart logo. I really needed a card case rather than stuffing a few in my wallet.

Griff smoothed out the corner before handing it to Paula. Then they ushered us into their living room and offered us chairs behind a wood coffee table with bowed legs that ended in tiny foot bumps. The chairs looked like something out of a horror movie and did not appear to be designed for comfort. I verified that as soon as I sat down.

"Lovely home. And a great view," Carla said.

"Yes, I've always loved the view," Paula said. "I grew up here. The house has been in the family for two generations." She smiled. "We make that the third generation."

"And the jewelry?" Paula asked. "I understand you recently inherited the pieces you want appraised."

"Yes, they were part of the estate." She turned to me. "My father died some years ago, but my mother only recently passed away."

That explained the décor. I murmured a few trite condolences, wondering if there was a back room with soft chairs and a television. Living in a small space like my houseboat didn't allow for any "show" rooms. Not that I needed one for entertaining. Except for hosting poker games for my buddies, I didn't have many guests.

"The necklace, ring, and earrings are right here," Paula said, pointing to three small blue velvet boxes on the coffee table.

Carla leaned over and opened the largest of the three, an oblong box with a hinged lid. Inside was an oval medallion decorated with what looked to me like diamonds and some pinkish stones I couldn't identify. It was hung on a flat, woven gold chain. All very ornate. "What a lovely piece." Carla held it up and turned it this way and that to view it from various angles.

"Yes," Paula said. "My understanding is that it was crafted in the 1940s. Pink sapphires were popular then."

"You understand that I can't make even a guess at value until I take a closer look at cut and quality," Carla said. She set the necklace aside and turned her attention to a square container that looked like a supersized ring box. It held an impressive wide-band ring sporting what I now knew was a large pink sapphire surrounded by small diamonds. Without comment, Carla opened the last blue velvet container, the smallest of the three. Inside the flat box were two gold earrings with small pink gemstones surrounded by tiny diamonds.

After examining each of the three pieces a second time, Carla snapped the boxes closed and smiled at the Jacobsons. "What a wonderful set," she said. "If the gemstones are authentic, I think you will be pleased with the valuation."

Griff and Paula grinned. "My mother certainly thought they were authentic."

"Jewelry values do fluctuate, though," Carla added. "Are you planning on selling them?"

"No, we would like to keep them in the family. That's why we want to insure them."

"Great." Carla pulled a small leather bag out of her large, expensive looking purse, put the three boxes in the bag and placed the bag back in her purse. "I'll take a closer look at cut and quality at my office where I have the equipment I need to make an assessment and will return these to you in a couple days. Is that alright?"

"I assume *you* are insured," Griff said with a smile.

"You don't have to worry. I am fully bonded. But I've never had a problem." She patted her purse. "I'll take good care of these. I know they have sentimental as well as commercial value."

Once outside, I turned to Carla and said, "I thought you were iffy about their jewelry."

"I was. It's unusual to have a complete vintage set like this. At first glance, they look pretty good though. But I'll have to have my partner take a look. Farley's the gemstone expert."

"Oh, I thought you told the Jacobsons that *you* would be the one making the assessment."

"It's too complicated to explain the process to people; and I always make the client contact. Farley prefers to remain in the office."

"Does he assess the paintings too?"

"He helps at times. And he maintains all of our records."

I decided not to ask whether the company knew about the arrangement; she might think I was questioning her professionalism. There was so much I didn't know about how things were done. I didn't even know the names of the gemstones and what an appraiser did to assess quality. "Does age have any impact on the value of the jewelry?"

"It depends."

"On what?"

"Cut and quality."

"Are those values that remain the same over time?"

"There are changing trends and varying availability of quality gemstones." We reached her car. "I'll tell you more in a day or two after I've had a chance to talk with Farley, okay?"

She got in her car before I could ask anything else. As I headed over to Bee, I realized that I had unwittingly revealed my lack of knowledge about jewelry with my questions. Although it probably didn't matter in the larger scheme of things, I wished I hadn't displayed my ignorance so readily to someone who didn't necessarily have my best interests at heart.

Bruno stood and gave me a hearty handshake when I arrived after work at our favorite tavern across the road from the lake. The place is a bit noisy and the lighting isn't the greatest, but the beer is priced right and the scattering of tiny tables makes you feel like you have territory of your own, even though there is no real privacy. He had a beer waiting for me. "You get the next round," he said.

When he sat down, I noticed him wince. "Hemorrhoids acting up?" I asked. We had that kind of relationship—I could ask about his hemorrhoids, but we didn't talk philosophy or deep feelings. Just men stuff.

"You weren't supposed to notice."

"Pretend I didn't. So, how's work?"

"Criminals keeping me busy. Job security. How about you?"

"Someone always wants to claim a loss on their insurance. Unless I screw up, I think I have job security too."

"You? Screw up?" Bruno started laughing. We'd grown up together, so he knew me as well as anyone, warts and all.

"Not funny."

"Come on, where's your sense of humor?"

"I left it at home with my cat."

"You have a cat?"

"If you call the monster living with me a cat. You can meet him next Saturday. After we talked, I realized it was time to have another poker party."

"Sounds good to me. I'll bring a six-pack."

"Better bring at least three." We laughed together, remembering past poker parties where players got tipsy and the game slid into revelry.

During the back-and-forth lightweight conversation, we both managed to finish off our beers, so I got up to go get us two more. When I returned, I decided to bring up Lonnie's death again. There was something about the way Bruno had responded to my question earlier that left me with even more questions. "About Lonnie Weller…" I began.

Bruno held up his hand: "No shop talk."

"This isn't business, just curiosity."

"You're not investigating anything related to his death?"

"No, I signed off on an appraisal for his neighbor, that's it."

"But your mother went to his funeral. Is she involved in some way?" He was familiar with Mother's fondness for mysteries and her irrepressible curiosity.

"Not that I know of. She had a friend who knew the family and needed a ride. Besides, if she wanted to put pressure on you to tell her something, she wouldn't hesitate to approach you directly. You know what she's like."

Bruno sighed; we *both* knew how stubborn and persistent she could be. "Okay. If it's just small talk…. Not that I know much. It's been written off as an accident, but…"

There was that "but" again. "But…?"

"I watched the drone footage—"

"I didn't think you were on the case."

"I'm not. But a couple of guys were talking about drones and someone decided to show what was on the camera right before he fell. Because it was interesting, no other reason."

"So, what did you see that gave you second thoughts?"

"There was a slight hesitation before he went over the edge. And the camera jerked around before he dropped the controls."

"Why is that strange?" It sounded about right to me.

"The other officers thought that when the ground started to slip away, he floundered a few seconds before he went over."

"That makes sense to me. The jerking may have happened as he was trying to regain his footing."

"It's also consistent with someone giving him a shove."

"So? Was there any indication of someone else being there?"

"There were several sets of footprints. But then, there were lots of footprints in the area generally."

"So, what makes you think it might not have been an accident?"

"I didn't say that's what I'm thinking."

"You implied it."

Bruno frowned. "Well, for one thing, he was experienced with drones and often flew them from the site where he fell."

"Isn't that the description of an accident?"

"What can I say—it's one of those gut feelings. But it's not my case."

"And no witnesses?"

"No witnesses that have come forward, at least."

"Well, if someone pushed him, they would have made sure no one was looking. And they certainly won't be volunteering as a witness."

Chapter Six: Neighborhood Spy

Tuesday morning, Carla called to tell me that it looked like the gems in all three pieces were authentic, and she thought she would be ready to return them on Wednesday. "I'm having Farley do a couple of other tests; I want to be absolutely certain of my assessment. They're rather pricey. At the top of the range for Universal."

All I had to work on was a small stack of non-urgent files, nothing pressing. So, when my mother called to ask if I would advise Lonnie's parents on how to submit a claim for their son's drone collection, I quickly agreed to pick her up in an hour.

Since I didn't want to explain to Emma what I was up to, I waited until she went down the hall, probably to the bathroom, maybe for coffee, before making a break for it. With luck, she wouldn't check on me until later in the day. But you could never tell with her. She was like a sheepdog, constantly watchful and keeping the sheep in line. Maybe I should ask Mother for a note just in case.

What Mother didn't mention until we were on our way to the Weller house was the reason the Wellers needed advice—their son's drone collection had been stolen, along with his laptop, cell phone and his TV.

"That's it?" I asked. "Just electronics? And only Lonnie's stuff?"

"That seems strange, doesn't it?"

"Did it happen during the funeral service?"

"Yes, now that you mention it, I think it did. What lowlife does that kind of thing?"

"The kind of lowlife that reads obituaries. I'm afraid it's not uncommon for thefts to happen when they know the family is away for a specific length of time. And it probably sounded like he had some high-end tech stuff."

"The Wellers are apparently pretty upset. First, they lose their son, now they've lost a collection that was extremely important to him. It's like losing him twice."

"Maybe we should give them Wild Thing to console them."

Mother gave me the stink eye, her supercharged mother version. "I thought you said it was working out."

"We have a fragile understanding. I feed him, let Valerie visit once a day, and he doesn't attack me. I guess you could call that 'working out.'"

"Come on, it can't be that bad."

"The landlord thinks I should pay the vet bill for the neighbor's dog Wild Thing savaged."

"Ludicrous. I'll talk to him."

"That won't be necessary, Mother."

"I gave you the kitten; I share responsibility."

"There's not much you can say, Mother. Remember, Valerie wanted to keep him, and her father made her give him back. He and my landlord both know what Wild Thing is capable of."

"Are you going to pay the vet bill?"

"I'm considering it. Valerie's father hasn't said anything to me about the bill, but he was pretty mad when it happened. And his daughter keeps Wild Thing happy and out of trouble. I should probably at least offer to split it."

"Well, I don't think you're under any obligation to pay his dog's vet bill. Imagine, a kitten hurting a full-grown dog, a German Shepherd no less; he ought to be too embarrassed to accept any reimbursement."

"I'm afraid they see Wild Thing as some sort of demon." Mother made a harrumph sound, dismissing the situation as absurd. In my mind I pictured some animal control person coming to investigate and insisting on checking out Wild Thing. I could end up paying for a hospital tab as well as a vet bill.

When we arrived at the Wellers', they offered us fresh coffee and just-out-ot-the-oven scones. The small kitchen was wrapped in the sweet scent of sugar mingled with caffeine. Mother and I eagerly sat down at the kitchen table to savor our snack while the Wellers filled us in on what had happened.

As Mother had explained, the theft occurred on Sunday during the funeral, and they had immediately reported the break-in to the police. At the time, they hadn't been able to tell the police exactly what was missing, and they still weren't entirely sure the list they'd compiled was complete. Nor were they certain about the value of the stolen articles, particularly about Lonnie's drone collection. That's why their friend had suggested they contact me through my mother.

"I'm sure John will be able to help you with your insurance claim," my mother said, turning to me for confirmation. I had devoured one scone and had my mouth stuffed with an overly ambitious bite of a second one. At the same time, I was distracted by trying to decide whether scones were classified as a pastry or a type of bread.

"He lived here full time?" Mother asked to give me time to swallow and focus.

"Like so many adult children these days, he lived with us to save money to buy a house of his own, eventually," his father said. "We were happy to have him here. He ate most of his meals with us, but we tried to give him some privacy."

"How familiar were you with his drone collection?" I asked, reluctantly setting aside what remained of my second scone.

"Neither of us was into the drone thing," his mother said.

"Well, I thought it was interesting, at first," his father said. "But after you get the hang of it, it's not that much fun. I mean, you just fly it around. Nothing too exciting happens."

"I think he checked out my car with one of his drones the day I was at your neighbors'," I said.

"Yes, he was a real neighborhood snoop." His mother smiled, shook her head, then sighed. "We warned him that could get him in trouble, but he seemed to enjoy knowing what was going on."

"I hope he didn't peek in people's windows with one of those," Mother said. "Just imagine."

"I don't think he was a peeping Tom or anything like that." Mrs. Weller sounded a bit put out at the suggestion.

"Of course not," my mother quickly assured her. "I didn't mean to imply anything like that, but I can see how tempting it would be to look around… perhaps a little more than you should. I mean, we're all a bit curious about our neighbors."

"Like if someone was sunbathing…" I began, but stopped when my mother gave me "the look."

"I understand what you're hinting at," Mrs. Weller said. "And if we'd had *any* indication that he was doing something he shouldn't have been doing, we would have put a stop to it. After all, even though he was an adult, he was living under our roof."

"It's not as if this is the kind of neighborhood where there's much happening," Mr. Weller added.

"I assume any recordings he'd made were taken along with the actual drones themselves," I said.

"I'm not sure what kinds of recordings he may have had. But whoever took the drones didn't leave anything behind."

"So, what you want help with is deciding how to estimate the actual loss since you don't have a list of everything that was taken, is that correct?"

"Yes, it's difficult to think about money right now, but we need to put in a claim. On the one hand, we don't want to ask for too much, but we don't want to undervalue what it was worth, either. That would be disrespectful to Lonnie."

After that, we got into the nitty gritty about what they could claim and what to expect from their insurance company. One thing they had going for them was all of the pictures they'd taken of their son with various drones and the equipment he used to operate them. They may not have been excited about drones, but based on the sheer number of pictures taken, they obviously loved their son.

I also took a look at their policy to make certain their son's property was covered. It was. Unfortunately, I had to warn them that they shouldn't expect to receive full value for the loss, in part because some of the drones may have been older and also because they had so little documentation.

Furthermore, they hadn't specifically listed his collection on their policy. Still, it was definitely worth filing a claim, especially with pictures to back it up.

"Once you make your list based on these pictures and your best recollections, you should also give the list—and copies of some of the pictures—to the police," I said. "It's possible they might turn up some of the drones once they have a better idea about what they're looking for."

Mrs. Weller was so thankful for the advice that she gave me a bag of scones to go. As we departed, I handed my card to Mr. Weller and told him to give me a call if they had any more questions. His lips moved as he read it. "The company with a heart," he said. "That's nice."

On the way home, Mother voiced what I'd been thinking: "I bet Lonnie snooped where he shouldn't have. His parents think it's a normal neighborhood, but you never know what's going on behind closed doors. Or in the alley. Maybe he saw a drug deal go down. Or caught someone sleeping with a woman who wasn't his wife."

"What about a woman sleeping with someone who wasn't her husband?"

"Either way." She dismissed her own misogynist remark with a wave of the hand. "But the point is, how would they know they'd been seen? You don't suppose Lonnie was a blackmailer, do you?"

I chewed on the idea. "They might have seen the drone watching them. Like I saw the one hovering over Bee. If they felt guilty enough about whatever they assumed he saw, I could see them breaking in to destroy evidence by stealing his equipment. I could even imagine someone roughing him up a bit to dissuade him from further snooping. But I'm with his father— what could he possibly have seen in *this* neighborhood that would make someone want to murder him?"

"Murder?" My mother sounded shocked. "I didn't know we were talking about murder."

"What were *you* talking about?"

"The theft. But murder, that's definitely worth looking into."

"No, Mother. We aren't looking into either a murder or a theft. We are going to let the police do that."

"Then why did you bring it up?"

"Because I thought *you* did."

"I was only thinking about the theft, but if there is a question of murder…" Her mystery book club antenna was on full alert.

"Mother, Bruno would throw a fit if either of us started poking our noses into a police investigation."

"But what if Lonnie really was blackmailing someone? Someone he caught in a criminal act. Bad people can live anywhere, you know."

"Of course, it's a possibility. But it's none of our business."

"Well, Bruno is like family. We owe it to him to let him know what we've learned. Besides, it's been a while since we've had him over to dinner. It's about time, don't you think? And after we tell him our suspicions, he can decide what to do next. I'm sure he'll do the right thing."

Chapter Seven: Is Someone Watching?

W hen I returned to the office, I was so distracted thinking about the conversation I'd had with my mother that I forgot I was supposed to sneak back in without letting Emma see me. Instead, I was ten feet away before I realized my mistake. She locked eyes with me, drawing me closer like a Siren luring a wayward sailor. There was no way to retreat.

"Where have you been?" The question sounded more like a reprimand than a request for information.

"I went out to get coffee."

She looked pointedly at my empty hands.

"And I drank it there," I said. "With a donut."

"Caffeine and sugar," she said disapprovingly. "What kind of donut?"

"The kind with a hole in the middle," I said, hoping my wit would sideline the discussion.

"The coffee shop on the corner doesn't have donuts."

"Maybe it was a scone."

"And I haven't left my desk in over an hour."

"Alright, I confess. My mother had an emergency, and I had to drive her to Urgent Care. But she's okay, and I stopped for coffee on the way back."

Emma eyed me suspiciously. Her perfectly coiffed hair was still as death.

A drip of nervous sweat rolled off my forehead into my left eye. I really needed to work on controlling my body's response to lying. Sidestepping the truth now and then didn't hurt anyone, and it avoided a lot of explaining. Although Mother would never admit it, that's something I'd learned from her.

"And I'm going to work late to make up for it," I added. There. I wasn't trying to take advantage, just being flexible. "Well, I'd better get back to work. Lots to do."

I was convinced Emma's eyes were boring tiny holes in my jacket as I fled to my office. Damn. Now I was going to have to stay late. She probably had a camera pointed at my door. Maybe there was even one in my office. Why hadn't I thought of that before? Was it legal for a business to spy on its employees? I started casually looking around. There were no visible cameras and no vents to hide them in. But these days, cameras could be pretty small. Had she been logging my naps? Monitoring my calls? Turning away in disgust when I cleaned out a nostril?

Well, one way or the other, I had to either put in an extra hour or two…or stay at least until Emma left for the day.

Shortly after what was normally quitting time, I made a couple trips to the bathroom to see if Emma was still there. She either thought I had a weak bladder or guessed my true purpose and was staying later than usual herself to keep tabs on me. If the latter was the case, there probably weren't any cameras. Still, there was no way to be sure.

On one of my fake bathroom runs, I noted that Emma was gone, and her jacket was no longer hanging on the back of her chair. In case it was a trick, I waited another five minutes. It was still possible that she might suddenly reappear, pretending to come back for something she'd *accidentally* left behind. But I really wanted to go home, so I finally decided it was worth the risk.

Instead of taking the elevator, however, I opted for the stairs. My fear was that if I took the elevator, Emma might be waiting for me on the ground floor. When the doors opened, there she would be, facing the elevator, staring at me with a "gotcha" look on her face. That was something my mother might have done.

Once safely beyond Emma's judgmental reach, Bee and I drove home to Bad Bunny rapping. I didn't understand a word, but I moved my shoulders back and forth to the beat, feeling cool. I was pumped for action by the time

47

I pulled into my parking spot, but there were no crows waiting for me. And when I got to my houseboat, Wild Thing almost seemed glad to see me. Well, maybe that's a bit of an exaggeration, but he didn't hiss while he impatiently paced back and forth in front of his food dish. I served up his meal with some unintelligible rap sounds accompanied by a few cool moves. Wild Thing didn't seem impressed. He remained focused on his food and started gobbling it up as soon as his bowl hit the floor. I was lucky to get my fingers back without toothmarks.

Then it was my turn. I stared at the sorry choices in my refrigerator, searched my cupboards for inspiration, and finally got a box of Eggos out of the freezer. My mother used to serve them with warm syrup. I didn't bother, but it would have been nice.

Wednesday morning, I met Carla outside Griff and Paula Jacobson's house, and we walked up their sidewalk together. "What kind of a name is 'Griff?'" I asked.

"I thought you would want to know about the jewelry."

"I do, of course." When she didn't say anything, I prompted her: "Well?"

"It's short for Griffith."

"I meant about the jewelry."

"It's fine." We were almost at the door.

"But I thought Griffith was a surname."

She gave me a look that would have made the petals drop off a daisy. "Think about it," she said as she rang the doorbell. "Or, look at your file on our clients if you can't figure it out."

I got the distinct impression that I had just flunked a test.

Paula and Griff were wearing their bell-bottom jeans, this time with matching shirts that looked like they had been made from authentic Indian bedspreads. I'd had one when I was in college. It was trendy at the time. The small shop that sold them had tiny ceramic holders with burning incense sticks protruding from them prominently placed on tables and shelves throughout the cramped space. To me, everything smelled like mildewed flowers, and I never managed to get the smell out of my bedspread. As I

48

shook hands with Griff, I stepped in close and took a deep breath to see if his shirt carried the scent I remembered. He smelled like peanut butter.

We took our seats at the same coffee table as before. Carla pulled the three blue velvet boxes out of the leather bag in her purse. Then she flipped open the lids and smiled—first at the pieces of jewelry and then at Griff and Paula. "Your mother was right," she began. "The gems are authentic. Not only that, but they are of exceptional quality." She delivered the good news as if she were telling the couple they had just won the grand prize in the Reader's Digest sweepstakes. Then she placed her report on the table and pointed to her valuation, glancing over her shoulder at me for approval.

I knew I should have asked to see the number earlier, before Carla showed it to our clients. That would have given me the opportunity to discuss and perhaps negotiate it with her before being forced to either agree or disagree with her valuation without having a chance to think about it. Oh well, she was the expert. Or Farley, the guy who actually did the valuation, was. With only a minor reservation, I nodded approval to the terms of the appraisal for their insurance coverage.

We were about to leave when I finally decided to look more closely at the necklace. In case there were questions later. I leaned over to study it, reaching out to run my fingers across the stones in the medallion. Then paused.

"I think one of the stones is loose," I said

All eyes turned to the necklace. Carla was the first to respond. She brushed my hand aside and picked up the box. After just a brief glance, she said, "I'm so sorry. I can't believe that I didn't notice. It might have been like that before, but it could have happened when I was running tests for the appraisal. Either way, I'll have this repaired and get it back to you later today." Then she gave the Jacobsons a warm smile. "We don't want you losing a stone."

No, "we" didn't. Not after agreeing to insure the piece at a fairly high price.

Carla was obviously embarrassed by the situation, but Griff and Paula didn't seem all that upset. They were clearly pleased with the appraisal and weren't concerned about placing blame for something so easily repaired. Especially since it was possible the gem had been loose all along.

On the way out to our respective cars, Carla thanked me for noticing the problem with the necklace. "You may have saved the company a claim. The sapphire could have fallen out and been lost."

A compliment from unsexy Ms. Bridges? Maybe I should ask for it in writing.

"You don't need to come back with me this afternoon," she added. "I'll let you know after I drop it off. Okay?"

"Okay." I couldn't see why I needed to be there. I'd already earned my brownie points for the day. Better not to press my luck.

The drive back to the office was slow, filled with honking horns and impatient pedestrians jaywalking instead of waiting at stoplights to cross the street. Once at my desk, I found a message to call Savannah. That surprised me. Wondering what she could possibly be calling me about, I pressed the return call symbol and got a message to leave a message. It was always tempting to say, "Tag, you're it." But I simply said that I was in the office and she could call any time.

While I was waiting for Savannah to call, I looked at the Jacobson file. His legal first name was Gruffudd. When I looked it up online, I discovered it was Welsh for Griffith. I wondered if he asked to be called Griff before or after middle school.

Savannah returned my call while I was paying a visit to the restroom.

I returned her call and got her voicemail again.

The next time she called I had gone to get a cup of coffee. She said she was headed out for a while and would try again later.

Chapter Eight: The Hottie Aunt

I was feeling hungry, so I decided to get something out of the company vending machines. The selections were all things I was pretty sure made the list of food items nutritionists warn against eating, but I somehow always managed to stifle the voice of reason in my head that said: "eat an apple." The voice sounds remarkably like my mother's.

When I returned, Emma glanced meaningfully at me before holding up one hand like a school crossing guard. In a voice dripping with disapproval, she informed me "There is a *person* waiting for you in your office." From the emphasis she gave the word "person," images of green aliens or a Shrek-like monster sent a tingle of trepidation down my spine.

I started to ask how the *person* got into my office in the first place, but Emma interrupted before I could think of a way to frame the question in a non-accusative manner.

"She said she had an appointment." Not an alien then, unless a female alien. Emma looked at me for confirmation, then added, "It wasn't on your calendar."

"That's because I don't have an appointment with anyone. You said 'she'—did she give a name?"

"Desiree Defelice." She said the name with a hint of scorn and a pinch of mocking accent. "Maybe a stage name?"

I had no doubt from her dramatic pronouncement what kind of "stage" she was referring to. My heart started beating a little faster. I wanted to ask if she looked like a "Desiree Defelice," but I would find out soon enough. My only question was why she told Emma she had an appointment.

51

As I opened the door to my office, I smelled a hint of lilac with a slight vanilla afterthought. Desiree was seated on the chair across from my desk. When she unwrapped her willowy figure and stood to greet me, I could almost feel the heat of her body seeping out of the plunging neckline of her formfitting dress. Her face was nice too. Bright red lips beneath blue eyes and long blond hair that looked too good to be real. Suddenly, I realized she was holding out her hand.

"You're Desiree Defelice," I said, meaning it.

"John, it's good to meet you."

Her handshake was so-so, but it hardly mattered. She didn't need to make any more of an impression.

I managed to get around her to my desk without brushing up against her breasts, although every fiber of my being wanted to do just that. "What can I do for you?" I asked somewhat huskily.

"You spoke with Savannah earlier, I believe."

"Actually, no, we've been playing phone tag."

"Oh, then you weren't expecting me?"

I almost said, "All my life." Instead, I managed a somewhat professional, "No, but my calendar is open. No appointments or anything." Did I sound like the lonely Maytag repairman with nothing but time on his hands?

"Well then, let me explain." She lowered her body into the chair, crossing her long legs and casually brushing the wrinkles out of her skirt that stopped far enough above her knees to make life interesting. I wanted to leap over the desk and offer to help smooth the remaining wrinkle.

I had to clear my throat before replying: "Please do explain." As I was getting a yellow pad out of my desk drawer, I accidentally dropped my pen on the floor. I bent down to pick it up and realized I had a tantalizing view of her legs under the shallow modesty panel between the two pedestals on either corner of my desk. They were very nice legs, ending in very high heels with ankle straps and open toes. Her toenails were painted bright red, like her lips. Be still my heart.

As I reluctantly sat up, my phone rang. I ignored it, but before we could restart our conversation, Emma poked her head in to tell me I had a client on line one. She glared at Desiree before withdrawing, leaving the door open a few inches.

"Do you mind?" I asked. Desiree shook her head no. "John Smith," I said into the old-fashioned receiver.

"This is Savannah. I wanted to tell you that my aunt would be coming by your office."

"Your aunt?" Desiree didn't look like anyone's aunt that I knew.

"Yes, she dropped in yesterday, and we decided she needed to talk to you." Desiree mouthed, "Is that Savannah?"

"I'll put you on speaker," I said, pushing the wrong button and ending the call. "It's Savannah," I said. "But I've cut her off."

The phone rang again, and I answered it. "Sorry, I said."

"What are you sorry about?" Emma's hard-edged voice said.

"Oh, I thought you were the client calling back. We got cut off." I didn't have to admit I was the cutter-offer.

"I just thought I should mention that your mother called and wants you to call her back."

"Thanks, Emma." As I hung up, the phone rang again. This time it was Savannah.

"Look, I have to go, but I just wanted to let you know that Desiree speaks for the whole family, okay?"

"Okay, thanks." I hung up and turned back to Desiree. "You were saying?"

"Yesterday, I went by to see my niece—at her request. She has some questions about the age of a painting your company has appraised."

"The one with the cow?"

"Yes, it's supposed to be quite old, but you can smell the paint." She paused. "Did you try smelling it?"

"No, I'm sorry, I didn't."

"Well, you'll have to take our word for it then."

"Of course."

"What we would like is a second opinion."

"But it was authenticated. And that means it got the benefit of a high evaluation, so I'm not sure why..." I stopped in mid-sentence because I realized I was about to say something a company person shouldn't.

Desiree frowned a red-lipped pout that looked sexy rather than disapproving. "The family admits it didn't give the painting the sniff test before accepting the appraisal. But we want to make sure the painting is what we think it is. I came to you to register our concerns because we would like another appraiser to take a look at them. A different appraiser from within the company is fine, or someone else you would recommend."

"Carla is an independent contractor, but she has been doing appraisals for us for some time, and she has a solid reputation." And a solid body, not soft and rounded like the one across the desk from me. "I have complete faith in her assessment," I added for good measure.

"But even good appraisers can be fooled. All we are asking for is a second opinion."

"Technically, we don't do that for clients."

"That's unfortunate." Her tone suggested she would not give us favorable marks on a customer service survey. "But surely you could help me find someone to do it, couldn't you? If not an appraiser—I know they can be expensive, perhaps a reputable artist who could take a look at the painting." She gave me an irresistible come-hither look accompanied by a toothy smile surrounded by those plump red lips. I suddenly remembered a camp song about lips "like two red wieners…" I've always liked hot dogs.

"Yes, of course. I will ask around to find someone for you. Ah, just to make sure. If that's what you want." I would be happy to fly to the moon and back for you, too.

She stood up. "It's settled then." She leaned across my desk and handed me a card. The view from where I was sitting was inspiring. I admit it took me a moment to make my eyes focus on the card. Her name in hot-pink script was in the center; her contact information to the left.

"You have an interesting name," I commented.

"Yes. It refers to desire and happiness. I chose it some years ago. To fit the image I try to project as an actress." She gave me another big smile before turning to leave. Belatedly taking my eyes off her voluptuous hips, I jumped up to see her out.

"Do you need to have me…" Emma was openly studying us as we emerged from my office.

"I know my way out," Desiree said. If Emma hadn't been right there, I would have insisted on at least walking her to the elevators. As it was, I reluctantly let her leave on her own, trailing the scent of lilacs, her lovely body swaying as the spindly heels on her shoes wobbled ever so slightly at each step.

I stopped by Emma's desk. "She's related to a client," I said. "They want a second opinion on a painting."

"Appraisal too low?"

"Something like that." I started backing away, then realized how stupid that must look, like trying to escape from a bear. So, I slowly spun around and sauntered back to my office to let Emma know I was unconcerned with her opinion, firmly closing my door behind me.

Before I made it to my chair, Emma poked her head in again: "Don't forget to call you mother back."

Round One went to me, but Emma had definitely won Round Two.

"Mother," I said when she answered. "I hope this is an emergency. I've asked you not to call me at work."

"So, you're hoping I have an emergency? What kind of thing is that for a son to say?"

"Sorry, I didn't mean it that way." I stopped talking, waiting for her to tell me why she called before I could irritate her more.

After what seemed like a long, punishing silence, she said: "Well, don't you want to know why I called?"

"Yes, Mother. Please tell me why you called."

"Bruno is coming to dinner on Friday."

"That's not until the day after tomorrow. Why call me at work to tell me that?"

"We need to strategize."

"Strategize?"

"On how we are going to get him to investigate Lonnie's death."

"He's already warned me to leave that alone."

"Oh, he doesn't mean it."

"I think he does."

"Well, we can talk about it before he comes on Friday. I'll expect you early to help me get everything ready."

Poor Bruno. When Mother makes up her mind about something, she holds on like a pit bull, not releasing her victim until she has what she wants. And poor me. I was about to be a co-conspirator in a game I really didn't want to play.

When I left for the day, Emma was still at her desk. I considered saying something about working late the day before, but I was still wary about the possibility that she had secret cameras tracking my movements. Instead, I kept it simple. "Have a nice evening."

"You call your mother?" she asked.

What was she, the new patron saint of mothers? "Yes, thanks."

"She good?"

"I wouldn't exactly describe her like that."

Chapter Nine: What's That Smell?

Thursday morning a strong wind from the northwest made my houseboat bounce enough to make me queasy. Lines squeaked as it tugged against its moorings. Wild Thing didn't like the movement one bit, and he made his displeasure known by yowling loudly before curling up on the couch with his tail tucked protectively around his small body.

The crows were too smart to be out in a summer storm, so at least I had a peaceful, if windy, walk to my car. Once at work, I went to the staff break room for a cup of coffee. The half-full pot looked and smelled suspiciously like it was left over from the day before. I doctored my coffee with some sugar and creamer, turning it to a disgusting beige color that probably had a fancy paint sample name like *canvas tan* or *baby spit.* It even smelled faintly like canvas or spit. I took one sip and poured it down the sink.

Back at my desk, I got out a pad of yellow-lined paper and chose a pen from the silver stein on my desk containing an assortment of pens, pencils, and markers. I'd picked it up at a garage sale. It had "first place, men's division" engraved on the front. There was no mention of the kind of competition. But it was nice to come in first.

Having a pad and pen ready for action was supposed to get me started. Like an appetizer that prepares your palate for the main course by getting your digestive juices flowing. Only my brain seemed in stuck mode. I needed something more to grease the skids and jumpstart my brain. I wasn't sure if that was a mixed metaphor, but I knew it meant I had to keep trying.

I wrote "goals" at the top of the page. Then I wrote *Number 1* below that. Since I was the only one who was going to see what I wrote, I could be honest. Still, it was hard to put in writing that my number one goal was to "learn enough about how the age of a painting is assessed in order to impress Desiree." That seemed shallow. But it was the truth. Okay, so when it comes to women, I *am* shallow.

Number 2 – Impress Desiree—a succinct, targeted version of *Number 1.*

Number 3 – While impressing Desiree, avoid ticking off Carla by suggesting that I had doubts about the accuracy of the appraisal. Unless I learned something that made me doubt the appraisal, of course. Then, I would be making a new goals list.

Number 4 - If I didn't learn enough to convince Desiree, I would have to come up with the name of an expert to recommend in order to stay in her good graces. That would definitely risk alienating Carla.

The four goals were clear enough, but challenging to execute. I especially didn't want to recommend another appraiser. There was no way Universal would spring for it without more than a teenager's sniff test to go on. And if the client had to pay for it, they wouldn't be happy. Furthermore, if I did make a recommendation, Carla was sure to find out, and there went goal number three. Besides, given Carla's reputation, I doubted another appraiser would disagree with her—or Farley's—conclusion about the painting's authenticity. It wasn't as if we were looking at a Rembrandt or some other big-time artist's masterpiece. In my opinion, the cow by the tree was a step above paint by numbers, but not by much. It seemed to me the best way to achieve goals one, two and three and avoid number four was to succeed with number one.

What I needed was someone who could educate me in a hurry. To make me *sound* knowledgeable. One option Desiree had mentioned as a cheap source of information was to get a real painter's assessment of the picture or what I should be looking for in it. Asking an art dealer might make more sense, but they would probably just point me to an appraiser. Talking to a painter as she suggested could help me to achieve my first goal while enabling me to quickly resolve the situation. The problem was that I didn't know any painters besides the guy who did the exterior of my houseboat a few years back.

I reluctantly turned to Google, the main source of all knowledge these days. If I could come up with the right phrase to do the search, I might get lucky. I tried "local artists," but that didn't narrow it enough. "Local painters" was a good source for hourly interior and exterior work. Then, there were specific mediums such as oil, watercolor, and acrylic. Affordable art. Art classes. Art for sale. There were too many options that didn't get me where I needed to be.

Finally, it occurred to me that one place to find the name of a painter was in a gallery where they displayed their works. I could call a local gallery and ask for a referral. Then I would be able to tell Desiree that such and such a gallery had recommended the artist. That should add some credibility to my choice and perhaps get a checkmark for goal *Number 2.*

Although I don't frequent art galleries, I knew there were several located within walking distance of each other in a somewhat dicey section of the city. I'd accompanied Mother and a friend of hers on a First Friday Art Walk once. As their male protector. Not my favorite night out, but at least nothing bad had happened. Except for the panhandling. I'm uncomfortable saying "no" to people who are down-and-out. But Mother insists that most of the homeless in that area of town are scam artists, and she disapproves of giving them any money. The night I played escort, she handed out "all-natural energy bars" instead. I didn't look back to see if they tossed them after the surprise of getting health food instead of money had worn off.

The first person I got on the line let me know that their clients were artists, not teachers. He suggested I contact the local community colleges for courses on art. That was probably a good suggestion, but I didn't have time to take a class, and it wouldn't necessarily focus on what I wanted to know anyway.

The second person put me on hold and played classical music that made me nod off. I jerked awake when they came back and told me that I would have to contact the artists directly. And, no, she couldn't supply me with a list. But she assured me, there were lots of excellent artists in the area. She made it sound like there was at least one on every streetcorner in the city, like Starbucks.

Feeling discouraged, I wandered over to Emma's desk and asked her if she knew of any local artists who could help me get up to speed on painting appraisals. It seemed to me it was okay to admit I didn't know everything there was to know about art to her. After all, a willingness to learn is a positive trait, right?

"I want to make sure I'm factoring in the most important considerations when committing Universal to insurance coverage," I said. I was pleased with how vague and yet impressive my explanation sounded.

"Have you talked with Cornell?" she asked.

"Cornell?"

"Your predecessor."

"No, I understand he left the company."

"He is very knowledgeable about art and the local art scene," she said.

That sounded promising. "Do you have contact information for him?"

Emma took out a small booklet and flipped through some pages. "I never understood why he left. I thought he enjoyed his job." She wrote down a number. "He works from home as an independent accountant now. I'm sure he won't mind if you call and ask for a recommendation. He's an art collector himself; very connected to the art community."

"Thank you." Cornell, huh? That was a name that would be hard to live with if you didn't have a British accent. I wondered if friends called him Corny.

When I called, Cornell at first seemed reluctant to talk. But after I identified myself as his "replacement" and told him what I wanted, he paused only a few seconds before giving me a name: Lars Lane. "He's very well-informed about art history as well as about appraisals and provenance. I'm sure he will be willing to help. Of course, he might try to sell you something. Most artists don't make all that much money."

"May I use your name when I contact him?"

"Please do. I've met him on several occasions, and I admire his work. I even have two of his pieces, one from his stylized phase and another a charcoal drawing."

"One other question…" I began.

"Sure."

"Did you ever meet Farley, Carla's partner?" I hadn't planned on asking him that. What I really wanted to know was how he got along with Carla and whether he had any tips for me, but that seemed too direct and revealing.

There was a moment of silence before he responded. "No, I never did. Carla was my contact." Before I could probe further, he said, "Well, it's been nice talking to you. Have to run."

Surprised at his abrupt end to our conversation, I briefly considered whether it had something to do with my mention of Farley. No, I was probably overreacting. Cornell was a busy man and had given me what I'd asked for: the name of a painter I could talk to about appraisals. And if the price of admission was purchasing a painting from him, well, that was okay. If it wasn't too pricey. There was lots of space next to the steering wheel on the wall in my living room. A painting of a boat on the open water would look nice there. Or one of a lighthouse. I've always liked lighthouses.

When I called Lars, I got his voice message. Keeping it brief, I told him where I got his name, what I needed, and asked him to call. An hour later, he did.

"I'd be happy to provide you with some information about authenticating paintings," he said. "Why don't you stop by my studio? I'll be here until around 6:00."

I'm not sure what I was expecting, maybe a loft in a trendy building or a barn-like structure with one large open space and paintings propped up along unpainted walls. Or an overcrowded space in a condo or apartment building filled to capacity with easels and tin cans with brushes in them. Something either funky or artsy, or both, like you see in the movies. And the artist would have long hair with splotches of paint on his clothes and maybe a few paint splatters on his face.

So, I was surprised to find the studio of Lars Lane in a middle-class neighborhood in a building in his back yard that looked like a mini version of his house. The door was standing open, so I knocked and stepped inside. My first impression was that everything was white—white walls, white ceiling, white tile floor. Everything nice and tidy. Like a house staged for sale.

There was a single row of paintings leaning against a windowless side wall with a number of others hung above them. An easel with a blank canvas stood next to a large window to the east with a table of neatly arranged paints and brushes next to it. A small table and a bookcase filled a corner at the back next to a door that looked like it led to another room. Maybe that was where the real work took place.

The second surprise was Lars. His hair would have passed the test for army regulations, his jeans were spotless, and he looked more like a poster boy for granola bars than an artist. "Hi, welcome to my studio," he said as he waved me in.

"So, this is where you create?" I asked, looking around for what he was currently working on.

"Yes, although I do rough drafts of ideas wherever I happen to be. I usually have a sketchpad handy. I've been known to doodle on a napkin at a restaurant or draw on the back of a grocery list."

"Ever use an etch-a-sketch?" I joked.

"Better than in the sand on a beach," he said with a smile.

I smiled back. I liked the man. "What's in back?" I asked. It was a random question, but he hesitated before replying.

"Supplies. And failures."

"Failures?"

"You can re-use canvases," he explained. "If I'm working with acrylics, I simply apply a fresh layer and start over. Oils may require some sanding before re-use."

"I think I remember reading about a masterpiece hidden under another painting." Actually, my mother had told me about it, but it sounded better to say I'd come across it on my own.

"That's what every art collector hopes to find. That or a priceless work of art being sold for a few bucks at a garage sale or flea market."

"Do you collect art?" I asked.

"The walls in my house are filled with unsold paintings. There's no room for anyone else's work." He smiled again.

"I'm lucky I guess—*my* failures are hidden away in filing cabinets." Then, not wanting to offend, I quickly added, "Not that an unsold painting is a failure."

"The market is saturated with amateur art," Lars said. "It's a competitive marketplace. Anyone who wants to paint for a living has to accept that frustrating fact. That's why I have a studio in my back yard."

Oh, oh. It sounded like he *was* going to hit me up to buy something from him. I took a longer look at the paintings lined up on the floor and the ones on the wall. There seemed to be a variety of styles represented, including a couple that looked like modern portraits. "You do paintings of people, don't you?" I asked. "I mean 'real' people?" Maybe my mother would like a portrait of herself. It would be a nice, personal present.

"Yes, all the time."

"Do they have to sit for it?" It wouldn't be a surprise if she had to pose.

"I can do it from a good photograph. Why, do you have someone in mind?"

"Yes, I'm thinking my mother might like a portrait of herself. How long does it take?"

"A couple of weeks would do it."

"That sounds good. I'll see if I can find the right photograph." Oh, oh, I didn't ask about price, like it was no object. "Ah…maybe I should ask about cost."

"We can discuss that when you bring in the photograph and decide what size canvas and the type of frame you want. Okay?"

"Okay." It was a ploy I was familiar with, the vague response intended to soften the impact of a price quote at the end of the discussion. But for now, I'd let it ride; my priority was to acquire information. "So, here's what I'm hoping you can help me with," I said. "As I explained on the phone, it's for a case I'm working on. Someone is questioning the appraisal value of a painting, and I would like to be able to sound like I know what I'm talking about." When I saw the amused grin flash across his face, I quickly amended my statement: "What I mean is that I would like to *know* what I'm talking about. I want to be accurate."

"I'm not sure I can make you an instant expert, but I can give you some of the basics. And answer any specific questions you may have."

"That sounds good."

"First, let me be clear—there's a distinction between tackling the issue of authenticity and determining value. A good appraiser will do both, but with moderately priced artwork, it can be challenging. There's often not good paperwork to verify provenance, especially if the piece is older. And information about the artist may be skimpy, depending on when and where the picture was purchased. Not all artists sell their paintings in galleries. Art purchased directly from the artist or at art fairs or exhibitions may not be as well documented.

"Some people consider art an investment, but most buy what they like and what they feel they can afford. These individuals are not necessarily thinking about insuring what they buy initially, so they aren't always scrupulous about keeping track of their purchases.

"Furthermore, families may hold onto paintings for generations but lose track of any documentation that once existed. The artist may or may not still be around, and his or her paintings may or may not have increased in value. It's complicated."

I was already feeling overwhelmed, and he hadn't started on specifics yet.

"What kind of paintings are you dealing with?" he asked.

I explained that I couldn't tell him much because I didn't know what I should be looking for, but that one was a cow by a stream, and the other consisted of random splotches of bright colors. No, I didn't remember the artists' names. No, I didn't know the medium. No, I didn't know when it was painted. No, I wasn't familiar with art styles or what was currently trending. At that point, he seemed to be suppressing either a grin or a gas pain, but I wasn't sure which. He led me over to the table by the bookcase and pulled out a couple of books.

"Let me show you a few topics you may want to discuss with your client." He opened a book to a section titled "Darkening of the Canvas."

"Assuming it's an oil painting, determining value is like solving a mystery. One place to start is by trying to determine its age. For instance, you can tell a lot by the back of the canvas." Lars pointed to some pictures of frames with dates next to them. "Older original canvases tend to darken with age."

"That looks pretty obvious, doesn't it?" Maybe I *could* sound well-informed.

"Unfortunately, there isn't always a direct correlation between color and age, and oftentimes a painting is relined."

"Oh."

"You have to look for several clues." He flipped a page. "Another thing to consider is that original paintings by established artists tend to have higher quality canvases. You can check for wear and tear. Like this." He flipped to some pictures that showed canvases that looked pretty sad.

"Then there's signatures and inscriptions. Placement, style, color—if you know what you're looking for, they can tell you a lot."

"That sounds complicated." Like in too complicated for me to assimilate in one fell swoop.

Lars smiled. "That's why people hire appraisers." He turned a few more pages. "In general, a lot of older original paintings tend to have a glossy finish. If a painting is dull or too perfect, it might be a fake. But it also depends on the age of the painting and the medium used. And how it's been stored."

"Can you Google stuff about specific paintings?" Maybe Google could save me.

"You can. But databases are limited. And even when you know what to look for, it's hard to assess authenticity with the naked eye. Appraisers start with a sound knowledge base, but they also use a variety of technical tools too. Infrared imaging, chemical analysis, X-ray fluorescence."

"Are there any *obvious* signs suggesting that a painting has been faked?"

"Supposedly, a lot of fakes have brush bristles stuck to them." Lars laughed. "That always seemed strange to me. A good forger should use quality brushes and check for that kind of thing."

"These people that find valuable paintings in flea markets, how do they recognize whether a painting might be worth something if authenticity is so difficult to prove?"

"First of all, there aren't that many great finds. The few that occur get a lot of attention. And I personally think the original purchase in most of these cases is based on unfounded optimism and guesswork rather than insight. And some very good luck, of course. Also, a lot of times what's *discovered* is a known painting that disappeared. It may have been stolen or simply changed hands without anyone knowing about it at the time. There's a tendency to want to believe these lost paintings exist and that they will turn up eventually. Once one is reclaimed, it's sometimes years later before they are actually proven to be fake."

I ran my eyes across the rows of books on painting and painters. There was no way I was going to sound smart when engaging in conversation about art with anyone who had even a smidgeon of knowledge. I don't know what I was thinking.

Lars interrupted my silent disappointment. "Can you tell me why the appraisal you got is being questioned?"

"It's mainly about smell," I said. "The owner's daughter thinks she can smell fresh paint."

"I hate to tell you this, but that's mostly myth. I mean, some aromas linger, but for the most part, after even a week you won't smell paint."

"Really?"

"Yeah. After they're dry, certain oil-based pigments may give off a faint odor, but it's one few people can actually detect. Acrylics and watercolors also emit a faint scent. So, depending on the medium used, your client's daughter may not be smelling fresh paint but the chemicals in whatever paint was used."

"That's good to know."

"It could even have been the chemicals used to test authenticity. Or mold from the frame. Something like that. What did you think it smelled like?"

"I didn't sniff it."

"Well, you're wise to consider any anomalies. But if the smell is the only thing—. I mean, I can't say definitively that it's probably okay, but that would be my guess."

"That's a relief. But if I can't convince my client to let it go, is there an appraiser you would recommend?"

"You might want to check with one of the galleries for a recommendation.

But if your own appraiser thought it was authentic, well, what can I say?"

"Thank you. You've put my mind at rest."

As I drove back to the office, I kept trying to remember the tune and lyrics to "Faking It." The beat felt wrong, and all I could remember was "not really makin' it." But I kept trying. Kinda like I was doing with Desiree.

Chapter Ten: "No" To Team Building

I stopped for lunch on the way back. After a Happy Meal and a large Coke, I was more full than happy. And I had a big grease spot conspicuously located in the center of my stomach. At least I'd thought to flip my tie over my shoulder while I ate. Oh, oh, my tie was still there. And from the way Emma was staring at my stomach, it was too late to use it to cover the spot. "Lunch," I said unnecessarily as I started to pass by her desk.

Emma motioned for me to stop. For a moment I had the sinking feeling that she was going to whip out some stain remover and rub my stomach. And not for good luck. Instead, she handed me a piece of paper.

"You're lucky they still had some spaces," she said.

"Spaces?" I echoed, scanning the paper she'd handed me, but not really understanding what it was all about.

"For the off-site team-building session you are scheduled for on Monday."

"Off-site?" Off-site team building didn't sound too bad. Maybe I would be spending the day at a fancy hotel.

"The outdoor facility is at a park not too far away from here."

"Outdoor?" My eyes darted down the page.

"Yes, they provide a variety of activities. It's a popular session. You'll have a chance to get to know some of the other claims adjusters better as well as meeting employees from other departments—finance, marketing, risk management, HR…"

"What kinds of activities?" There were no specific activities listed on what she had handed to me, but I could feel the sweat beads gathering in the middle of my back.

"The usual."

"I don't know what the 'usual' is."

"Oh, this will be your first team-building session?" Her expression told me she wasn't surprised by that little fact.

"You're not going to tell me, are you?" The sweat was now starting to run. If she wouldn't tell me, that meant she thought it was something I wasn't going to like. And she was gloating.

"You'll find out soon enough." She dismissed me with a cat-eating-cream smile.

"Do I, ah, have a choice?" I asked, although I was certain of the answer.

"No, it's mandatory," she replied with a sly grin. Then she added, "Mr. Van Droop suggested I sign you up."

I wasn't sure I believed her. She might be doing it to get back at me for something. But until I knew more about the company's workshop requirements and what this particular one involved, I would pretend to go along.

Once back at my desk, I quickly Googled "outdoor team-building activities." A long list of things popped up. Maybe Monday's session would be a team *scavenger hunt*. That wouldn't be too bad. *Trust walks* didn't sound all that hard, but not very appealing. I don't like being blindfolded. Although I couldn't actually remember a time when I had been. But I definitely didn't like the idea. *Tug-of-wars* would be okay. I would have help. Or a bike *buildathon*. That almost sounded like fun, although I'm not particularly mechanically inclined.

Then my heart started racing at the thought that the session might involve *horses*. But Emma wouldn't know I was afraid of horses. And it had to be something she thought I would hate for her to be so pleased.

Then I found it—my gut said that she had signed me up for a *ropes course*. Climbing obstacles, low and high rope walks, zip line rides, rock climbing… all things physical and terrifying. I got on the phone and called HR. The sweet young thing that answered said that, yes, I was signed up for a Team Building session on Monday. I could hear the capital "T" and "B" in her voice.

"Is it mandatory?" I asked.

"It's strongly recommended by our executive team. And it looks as though your boss recommended this for you. It's not inexpensive; you should be pleased."

"But could I postpone doing it?" I heard the panic in my voice and hoped she didn't.

"You should do one team-building session a year, and it looks like you've been here a year."

"Are they all the same?"

"No, you're lucky. This is the first ropes course that has come up since last year. You'll have a great time."

At the phrase "ropes course," all the fight drained out of me, replaced by fear gripping my internal organs, twisting and grinding. I was fairly certain that I wouldn't have a great time, not even a lousy time; no, it would be a disaster.

I spent the rest of the afternoon worrying about what was going to happen on Monday, just three days away. It almost felt like a death sentence. At the very least, I would be subjected to some act of total humiliation in front of colleagues. I had visions of falling through space, getting tangled in a net halfway up a wood wall, or being so slow to make my way through an obstacle course that everyone would be standing there laughing when I got to the finish line...IF I made it to the finish line. I told myself that my colleagues weren't middle-grade boys seeking to build their own egos by putting others down. But I couldn't shake the feeling of dread.

I left about fifteen minutes early, stopping to tell Emma I had a pain in my stomach. "Maybe I'm coming down with the flu," I said, coughing into my hand to prove it.

"I'm certain you will be fine by Monday," she assured me pointedly. "If you need to take a sick day tomorrow, be sure you see a doctor." Her words were definitely a threat. I wondered if I could get some doctor to sign off on flu without actually examining me. Maybe I could find some frail or wimpy doctor who would understand my plight and give me a free pass. But by

Monday? I wondered if a note from Mother would do.

"I certainly hope so," I said, trying to sound like I meant it. Her eyes-wide stare told me she saw through my subterfuge. Damn. Even if I managed to come down with the flu, it was going to be a hard sell to legitimately avoid attending the session. Especially one recommended by my boss. Maybe I could get through it by taking a couple of shots of vodka at the start, with some extra reinforcement in a water bottle to take as needed. Combined with a few breath mints, I might be able to survive the day.

The way my current day was going, it should have come as no surprise to find I had a welcoming party at The Haven. On the sprint from parking spot to door, one badass crow targeted my umbrella with a poop bomb. I heard it splat and saw the crow speed upward and away, like a World War Two Luftwaffe pilot after dropping a load. For not the first time I wondered if shooting crows was illegal. Not that I thought I had a chance of actually hitting one with a gun, which I didn't have.

When I let myself in, it was clear that Wild Thing didn't like me coming home early. He circled me, hissing and making a sound like a ghost moaning. Then he went to stand by his dinner bowl, barring his teeth when I didn't immediately serve him. "It's too early," I told him. "Let me have a drink first, okay?" OMG, I was becoming the equivalent of a cat lady. Was there such a thing as a "cat-man"?

Admittedly, I had a little too much to drink with dinner and was feeling no pain when my mother called. She immediately accused me of being drunk.

"No way," I said. "I've had just a little something to ward off the flu."

"It isn't flu season."

"Then what should I come down with before Monday?" I needed to know.

"What's happening on Monday?"

"*TEAM BUILDING.*" I felt my stomach churn.

"That sounds like fun," she said.

"It's outdoors," I countered. "Do you know what that means?"

"Yes, I'm familiar with the term."

"You don't want your son to be injured, do you?"

"John, you need to get a grip. Maybe have a cup of black coffee. You're not making sense."

"They climb up things. Walk on ropes in the air. I don't wanna do that."

"You were never very athletic."

"Never," I agreed, although it pained me to say it out loud.

"But you will be all right. There must be people with all levels of physical agility participating. Young people, older people. People who work out regularly as well as those who don't. Like you. Maybe you'll meet a nice girl."

"Swinging from a rope?!"

"Maybe there will be a nice nurse there."

"Great. My own mother wants me to get injured so I can meet a nurse. Thanks a lot."

"John, have some coffee and call me back. I want to talk about tomorrow's dinner."

"That's what we're doing, talking."

"You need to be a bit more focused. We need a plan."

"I will probably be sick."

"John, I repeat, have some coffee and call me back." She hung up. My mother hung up on me. She must be taking lessons from Emma.

I lapsed into self-pity before falling asleep on the couch. And I didn't wake up until the phone rang. After I finally located it, I managed a slurred and sleepy "Hellloo."

"You didn't call me back," my mother complained. "We need to talk about tomorrow evening."

"I'm skipping tomorrow in anticipation of ending it all on Monday."

"Don't be ridiculous. You can skip work if you want, but you are coming to dinner tomorrow evening." She sounded like she did when I was young and she was telling me to eat my carrots.

"If I'm still alive."

"Oh, John. Why are you so worried about playing a few silly games with colleagues? Get over it. Everything will be fine."

"Promise?"

"Yes, I promise."

The entire world, including my mother, was against me.

"Now then, let's talk about tomorrow's dinner conversation. How do we get Bruno to agree to talk to Lonnie's neighbors about whether he was blackmailing them or not?"

My mind was foggy, but not so foggy that I didn't state the obvious: "No one is going to admit to being blackmailed. Especially by someone who's dead."

"Don't be silly. You don't ask the person whether they were being blackmailed. You get neighbors to talk about their neighbors, find out whether they think someone was misbehaving in a way Lonnie's drone could have discovered. Then you confront the potential criminals with the evidence."

"But there is no evidence. It was stolen."

"You bluff then. I know you know how to do that."

There was no arguing with her; she was determined to make this happen. It was up to Bruno to say "no." It wasn't *his* mother, after all.

I dozed off while talking to Mother and woke up when I dropped the phone. She had already hung up.

Suddenly Wild Thing jumped up on the coach and settled in near my feet. Was he sensing I wasn't long for this world and therefore there was no use plaguing me anymore? Maybe the crows would be nice for the next couple of days too.

Chapter Eleven: Two Down

Friday morning, the truce with Wild Thing was apparently over. He swatted me awake, fortunately with claws retracted. But I had the distinct impression that I was only one swat away from being scratched. Maybe it was his hangover remedy. As long as he kept his claws in, it beat drinking some concoction with a raw egg in it. Nevertheless, I made a note to make sure that, in the future, my door was shut when I went to bed.

"Just this once," I told him as I dragged myself out of bed, my head pounding in protest. "In the future, you get your breakfast *after* I'm up and dressed and have a cup of coffee in hand. Do you understand?"

Instead of mewing like most kittens, he hissed like an angry serpent. I was afraid to think of how he would communicate when he was older.

Wild Thing ate while I made myself a cup of coffee. As soon as he'd licked his bowl to retrieve every tiny scrap of food, Wild Thing disappeared. There aren't many hiding places on a houseboat, so I worried about where he spent his days. He obviously didn't "hang out" on his scratching post tree like the clerk had assured me he would. He preferred "hiding out." But until I found him alternative living accommodations, I was stuck. And so was he.

I popped a couple of aspirins and washed them down with the rest of my coffee. No time for breakfast; I was running late.

The umbrella was on the deck where I'd left it, but I'd forgotten to clean the crow poo off of it. A nasty-looking chunk fell on my porch as I popped the umbrella open. Then I came close to stepping in the crust-on-the-outside and soft-on-the-inside blob as I whirled the umbrella around to protect myself from an aerial attack. It turned out to be a seagull and not a crow swooping by. The quick defensive movement intensified the throbbing in my temples. Was the seagull in league with the crows? Was he on his way to warn them that I was coming?

Holding the umbrella at ready, I didn't even slow down as I hurried past my landlord, who was once again trimming some bushes in front of his house. He definitely needed more yard. Or more plants that needed care.

"What did you do to them?" he yelled after me as the crows tag teamed me on the race to my car.

Half way to the office I realized I would need more than two aspirin to get me through the day, so I made a quick stop at a local pharmacy and bought a 500-tablet bottle. That seemed like more than enough to cover all of the hangovers in my future. And hopefully enough for the injuries I was sure to incur on Monday.

By the time I got to the office, I truly didn't feel good. But I could hardly say anything to Emma about it, because if she took a good look at my bloodshot eyes, she might guess it was a hangover and not the flu. I nodded as I rushed past her, trying to hide the small sack with the Pill Party's bold orange logo on the side. Perhaps I should have put the aspirin container in my pocket.

Since I hadn't reported back to Desiree to tell her what I had learned from Lars, I decided to call her before I did anything else. At first her voice was all honey and spice, and I immediately felt better. But when I told her that based on what I had learned that I was satisfied with Carla's appraisal, the honey lost its sweetness. It became almost as acidic as the double espresso I was craving.

"In some ways, it's good news," I said. "The appraisal value is actually more than your sister thought the painting was worth."

"Savannah is so certain," she said, as if that was all the proof anyone should need.

"The artist who advised me really seemed to know what he was talking about," I said.

"You may be right. But I'd like to hear it directly from him. Can you make that happen?"

I wasn't in a fighting mood. Especially if it meant I'd be seeing Desiree again. A dying man's last wish. "I can meet you at his workshop at 11:00."

"Email me the address, and I'll be there."

When I called, Lars didn't answer, but his voicemail said his hours were from 10:00 am to 4:00 pm daily, so I left him a message to let him know when to expect us. He was probably totally engrossed in a painting or had gone to his house for a cup of coffee or a rest break.

Between 9:00 and 10:15, I took four more aspirin, washed them down with several cups of strong coffee, and made more than my usual number of trips to the restroom. When the time came to depart, I tried to get past Emma without explaining where I was going by walking fast and not giving her eye contact. No such luck. She waved me to a stop and asked where I was going. I paused long enough to admit I was tying up some loose ends on the Winslow case. Before she could ask for details, I looked at my watch, murmured something about not wanting to be late, and hurried off. Not that I would know if I was late or not any time soon—my watch had stopped. It apparently needed a new battery. Last time I'd needed a battery, I'd damaged the watch while trying to get the back off and had to buy a new one. I hoped this watch was easier to put batteries in.

Desiree was standing beside a bright red sports car looking peeved when I pulled up. "You're late," she said, without so much as a drop of honey in her tone. "And what's with the yellow car?"

"My watch quit on me," I said. "And I like yellow."

Her eyes flicked over Bee. "Yellow is good for kitchen walls. Well, let's go talk to this artist you've found."

We walked around back to his workshop. The door was open slightly. I knocked and called out his name. There was no answer.

"Did you make an appointment?" she asked.

"I called and left a message. His hours are 10 to 4. Maybe he just stepped out for a few minutes. Or he's in his house getting something to eat."

"Well, let's check out his studio first." She pushed open the door and went inside. There was no one there. The row of paintings on the floor and the ones on the wall looked like the same ones as before, but I couldn't swear to it. Everything else looked the same, too.

Desiree walked around, stopping every few feet to study a painting, and I followed, hoping Lars would magically appear soon. "He's pretty good," Desiree said.

"I'm thinking of having him do a portrait of my mother," I said.

"That's nice."

"As a surprise. He says he can do it from a photo." There was something nagging at the back of my mind. When I talked with Mother last night, had I let slip the bit about asking Lars to paint her picture? Nah, I wouldn't have done that...would I?

"What's in back?"

"He said it was for supplies."

She went over and opened the door, stopping at the entrance. I peeked around her. "Not many supplies," she said.

The room had a table, some paints, and a few blank canvases propped against the wall. The shelves were empty. Why had he told me the room was for supplies if there was next to nothing in it?

We took one more swing around the paintings in the outer room before Desiree suggested we go see if he was at his house.

Since we were already in the back yard, we knocked on his back door instead of going around front. There was no answer. Desiree started peeking in the windows. "Can't see much," she said.

"I'm not sure you should be doing that. I mean, what if he's, ah, naked?"

"I've seen naked men before."

Probably fit specimens who would excel at ropes training, I couldn't help thinking. "Let's try the front door."

We worked our way around to the front, Desiree looking in each window we passed. "He has a lot of art on the walls. They look like his work."

"He told me he hangs up paintings in his house when he can't sell them."

"What a shame—I really like some of these."

"He seems really savvy, about painting and about marketing. He said there's a ton of competition though."

There was no answer at the front door either. I called his phone but didn't get an answer.

"Well, I would prefer talking to him, but I like what I've seen. And you got a recommendation for him from a collector, right?"

"Right." She didn't need to know that the "collector" was my predecessor.

"Okay, I'll break the bad news to Savannah. See what she wants to do."

"Thank you." She headed for her car. "Ah, Desiree," I called after her, hurrying to catch up, ignoring the faint throbbing in my head. All those aspirin and that headache were still lurking, threatening to take over my entire head. "Since you drove all the way out here for nothing, could I make up for it by buying you lunch?" I actually surprised myself. It was a bold move on my part. Having only two days left before my team-building demise left me with a "what the hell" approach to living.

"That's nice of you, but I don't eat lunch. Too many calories."

"Okay." *If at first, you don't succeed, give up.* Was that on a Demotivators Calendar in the office? Perhaps when it came to Desiree, it might be good advice. Besides, who wants to be with a woman who doesn't eat lunch?

"How'd it go?" Emma asked as I once again tried and failed to slip past without having to provide any details.

"I think it's settled," I said, slowing but not stopping.

As soon as I sat down at my desk, I remembered that my watch wasn't working. I know most people use their cell phones to tell time these days, but I like the convenience of glancing at my wrist for the time. I got out a paperclip, straightened it, and tried to take the back off so I could see what kind of battery I needed. That didn't work. I tried using the narrow blade on my scissors, but that didn't work either. Nor did my fingernails or the clip on one of my pens. At that point, if I'd had a hammer, I would have smashed it.

I was feeling so low and so desperate that I went to see if Emma had a tool that would work on my watch.

"Let me see it," she said. I obediently handed my watch over. "I think all you need to do is…" She took out a paper clip and straightened it just like I had. Then she popped the back off on her first try.

"Thank you. You're really good at that," I said.

"These batteries are hard to find." She was peering at the tiny numbers on the bottom of the teensy disk. "You will probably have to order it online."

"Thanks," I said again. "I'll do that."

I took the watch back to my office and tried to read the numbers but failed. Maybe with a magnifying glass…which I didn't have. Of course, I could have asked Emma for her help again. Or, I could buy a magnifying glass. Or I could buy a new watch on my way home. I decided on the latter. I would need a watch on Monday to record my life on earth ticking away.

Just when I thought things couldn't get any worse, Carla came storming into my office. "You back-stabbing little dweeb," she said loudly. She hadn't closed the door, so I was fairly certain Emma was able to hear Carla's tongue-lashing.

"What did I do?"

She leaned over my desk until her narrow nose was inches from my face. "You know what you did. You went behind my back to challenge my appraisal of the Winslow paintings."

"No, I didn't."

"Don't add lies on top of everything else."

"I was just trying to satisfy our client."

"That wasn't what you were trying to do. You were trying to show me up. Well, it won't do you any good, because I was right. So, challenge away. You'll be sorry." She turned around, pausing in the doorway with one final volley: "And don't expect me to do any appraisals for you in the future. Ever again."

Before I could defend myself, she was gone.

It seemed to me that Carla shouldn't have been all that upset. Particularly not at the name-calling level. After all, it was the client who had asked for a second opinion. The request hadn't originated with me. And Lars had basically dismissed the need for a second opinion. Even the follow-up visit to his studio with Desiree had turned out okay. Carla hadn't been harmed in any way. One thing puzzled me, though—who had told Carla that I was getting a second opinion? No one but Desiree knew. Unless Emma had overheard something. But even disliking me as much as she did, why would Emma have told Carla?

One thing for sure—that was the second relationship that had ended abruptly, and badly, in a single day. A record even for me.

Chapter Twelve: Dinner Is Served

Wild Thing was watching TV when I got home. At least, that's what I thought at first. Did he know how to use the remote? Then I saw Valerie stretched out on the couch next to him. Her thin legs were encased in knee socks covered with cats of various shapes and colors. She glanced over at me for a second before turning back to the screen. There was a lot of fighting going on, people shooting at people, blood dripping from bodies and pooling next to bullet wounds and crushed body parts.

"Valerie. Valerie." I had to say her name twice for her to hit pause. "This does not look like something you should be watching with Wild Thing."

"He's okay with it."

"That isn't what I meant."

"My dad won't let me watch things like this at home."

"Then you shouldn't be watching them here, either."

"Why not? It's not real. I mean, they're all stunt people, and the blood and severed heads and limbs are fake."

That seemed pretty cynical for an eight-year-old. And her use of the word "severed" was both impressive and scary. "But if your dad finds out, he won't let you come by and visit Wild Thing." The implicit message was that Wild Thing would then go to "the farm."

She flicked off the TV and sat up. "I suppose you're right. But I still don't see why adults get so upset about a few people getting whacked."

"Whacked?"

"You know, smoked, taking a dirt nap, light's out, food for worms…"

"Stop, I get the idea." I almost asked where she learned that kind of language, then realized it was probably from my TV. "I wouldn't talk like that around your father if I were you."

She got up. One knee sock started to droop, and she had to tug it back into place. "I'm not stupid."

"Well, you'd better leave now anyway. I have to get ready; I'm going out to dinner."

"Do you have a date?"

"No, not exactly."

"It's a yes or no question."

"Then no. A friend and I are having dinner with my mother."

"You need a girlfriend," she said as she headed for the door. "That's what your mother says."

"When did you talk to my mother?"

"When she called earlier to remind you to bring wine tonight."

"You answered my phone and took a message from my mother?"

"Yeah. That's how I knew you didn't have a date."

With that, she left. A diabolical little girl who sounded much older than she actually was and someone I was entrusting with a key to my houseboat. What was I thinking?!

Wild Thing yowled and butted his head against my leg before pointedly walking over to his food dish. "Didn't she feed you?" He looked back at me with a "let's get on with this" glare. Oh well, at least he seemed calm. I served him his dinner and went to take a shower. I needed to hurry if I wanted to stop for wine and still be on time.

Bruno was already there when I arrived. He and my mother were chuckling about something and didn't even say hello when I joined them in the kitchen with a bottle of red and a six-pack. Bruno kept right on telling Mother a story that involved two parrots, a farmer, and a city visitor. Mother kept interrupting with guffaws and chortles. Bruno grabbed a bottle of beer, tried to twist the cap off, and handed it back for me to open. It wasn't a screw cap. I wished I could have struck it on a corner of a table to remove the cap like

I'd seen done in movies. Instead, I rummaged through several drawers until I found a bottle opener. Redwing Casino was etched on the top. I popped off the cap, spilling some foam on the table, and handed it to him.

Mother took time out to look at the spill and motion for me to clean it up.

During the clean-up, I missed the point of the story. But when Bruno delivered the punchline, and the two roared with laughter, I laughed too, and almost as heartily.

Mother and Bruno stopped laughing and turned to me. "What's so funny?" Bruno asked.

"Your story about—"

"You didn't even hear the set-up," Bruno complained.

"Well, laughter is contagious. I couldn't help myself."

Mother shook her head, her way of indicating that I was beyond help. Then she opened the wine with an efficiency that suggested she knew what she was doing and poured herself a hefty amount.

"Sorry," I said, although I wasn't sure what I had to be sorry for—missing the first part of his joke or laughing at a punchline I didn't understand. It wasn't the first time I'd done that.

We made small talk for a few minutes, then Mother announced that dinner was served. It wasn't long before food was on the table, and we were all digging in.

Mother's timing was perfect. Bruno had just forked a large hunk of meatloaf into his mouth when she brought up the real purpose behind her dinner invitation. "Bruno, you need to look into Lonnie Weller's death," she said with conviction.

There was a slight pause while Mother and I watched him chew, then swallow. "This is really good," he said. I could have told him that no amount of flattery was going to distract Mother from her objective. Like a salmon swimming upstream to spawn, nothing short of death was going to stop her.

Mother didn't say anything; she just sat there staring at him.

"Really good. Isn't it, John?" He was trying to rope me into the war of wills, but we both knew it wasn't going to dissuade her.

"Really good, yeah." I took another bite, chewing slowly while I watched the drama unfolding at our dinner table.

Mother still didn't say anything. She's good at letting pressure build.

Bruno put his fork down in defeat. "Okay, what do you want me to do?"

That was her cue; she didn't miss a beat. "I've given it some thought, and I want you to interview neighbors, find out who Lonnie was spying on. Then prove he was murdered."

"That's all?"

"One thing leads to another."

"His death has been ruled an accident."

"But we all know it wasn't."

"And how do *we* all *know* that?"

"Come on, Bruno, are you seriously saying you believe he simply slipped over the edge?"

"Even if I don't buy it completely, it isn't my case."

"But you could still poke around a little, couldn't you?"

"Not without getting permission."

"So, get permission. And take John with you."

Bruno raised his eyebrows and hands simultaneously, as if he was a puppet and they were connected by strings. It was a classic "Why would I do that?" gesture.

"Mother, I can't go around interviewing neighbors with a cop," I said, trying to offer Bruno some support against Mother's request in a backhanded sort of way.

"He's not a 'cop,' he's a Sergeant."

I felt the ground beneath my arguments slipping away, like the top of the cliff under Lonnie's feet. Bruno might not want to, but he would somehow get the person in charge of the case to agree to let him ask neighbors a few questions, and I would end up spending non-work time making a pointless effort to get at some truth that might not even be there.

Bruno and I exchanged looks and silently admitted that we'd lost the battle of wills. "What's for dessert?" he asked.

Dessert was Bruno's favorite—red velvet cake with fudge frosting. Mother was going all out to seal the deal.

Just before we'd finished seconds of cake, I asked Mother if she had a picture of herself that I could borrow."

"For that portrait you're going to have done?"

Apparently, my fears about the other night were justified: I'd blabbed about the portrait. "It was going to be a surprise," I said.

"Then you shouldn't have said anything to me about it." She stood up, her gray curls bouncing with energy. "I put aside a couple of pictures that I think might be good for it. Be right back."

"You're having a portrait done of your mother?" Bruno asked. I nodded. "That's really nice."

"It was supposed to be a surprise," I repeated.

"Then why did you tell her about it?" Bruno sounded sincerely confused.

"Too much to drink," I admitted.

"Ah."

Mother returned with an envelope and handed it to me. "How long will it take?"

"It depends." I didn't want to admit I hadn't been able to get in touch with Lars for several days. "I'll let you know."

"If you want me to, I can act surprised when you give it to me." She and Bruno laughed. I didn't.

Bruno and I left together. Full of good food but also aware that we had been bribed and manipulated.

"Let's get it out of the way tomorrow," Bruno said. "People are usually home on weekends, and we may not feel like interviewing anyone on Sunday if your poker game tomorrow night is anything like ones in the past."

"This time, I'm going to win," I said to distinguish it from past game nights.

"Who's coming?"

"The usuals plus someone from work who mentioned he liked to play poker."

"Is he a good player?"

"I didn't ask for his gaming history or make him take a test. But he seems nice enough."

"We need some fresh blood."

"By fresh blood, you mean someone who may lose more than he wins?"

"Like you."

"Not this time." I was determined to make what could be my "last" poker game profitable. Although if I wasn't around after Monday to enjoy my winnings, I wasn't sure why I cared.

Chapter Thirteen: Let's Play

Saturday morning I met Bruno at a diner near where the Winslows and the Wellers lived. We both ordered a full stack of pancakes with bacon and extra syrup in an attempt to fortify ourselves for the task ahead. Neither of us was pleased with the situation, but we had no choice. Saying "no" to my mother just wasn't an option. For me, because I'm her son. For Bruno, deep down, he's a softie with a special soft spot for my mother. Not that he lets it show most of the time.

"So, what did you tell your boss about what we're doing today?" I asked.

"You've got a drool of syrup on your left cheek."

My napkin had fallen on the floor, so I wiped it with a finger. "So…?

"I told them I was accompanying a claims adjuster doing some follow-up that might be a bit dicey under the circumstances."

"What 'circumstances'?"

"I acknowledged it was a closed case but explained that there were rumors that the *accident* might have been a murder. And that you were determined to ask questions that could easily get you into trouble."

"And that did it? He was okay with you possibly stepping on another team's toes to help out a claims adjuster doing some follow-up?" I'd been hoping we'd be forced to back off.

"Actually, he said something like, 'If you want to waste your day off chasing shadows, go for it. Just don't upset anyone in the community by hinting that the death might be anything other than an accident.'"

"Well, that's more like it. But I can't imagine we'll ruffle any feathers. I mean, we don't actually expect to uncover any criminal acts or get confrontational with any suspects…do we?" I hoped he and I were on the same page.

"One thing I've learned over the years is that you never know what you might find if you ask the right questions. No, make that *two* things I've learned—your mother's instincts are often right on. That's partly why I agreed to do this."

"She does have good instincts—usually. But this time I think she's off base. She's seen a few spy movies where drones were used, but that doesn't prove anything in this instance. In my opinion, Lonnie was little more than a mischievous hobbyist. Possibly a bit of a letch."

"You may be right, but if we don't canvass the neighborhood, we'll never hear the end of it. And your mother has always been a human lie detector where you're concerned, so we can't just say we did it; we have to actually do it." Bruno pushed away his empty plate.

"You aren't so good at lying to her either," I pointed out.

"Hey, I haven't tried since we were kids."

"Because you know she'll catch you. Remember one Halloween when we toilet papered old man Crowley's house?"

"Yeah, we would have gotten away with it if your mother hadn't suspected us. I can still remember her staring me down."

We were both quiet a moment, savoring memories of the mischief we got into as kids. Then I stood up. "Okay, let's do it."

"You pay," Bruno said. "She's your mother."

We took both cars so we could go our separate ways once we'd questioned enough neighbors to satisfy Mother. I was thoroughly convinced we wouldn't discover anything significant. You'd need to do more than ask a few questions to uncover deep, dark secrets. The kinds of things worth murdering someone for. Knowing Lonnie had spied on his neighbors was a start, but without something more specific, it seemed to me that we were destined to fail. Maybe if we had access to an FBI database to identify potential suspects in advance, or if we'd discovered the actual drone photos Lonnie took, then, maybe. But for this hit-and-miss assignment, the highlight was probably breakfast.

We parked at the end of the block and approached the first house together. "Hey, remember the year in middle school when we had to sell nuts to raise money for new band uniforms?" I said.

"I hated it."

"Me too."

"But we did it."

"Together."

"Let's hope this turns out better than that did." After spending most of our spare time for months selling nuts, we decided the new uniforms made us look stupid, like British guards at the Queen's palace. Not something to attract girls, which, at the time, was a primary interest. So, we'd both quit band. *Not* being in band hadn't helped me win any girlfriends either, but in high school Bruno started playing football. That made *him* popular with all the girls.

At the first few houses, we tried a fairly innocuous approach, attempting to establish a reason for being there in the first place without asking anything inflammatory. Bruno introduced us, said something vague about following up on a complaint, then asked: "One of your neighbors spent a lot of time surveilling the neighborhood with his drones—any idea what he was looking for?" In response, we got a variety of answers, none of them helpful: *"Nope, no idea." "I didn't really pay any attention, but it irritated my dog." "He was a nice kid. Just having a bit of fun."*

The most passionate response we got admitted some animosity toward Lonnie: *"Those damn drones were always hovering overhead. I warned him to keep them away from me."* We might have considered the implicit threat something to follow up on, but the man was at least in his late 80s, thin enough to be called "string bean," wrinkled like a raisin and bent over like a curved zucchini—a veritable garden of decrepitude. Not a likely suspect, given the location and nature of the incident.

It didn't take many awkward and unproductive interviews and houses where no one was home—or at least not answering—before we started thinking about a long lunch. "One more," Bruno said. "Then let's take a break."

"You don't think Mother will ask for the number of neighbors we interviewed, do you?"

"Let's plan on telling her how many houses we stop at—if you can avoid not blurting out something about people not being at home."

"She'll know I'm hiding something."

Bruno sighed. "Okay. Let's get on with it."

Our next stop was a small house across the street from where we'd started. There were lots of flowers in the yard in well-tended flower beds. The house, however, needed some maintenance work. There were several tiny trees growing out of the gutters along the moss-covered roof, and the paint on the handrails leading to the front door was peeling, an extreme case of paint eczema sans the itching. The older woman who answered just as we were about to give up was the first person to suggest that Lonnie might have been crossing the line with his drone activities. "Some evenings, I would see one of them lingering near the back windows in the Gillmor house," she said.

"Any idea why?"

"Well, I don't like to tell tales…" When someone says that, you always know they have something juicy to share…with a little prompting. In this instance, all we had to do was remain silent a few seconds. "But it was usually when Mr. Gillmor's car wasn't in the driveway. I wouldn't have noticed, except her visitor always parks in front of my house rather than theirs."

"Do you know the identity of the visitor?" Bruno asked.

"All I know is that he is a man who visits Mrs. Gillmor until the early hours and only when her husband isn't home." She quickly added, "I'm a light sleeper. I hear him start up his car when he takes off."

We thanked her for the information and left.

"Well," I said to Bruno, "…maybe Mother's instincts were right, after all. Lonnie peeked in windows with his drones, and he apparently had some notion about which windows had the best show."

"It all depends on why he was doing it—to get his jollies or to blackmail someone."

"Maybe both. But even if we find other neighbors who confirm *what* he was doing, that won't tell us whether the people he was spying on knew what was going on. And if they did, I doubt they're going to confess to being blackmailed."

"At least now we have a lead. At some point we'll have to talk to Mrs. Gillmor."

"Let's interview a few more neighbors first. See what they have to say."

The next neighbor we talked to reinforced the notion that Lonnie was getting his jollies with his drone spying. "I told him to quit it, or I would report him to the police. But he thought it was funny. Said it was like watching a Rom Com. Every time my daughter returned from a date, that drone would be there. If they stayed in the car, it peered in at them. If they waited to kiss goodnight on the doorstep, it was right there watching. Rom Com—harumph. An invasion of privacy is what it was."

Still another neighbor complained that she couldn't sunbathe in her own back yard without some drone overhead. "He was a pervert," she said.

"Well," I said as we walked to the next house. "I guess he was definitely using the drone to fulfill sexual fantasies."

"A lot of guys in his age range check out online porn. He just used a different medium."

"Well, it sounds as though he either wasn't very good at hiding what he was doing or enjoyed irritating the people he was watching."

There was loud music coming from a square beige house on the corner. When we knocked, the music was turned down, and a dog started barking. "Quiet Brute," a male voice commanded. Bruno and I glanced uneasily at each other. "Brute?" I whispered. I was ready to make a run for it when a clean-cut teenager wearing trendy clothes and a teen swagger answered the door alongside a tail-wagging chihuahua. Really?

It didn't take long for the teenager to admit—off the record, that Lonnie caught him smoking weed with a group of friends behind their garage. "He said he'd show my parents if I didn't give him fifty bucks."

"And did you?"

"I would have been grounded for a month, so yeah, I gave him the money. And I made him show me that he'd deleted the pictures he took. Although I was worried about backup photos."

"Did he ask you for money after that first time?"

"No, I think he believed me when I said I'd beat the crap out of him if there was a next time."

"You shouldn't be threatening anyone with violence," Bruno said.

"I wouldn't have done it. I just needed him to believe I would."

Bruno gave him a hard glare. "Okay, your secret is safe…for now." The implicit message was that he'd better not get in any trouble, or Bruno's promise of confidentiality was moot.

"I get it," he said. "And I feel bad about Lonnie's accident. I didn't like him, but that was a nasty way to go."

We decided a lunch break was in order. On the way to a local café, we discussed what we had learned. First, Lonnie was definitely using the drone to spy on his neighbors. Some of it may have been innocent enough. I mean, who wouldn't want to check out a shapely sunbather? But in at least one instance that we knew of, he had actually exchanged photos for money. Neither of us thought the kid caught smoking weed was a serious candidate for pushing Lonnie to his death. But the fact that Lonnie had blackmailed him meant he could have been blackmailing others in the neighborhood. And maybe someone had a bigger secret to hide. Like being an adulteress.

The restaurant was busy, but we were served quickly. Bruno took a huge bite of his hamburger, a tiny piece of onion dripping with sauce not quite captured by his mouth. It fortunately landed on his plate. My fish and chips were easier to eat while carrying on a conversation.

"Any chance the police will catch up with the thieves?" I asked after swallowing a French fry.

"Darfle," Bruno said while chewing.

"Darfle?" I asked.

Bruno swallowed. "Right."

"What does 'darfle' mean?"

"You weren't listening. I said it was *doubtful*. If it hasn't happened yet, it's not going to happen."

"Then we'll never see what he filmed."

"It's darfle," Bruno said with a grin before taking another huge bite.

"Thzzgd."

"I got that—your hamburger is good." He nodded.

"So, without proof, knowing Lonnie was spying on people in the neighborhood doesn't do us much good."

Bruno shook his head in agreement.

"I guess we knew that when we started. But it's disappointing to think that there might actually have been evidence to suggest who wanted him eliminated."

"I can tell the lead on the case, but with the case closed, and without more to go on..."

"Mother will have to be satisfied knowing that she could be right. And maybe I can convince her that poking around will only make it worse for Lonnie's parents."

"Just don't let her go snooping around on her own."

"She will probably insist on talking to the woman who's been having the affair. If we don't, that is."

"You're right—not a good idea. Okay, we can make one more stop before we call it quits. But then I'm through."

When Mrs. Gillmor answered the door, we could hear young kids playing in the background, so Bruno asked if she would step outside for a minute to answer a couple of questions. She only hesitated briefly. "I can't leave the kids alone for long," she said.

We had decided on the direct approach, so Bruno quickly highlighted what we knew about Lonnie's use of the drone to spy on her. She looked so sincerely shocked that I was immediately convinced of her innocence. At least in connection with Lonnie's death. "No," she said. "I can't believe he'd do that."

"He did," Bruno said. "Sorry."

"But he seemed so nice. He used to help me carry in groceries. And he showed my oldest how to fly a drone."

"Did he ever mention anything about your, ah, affair?"

At first she denied that she was having an affair, then she broke down and confessed, all teary-eyed, and begged us not to tell her husband. "It just happened. My husband's away a lot, and, oh, I realize there's no excuse for what I've done. But please don't tell my husband. It would ruin my marriage."

I felt like pointing out that *she* was already ruining her marriage by having an affair, but I know there are always two sides in situations like this. At least, that's what my mother says.

Bruno had apparently come to the same conclusion about her culpability. "I don't see any reason at this time why we will need to talk to anyone else about this." He paused and leaned toward her, an intimidating presence, done intentionally, I guessed. "You swear Lonnie wasn't blackmailing you to keep your secret?"

Again, she looked shocked. This time, the red faded, leaving her face almost true white. "No, OMG, no," she said.

Bruno didn't press. Instead, he said, "If you think of anyone else Lonnie might have been spying on, please let me know." He gave her his card. "And don't tell anyone we asked about blackmail. If you do, then I can't guarantee that your, ah, secret won't get out. Do we have an understanding?"

She nodded and thanked both of us profusely for our discretion before disappearing back inside her happy home.

"Sad," I said to Bruno.

"You never know what goes on behind closed doors," Bruno said.

"Unless you have a drone to look inside."

"You got the same impression as me, didn't you?"

"I think we took her totally by surprise. If not, she could win an Oscar. Or at least a Golden Globe."

Bruno was silent for a moment. "I don't think I'm going to include any names on my report. Simply comment that he was doing some spying on sunbathers, kids making out and underage kids smoking. If they want to canvass the neighborhood looking for something to support a murder charge, they are welcome to try."

"Is that why you told her not to mention to anyone that we asked about blackmail?"

"In part. But if Lonnie *was* pushed over the edge by someone he was trying to extort money from, then whoever did it might not take kindly to anyone bringing up the topic."

"It was for her protection then."

"Best to keep her out of it. Assuming she's innocent, of course."

"I bet she breaks it off."

"I would hope so—for her kids' sake."

The interviews at an end, Bruno said he'd call Mother tomorrow and report so I didn't have to deal with it. He probably thought it would be easier for her to push back on me, and he was of course right. It was better for both of us if he handled it.

I headed home to get my place ready for the poker game, stopping on the way to load up on snacks and drinks. I was hoping to earn back what I was spending by winning a few hands.

No one from The Haven was invited to the poker party. There were no other single men in the houseboat community, and my poker parties were for single men only. If there is a name for excluding married men from something, I don't know what it is. But my reason for the rule was that I didn't want to cause problems between married couples by having a spouse come home drunk and with an empty wallet. Nor was I being intentionally sexist by excluding women; I simply didn't know any women who liked playing poker while chugging beers all evening.

Wally Conklin was the first to arrive. He's an insurance agent from a large downtown firm. At one time, I suspected him of murder, but I'm glad he wasn't guilty—he's the only player who loses as frequently as I do. Next came Milton Davenport, an underwriter from a firm specializing in malpractice cases, a business acquaintance I have lunch with from time to time. He's fairly conservative, but he likes to drink and play poker. Bruno showed up on Milton's heels with a former football buddy, Louie, a mediocre poker player who looks like a football player who quit exercising about ten years ago. Jack, a claims adjuster from the office, was right behind them. Jack was the only new guy. We'd got to talking one day in the break room at work and he'd told me he liked to play poker and that he was divorced. The right combination for our little group. Last to arrive was a kinda friend of mine from high school. I say "kinda" cuz I never liked Tony very much, but our paths have a way of continuing to cross. Currently, he works for a rival insurance agency, so we have jobs in common. That's partly how he ended up as one of the "regulars."

Everyone got something to drink and grabbed a plateful of snacks while I introduced Jack all round. Then we sat down to play. It was party time.

I lost at first. It wasn't intentional, but it seemed like the kind of thing a good host should do. Unfortunately, I continued to lose for the rest of the evening. At least, I assume I did. I also had a little too much to drink, so some of what happened was a bit fuzzy. I remember Jack and Tony complaining about their respective jobs and someone insisting they should quit rather than put up with shit. I also remember Wally saying something about a murder of crows threatening him when he parked. And I remember Bruno and Jack being locked in a two-man contest of wills several times while the rest of us drank and watched. Too much drinking for me, so the watching was done in a half stupor.

Wild Thing had done a lot of chuffing and growling when my guests first started arriving. Jack tried to make friends, and Wild Thing swiped his outstretched hand with claws out. After that, everyone kidded me about having a vicious cat. At some point, they started calling me a cat-chelor. That's apparently someone who has a cat instead of a girlfriend. It didn't help when I tried to explain that Wild Thing was a gift from my mother.

It was getting late, and we were all a bit drunk when someone, Tony, I think, said that I needed a girlfriend instead of a cat. Wild Thing had come in during the last hand and jumped on the table, messing everything up as we tried to remove him. I thought I heard him snickering as he leapt over my shoulder and ran off. I was pretty upset. It was the first hand I'd had a chance of winning.

There was another showdown between Bruno and Jack, and while we were waiting for them to finish, I vaguely remember someone suggesting they put up a profile of me on some dating app. Louie snapped a picture that didn't look half bad. Of course, the other half looked kinda drunk. When they started working on my profile, I assumed it was a joke, a way to pass the time until either Bruno or Jack won the pot, so I stayed out of it and let them have their fun. Besides, I wasn't feeling that great, and my lens on the world was a bit foggy.

I vaguely remember someone mentioning my obsession with drones. I must have said something about Lonnie's drones, or maybe Bruno had. I thought about telling them I didn't really have any interest in drones, but my tongue was numb, and before I could speak up, I forgot what I was going to say.

Then Wally made a snide comment about how much I loved Wild Thing, and they all started laughing. The next thing I knew, the four men started hunting for Wild Thing, calling "Here, kitty, kitty. We want to take your picture." There were several Wild Thing sightings—someone would shout his name, and everyone would go tripping off after him. But Wild Thing was sober and always managed to elude his pursuers. "We need to put you online with Johnnie. Here, pretty kitty." I hate to think what might have happened if they'd cornered him. Several drunken men versus a Wild Thing with sharp claws—it was no contest.

When we ran out of beer, everyone started complaining. About no more beer. About losing. About their love lives. About money. About their relatives. About their work. It was the slow process of losing the euphoria that comes from a drinking high and believing you are going to win big time before reality slowly descends like a cold snowfall.

Then, the complaints got more specific.

"Everyone wants to do away with cops," Bruno said. "Defund us."

"The company doesn't even give us good health insurance," Louie whined.

"You're lucky to have *any* health insurance," Tony said.

"Mine's good," Milton said. "But my boss sucks."

"I had a sucky boss," Wally said. "But someone stabbed her."

There were murmurs of approval as if that was a good way to get rid of someone you didn't like at work.

"I'm glad to have a job," I said. My voice sounded like I was underwater, and everyone stopped talking. I was just sober enough to realize I'd violated a rule of poker-night conversation. When the liquor runs out, the losers are unhappy, and complaints replace card playing. "But I have a nosy, uptight office manager," I hastily added, if slurring my comment a little.

"You're lucky you don't have an ex-wife who thinks you should send your kids to private schools," Jack said.

"Yeah," Tony said. "My ex thinks every penny I earn should go to her to support the kids she won't let me see more than a couple times a month."

"The CEO makes tons more than I do, and all he does is go out to lunch with other CEOs and direct work from on high." Jack's complaint was received with some derisive comments about the wealthy, accompanied by a few confirming swear words. Tony badmouthing insurance company executives in particular.

It was time to call it a night. As the door closed behind the last poker buddy, I had a momentary flash of sobriety when noticing the mess I would have to clean up tomorrow. Their boisterous departure echoed like tympani clanging as they stumbled and shouted back and forth as if they'd suffered hearing losses from the evening's activities. My landlord would probably complain tomorrow about the racket. And I had no doubt Wild Thing was unhappy about the entire evening. Unhappier than usual, that is.

In addition, Jack had won the last big jackpot and made a show of piling up his money, so none of my regulars were going to thank me for inviting him. Especially Bruno, who had lost big on the final hand and was walking funny when he left. He hadn't wanted to sit on a donut in front of the guys, so his hemorrhoids were no doubt acting up. I sincerely hoped no one wanted a rematch any time soon. I knew I couldn't afford one.

Chapter Fourteen: Cat-chelor

I woke up to pounding. In my head, and, as I finally realized, on my door. Then I heard my landlord yelling, "Come get that damn cat of yours, or I'll shoot him."

Groaning, I rolled out of bed and managed to pull on a robe over my underwear. I had apparently not bothered with PJs. My mother had given me the robe one Christmas. It had tiny white sheep all over it against a background of clouds and blue sky.

My landlord's bib overalls covered part of what was written on his T-shirt. I wanted to ask what "Karmasutra" was, when it hit me that he was standing in the middle of my living room. "How did you get in here?"

"Your door was open. That's probably how your cat got out. He's out there digging up my flowers and terrorizing Glen's dog. I want you to go get him NOW. Or else."

"You wouldn't really shoot him, would you?" He might deserve to be shot, but he was still only a kitten. He had a lifetime of making people miserable ahead of him.

At that moment, Valerie appeared in the doorway. She had Wild Thing in her arms. He looked almost angelic as he gazed fondly up at her.

"I found him outside," she said.

"You should have him put down," my landlord said as he headed for the door. He paused before exiting and said, "And your bathrobe is wimpy."

Valerie looked at my robe. "I like it. The sheep are cute."

My head felt like it was about to explode. "Look, Val…"

"Valerie," she corrected.

"Look, Valerie, I was up late and don't feel too hot. If you wouldn't mind putting Wild Thing in the back bedroom…" I pointed.

"I know where it is. But you can't leave him locked up in there."

"Just until I have a chance to have some coffee."

"Why don't I put him down here." She bent down and released Wild Thing. He rubbed up against her leg, then turned toward me and hissed.

"He's upset because I had a party last night."

"I have to go; my dad will be looking for me. And it smells in here." She rushed off, leaving the door slightly ajar. I barely made it ahead of Wild Thing, and it cost me. My head threatened to explode, and he swiped at my ankle, drawing blood, before running off.

I headed for the kitchen to make coffee, sidestepping some bottles on the floor, checking out the mess on the couch, picking up a few plates of mostly eaten food left here and there, noting a few personal items left behind. What a mess. While my coffee was brewing, I wet a paper towel and dabbed at the wound on my ankle. The meandering route I'd taken since the attack was marked by tiny red spots on the floor. It could have been a diagram of a murder scene from the Family Circus comic strip, drops of blood next to the footprints of a distracted child taking detour after detour. I bent down to start wiping up the blood, then quickly realized bending over wasn't such a smart idea. Coffee first; clean-up later.

Mother called when I was pouring my coffee. I was tempted not to answer, but I knew she would just call back.

"Hello." I took my first sip of coffee and burned my tongue. "Ow," I added involuntarily.

"John, are you alright?"

"Burned my tongue."

"I heard you slurp. Coffee too hot?"

"Yes."

"How was your poker game?"

"Not great."

"You lost money." She didn't sound surprised.

"And Wild Thing got out."

"Oh no. Have you found him?"

"Valerie did. But the landlord isn't happy. Wild Thing went after Glen's dog again."

"The cat is gutsy, you have to admit."

"Well, the problem is that there's *good* gutsy and *bad* gutsy."

"Your landlord is just upset because a tenant's German Shepherd is afraid of a tiny kitty."

I took another sip of coffee, ignoring her last remark. It was still too hot. "You call for a reason?"

"That's not very kind."

"Sorry, but I know you must have a reason for calling this early the day after a poker game."

"It's 10:00."

"Oh." In my opinion, that was still early the day after a poker game.

"I was wondering what you and Bruno found out from Lonnie's neighbors. I thought you would call yesterday."

"We spent most of the day interviewing neighbors, and you had your book club in the afternoon, so we thought we'd wait until today. Bruno is going to call you with the official report."

"Oh. Well, why don't you give me a preview. I wouldn't want to bother Bruno at this hour."

"He lost, too," I said.

"Poor Bruno."

Poor Bruno? What about me? I wanted to ask, but even with a brain fogged from drink and an abrupt awakening, I knew it was best to get it over with. I managed a brief and fairly accurate overview of what we'd heard from neighbors, leaving out the part about Lonnie spying on the woman cheating on her husband.

"So, he was poking his drone's nose in places where it wasn't wanted," Mother concluded. "Doesn't that suggest one of his neighbors may have had a motive for wanting him stopped? Maybe more than one. Maybe they all got together—"

"Like in an Agatha Christie book? They all sneaked up on him at the edge of the cliff and together they shoved him over? Seems a bit unlikely."

"I grant you that neither the location nor method lends itself to multiple suspects."

"Bruno and I agree he may have seen a few things he shouldn't have, but that doesn't prove his death wasn't an accident."

"I still think there's something there."

"Let it go, Mother. Bruno needs proof of something other than Lonnie spying on sunbathers before he can do any more. He's already stuck his neck out at work to get this far."

"Okay, I'll think about that."

"Meanwhile, I need to clean this place up. Talk to you later."

The fact that Mother wasn't giving up was bad news. Maybe after she thought about it for a while, she'd change her mind. Or maybe Bruno would make it clear why he couldn't go any further with an investigation that wasn't his to begin with.

The morning became a blur of cleaning and trying to calm Wild Thing when he objected to my efforts to get the houseboat back to normal. First, he attacked the vacuum. Then he started following me around, making unfriendly noises as I picked up debris and wiped up unidentifiable spots on the floor and off of cabinets. How had we managed to splash what I hoped was ranch dip on the wall? I continued to mop up the mess, and Wild Thing continued to protest. Finally, I gave him some sardines I'd been saving for lunch. That settled him down for a little while. But it wasn't until I quit making clean-up noises that he quit taunting me and stretched out on the couch for a nap, one leg hanging over the edge. I wanted to lie down on the couch myself, but I was reluctant to try to move him.

It was really too bad he couldn't be trusted outside; I could have put in a cat door. Then he would be able to visit Valerie whenever he wanted. Another option was to completely enclose my back deck. But that would make sitting outside undesirable. And he'd probably dig in my planters. No, until I figured out how to pawn him off on someone, he and I were stuck *inside* with each other.

I was going to send Bruno a text to find out if he'd talked with Mother yet when I noticed I had quite a few emails. To my surprise, most of them were responses to a dating app exchange. I suddenly remembered my poker buddies teasing me about being a cat-chelor and saying that I needed a girlfriend. They'd apparently used the picture they'd taken to set up a profile. I couldn't recall any of the details about what they'd done, but nervous butterflies began fluttering in the pit of my stomach. On the other hand, maybe it wouldn't be such a bad thing. My love life wasn't exactly hopping.

The first email I clicked on thanked me for responding and said that she looked forward to meeting me...TODAY for coffee at 4:00. What? Not only had they listed me on the dating app, they'd replied to at least one respondent and set up a date? Her name was Laney Drew. She said that she, too, was a cat lover and had quite a few drones of various sizes and types and that she looked forward to comparing notes on our collections. There was also a picture of Laney. She looked normal, someone I would describe as pretty in a wholesome way, with deep dimples on both cheeks accentuating her smile. Someone I would like as a sister or a colleague, but not necessarily as a date. Especially not as a date who expected me to love cats and drones.

My first thought was to email her and tell her it was all a mistake, but that required a lot of explaining. I finally decided it would be better to buy her coffee and tell her in person about the joke my friends had played on me. When she found out we didn't have cats and drones in common, she would probably be relieved not to see me again. Maybe she would even be willing to take Wild Thing off my hands.

The second date they had set up for me was with someone who looked like a praying mantis. No, that wasn't fair. She was just thin and spindly looking, and she had a nice enough face. Betty Noland. In her picture, she had a cat in her lap, a large furry creature that looked like he weighed almost as much as she did. I was set up to buy her lunch on Tuesday. She would probably be a cheap date. Assuming I lived through Monday's ropes session and could still eat lunch on Tuesday.

I scrolled through the rest of the respondents. One in particular caught my eye, a blond holding a cat next to her face. Both were attractive. I considered contacting her; after all, I didn't dislike cats, just my particular animal. Her name—Sherri Sherman—sounded kinda romantic. And she didn't comment on my drone collection. But she liked my interest in science and technology. Well, I wasn't disinterested, was I? I sent Sherri a message asking if she would be able to meet me for lunch on Friday. At a place of her choosing. If Sherri and I hit it off, I'd forgive my poker buddies for setting up a misleading profile on a dating app.

Looking one last time at my profile and picture, I was surprised anyone had responded. Maybe Laney and Betty were scam artists, and I looked like a patsy. I certainly didn't look like someone I would want to date if I was a female. Could the dating pool possibly be that small?

I had trouble getting my hair to lay down for my coffee date. It kept poking up, like a crocus in the spring. Maybe she would think it was on purpose. A fashion statement. Although my mirror sent the message that spiky hair was better suited to someone with a face like Zac Efron. I kinda resembled a human roadrunner. At least the bald spot on the side of my head was filling in.

Unfortunately, my eyes were still a bit red from my evening of poker and beer. And the scratch on my ankle had bled through the Band-Aid, leaving a bright red splotch on my white socks. I knew I wasn't supposed to wear white socks with sandals, but the sandals weren't comfortable without socks, and I hadn't done the laundry for a while. Maybe I needed to buy more socks. Poor Laney; she was going to be disappointed in so many ways.

The coffee shop where we were to meet was only about fifteen minutes away. I arrived right on time and found a table in the corner near a window. Laney showed up a few minutes later, and I stood up and waved her over. She looked just like her picture. I had hoped maybe she was sexier in real life.

"You look just like your picture," she said, obviously trying not to stare at my topnotch.

"You do, too," I said. We stood awkwardly for a moment before I found my tongue and suggested she sit while I get us coffee.

"Chai tea, please."

I wasn't sure what it was, but that was okay. "Would you like a cookie?" I sounded like I was talking to a parrot: *Laney want a cookie?*

"That would be nice. Peanut butter."

"One Chai tea and one peanut butter cookie coming up." Now I sounded like a demented waiter.

I had to make two trips in order not to spill or drop anything. Then, as I sat down, I bumped the table with my hip, and some of her tea sloshed out of the mug. "No problem," she said as I ran to get some napkins.

When we were finally settled in, I took a deep breath and prepared myself for breaking the bad news. But she beat me to it.

"I have a confession to make."

"Oh?" Had she lied on her profile? Even if she had, I couldn't imagine *her* lies could top mine. "Please, confess." I smiled, then immediately wondered if that was an appropriate nonverbal response. Did priests smile behind the screen in the confessional booth?

"I'm not actually interested in finding a boyfriend; I just want someone to fly drones with. Maybe go for walks, that sort of thing." She broke off a chunk of peanut butter cookie and tapped it up and down on the plate. She was obviously as nervous as I was. Although her implicit lie wasn't nearly as egregious as my outright one.

"Then what I have to tell you will be disappointing. You see, I don't have a drone, not a single one."

She looked surprised. "Then why...?"

"My poker buddies put it in my profile. They'd had a little too much to drink and thought of it as a lark."

"I like poker," she said. "But I still don't understand."

"You like poker?"

"Yes, my dad taught me when I was young. I would like to think I'm pretty good."

"Well, about the drone thing. I've been working on a case that involved drones, and I talked about it so much my poker friends thought it would be funny to put that in my profile."

"Oh, so flying drones with me is out?"

"Well, not necessarily. I mean, it could be fun." I wasn't sure why I said it, but I kinda liked Laney. "If you don't mind that I don't have my own, that is."

"I could teach you," she said. Then she looked serious. "You do have a cat, don't you?"

"Yes, I have a cat. He was a gift."

"A gift? Oh, I don't believe in giving animals as gifts." She flushed. "Sorry, I didn't mean to be critical."

"It was from my mother," I said, as if that explained everything. "It was headed for the shelter and possible extinction, so she gave it to me."

"It?"

"He, him, Wild Thing."

"Oh, great name."

"Actually, it's descriptive. And to be honest, he hates me. But my neighbor's young daughter and he have hit it off. She comes by each day to play with him."

"That's sweet."

"She used to put dead fish and gum in my mailbox."

"Not sweet then." Laney laughed, deepening her dimples. "Dead fish and gum?"

"Among other things. It's a long story. But we have a truce now that Wild Thing lives with me. Her father won't let her keep him."

"That's a shame. Although you may slowly develop a relationship with Wild Thing. Sometimes, it takes a while for a cat to trust you."

"It was instantaneous with Valerie," I said, feeling a twinge of jealousy.

"Well, maybe I can suggest some things. Assuming I meet Wild Thing, that is."

"Laney, I would love some advice on how to get along with Wild Thing, and I'm sure I would enjoy flying drones with you."

She gave me a warm smile. "I have a feeling we are going to be great friends."

I had the same feeling.

Chapter Fifteen: Survival

As much as I'd been hoping the universe would skip Monday this week, it arrived right on schedule. I'd been instructed to wear clothes appropriate for outdoor activities, whatever that meant. I wear all of my clothes outdoors. Okay, so I knew what they wanted—the kind of resilient and trendy clothes outdoorsy people buy at REI. And I also knew what I personally needed to wear—clothes I didn't mind ripping or getting blood all over but with clean underwear in case I ended up going to the hospital. For as long as I could remember, my mother had been warning me about that.

I compromised by wearing a sweatsuit outfit Mother had given me one Christmas so I would have something acceptable to wear when I went jogging. Which I never did before or after having the right clothes for it. The sweatsuit was dark blue with white strips down the outside of the sleeves and pants. Like a skunk turned sideways.

Traffic was light and the directions for getting there were far too easy. The Fates were against me; Atropos poised—and eager—to cut my thread of life. The three Fates and talk of destiny was about all I remembered from a course I'd taken on Greek and Roman mythology, chosen after seeing a movie filled with chariot races and Roman infantry. All I can say is that the movie was far better than either the textbook or the lectures.

I reluctantly pulled into the large parking lot, already half filled with cars—Ford Mustangs, Jeep Wranglers, Dodge Rams and several other trucks with big wheels, along with a few Subaru Outbacks and a couple hybrids. Functional vehicles used for outdoor activities. Bee was the only yellow car in the lot.

Just beyond the parking area was an expanse of open terrain that ended in a wall of tall trees. It was a large park, especially given its urban location. As a city boy, I like my parks filled with sparse vegetation, ponds with ducks in them, and lots of benches.

There was a crowd gathered around a tent near the edge of the clearing to the left of the parking area. As I walked toward it, I tried not to look too closely at the platforms and other equipment in place for the various activities. Did a French prisoner stare at the guillotine on the way to his death?

There were about fifteen people there ahead of me, with more rushing up from behind as if eager to get started. Before I had a chance to mingle, a smiling woman approached, coming close and leaning toward me as if she wanted to whisper in my ear. And she did.

"I'm going to reach behind your neck and pull off the price tag, okay?"

It was a very disappointing come-on. She didn't wait for a reply but jerked my collar so hard it almost cut off my breathing. Then she handed the tag to me.

"Good bargain," she said.

I looked at the tag. My mother had purchased my suit on sale, marked down 70 percent. She could at least have removed the tag so I wouldn't know. "Thank you," I said.

"I'm Audrey. Accounting."

"John, Claims."

"Nice meeting you. Aren't you excited?"

"Not especially," I said truthfully. "A bit nervous, actually. I'm not, ah, very athletic."

She gave me a once-over. "Then why did you sign up for a Level 3 ropes class?"

"Level 3?"

"Oh, you didn't know? Well, I'm sure you will be okay. Just relax and listen to the instructions."

"Level 3?" I repeated.

"It assumes you've done other lower-level activities, but don't worry. I took a trapeze class last year with no previous experience, and I was fine."

"You actually did airborne stuff, like in a circus?"

"The aerial arts from take-off techniques, flight, and dismount. Although nothing fancy like in a real circus."

"Weren't you afraid of falling?"

"There were nets. Like there will be here. If you fall, just go limp." She waved at someone coming from the parking lot and said, "Gotta go. Good luck."

Somehow her little pep talk hadn't calmed me down. Go limp, huh? As easy as falling off a log. Sure. But who wants to fall off a log? And why had Van Droop recommended signing me up for a Level 3 session?

I checked out the rest of the group. None of them were wearing clothes that looked like they had never been worn before. I should have rolled around in the grass or something so I wouldn't stand out so much. Then I saw someone I recognized. I hadn't realized Jack was coming today. He didn't look very athletic either. I quickly hurried over to him.

"Hi, Jack. I didn't know you were taking this course."

"John, good to see you." He shook my hand with exact company protocol. "They sent you to mingle, huh? Too bad you aren't with the rest of us in the cubicles. You'd already know a lot of the people here."

"Well, I like having a door."

"That would be nice," he said. "But it's also nice to feel like part of the team."

"I guess that's why I'm here today." I tried to say it like a joke, but it sounded flat. "What about you, did they sign you up, or did you choose this on your own?"

"I've always wanted the challenge of doing an advanced ropes course."

When you only know someone in a work context, or from a single poker game night, you don't necessarily think about how fit they look—unless they are exceptionally muscular, like they spend a lot of time at the gym. Jack didn't appear to be in much better shape than me. If he thought he could handle the day's activities, maybe I could too.

Before I had time to work on psyching myself up for the challenge, the instructors called for us to "gather round." I obeyed, lagging behind the others, my psyche resisting being psyched.

I got through roll call just fine, ignoring the cutesy comments about my name. I've heard all of the Pocahontas jokes before, and I no longer felt an obligation to explain how John Smith became such a common name that it is considered synonymous with anonymity. I was actually named after an uncle who had died before I had a chance to complain to him about being his namesake.

After a brief introduction of the instructors, the schedule for the day, and the location of the restrooms, we were paired up for what they referred to as a warm-up exercise. "Remember, today isn't a competition," one of the buff-looking male instructors said. I'd already forgotten his name. "We are here to help you learn how to work together better by participating in some challenging physical activities." Challenging physical activities? That didn't sound good. "With that in mind, we want to start with a trust exercise. The instructions are simple. Who would like to demonstrate this with me?"

The trapeze woman stepped forward, and the instructor continued his explanation. "The *faller* stands about three feet in front of the *catcher*." They got in position, and the instructor used his hands to illustrate what three feet looked like. "The faller keeps their feet together, arms folded across their chest, eyes closed." The trapeze woman put her feet together, folded her arms across her chest, and closed her eyes. It looked to me like a "coffin position."

"The catcher stands with one leg back and straight and the other forward and bent. Like this." He took the described stance. "Both arms out, palms up. Then, on the count of three...one, two, three." The woman obediently fell back, and the instructor caught her and quickly returned her to an upright position. Everyone applauded.

When I found myself paired with a healthy-looking young man who appeared more than capable of catching me, I started feeling more confident. Although I wasn't so sure how well I could perform the role of catcher in return. But my partner was young. He could undoubtedly spring back from a partially failed catch. I mean, I would try; I just wasn't sure I was strong enough to take his full weight and prop him back up. Although maybe it wasn't any more taxing than swinging a bowling ball.

We were instructed to get in position. I was the designated faller for round one. I got prepared—feet together, arms crossed, one eye closed. "One...two..." I was just starting to lean back when I heard a barking dog racing in our direction. I kept leaning back further and further. I could do this.

As I hit the ground, a sharp pain shot up my leg and ended somewhere along my spine. "Ow," I screamed, "Oooh." I had turned slightly to look at the barking dog and had fallen twisted instead of flat. My last thought before hitting the ground was to ask myself why my "partner" was chasing down the dog instead of catching me.

Two instructors were suddenly standing over me, witnesses to my pain. "Don't move," the woman said.

"I don't think I can."

My untrustworthy teammate reappeared. "Oh, hey, man. Sorry about that."

Then there was someone poking at me. Each jab intensified the pain. I tried to get away, but a voice said: "Hold still. I'm a nurse." I stopped moving. "Tell me, does this hurt?"

I yelped. "Yes."

"And this?"

"Yes!" Why was she trying to hurt me? Hadn't they already done enough damage?

"Can you sit up?"

"Here, I'll help," my teammate said as he put an arm around my shoulders.

"No," I practically screamed as they forced me into a sitting position. I thought you weren't supposed to move people with possible back injuries. One of the instructors came over to assist the nurse, and I saw my teammate wander away in the direction of a young blond woman.

"Okay, on a count of three, let's pull him to his feet. One, two..."

Since no one was paying any attention to what I wanted, I braced myself for what was to come. "Three." They catapulted me into the air, almost pushing me over in the other direction. At the last instant, the nurse caught me and held me upright.

"Take a deep breath," she ordered.

I did.

"Now, can you walk?"

I wasn't sure. When they let go, I took a tentative step and found that my feet were functional. "Yes, I think I can." Then, my mind cleared sufficiently to realize that this was an opportunity. "But I need some help." Leaning heavily on my two helpers, I let them take me over to a bench off to the side of the field. By then, I was hurting less, but I pretended I was suffering from agonizing injuries.

"Do you think we should call an ambulance?" the instructor asked the nurse.

"Let's give it some time first," she said. "I'll sit here with him a while."

Meanwhile, I was no longer the center of attention. Everyone had gone back to team building. Leaving their injured teammate behind. Even a goose that is injured and goes down has two others drop out of formation and stay with it until it dies.

"Don't move," the nurse said. "I'm going to go get you something for pain." She rushed off and returned before I had time to wiggle my toes long enough to make sure they were in working order. She handed me a bottle of water and a green pill. "This will dull the pain and reduce swelling."

"Do I have swelling?" I was starting to panic. Maybe I wasn't pretending. Maybe I was really seriously injured, my brain numbed by the shock.

"Traumatized muscles tend to swell. This will help."

I obediently downed the pill, followed by a healthy swig of water. Failing the trust test makes you thirsty. "How long will it take?" I asked. Even though I was no longer feeling any pain, I was much happier on the bench than headed for the first obstacle course with the others.

"Maybe a half hour at most."

"Will I, ah, be able to finish the activities today?" Please, please say "no."

"Given what you've experienced so far, I advise against it. I'm sorry."

I tried to keep the relief out of my voice. "That's alright. It isn't your fault." Nor mine, I was pleased to say. Emma couldn't blame me for an accident someone else caused. I wondered if I could get credit for the course if I didn't complete it.

The nurse was called away when someone hurt a finger in the net climbing over a high wooden wall. I assured her I would be fine. In fact, I was not only feeling no pain, I was feeling like I'd had a few stiff drinks. It must have been a powerful pain pill.

I was trying to assess what I should do next when a female instructor whose nametag said "Winnie" came over to see how I was doing. "I'm feeling okay, Winnie," I said. "I may skip my dance lessons tonight, though."

Instead of laughing, she said, "I'm so sorry." Then, before I could say I was kidding, she added, "Do you have a copy of your disclaimer?" Winnie sounded sooo innocent, but my claims adjuster antenna immediately went up. Even sedated, I knew why she was asking.

"I don't remember any disclaimer. My office manager signed me up for the course." *Thank you, Emma.*

"Oh, that's right. We were asked to add you at the last minute." Now, she was visibly worried.

I felt slightly lightheaded, but at the same time, I was very clearheaded about my position of power. "The nurse said I will be fine but that I shouldn't participate in more activities today. But I really need the credits. Is there any way I can complete the day without actually doing some of the more physical stuff?"

"I'm afraid it's all physical." She frowned. "But your boss obviously wanted you to participate." I could almost see her thinking about how to handle the situation to make sure she didn't disappoint an important client or make me unhappy or upset enough to sue. "Maybe you could do some timekeeping or help keep track of people as they finish each activity. Cheer teammates on. How would that be?" It was obvious she wanted me to say yes, and, from my point of view, her suggestions were a huge relief. I had to remind myself that I was not only hurting but extremely disappointed not to be able to finish the course. It was hard, but I managed to keep my enthusiasm for Plan B in check.

"As long as I get credit for the course," I said. "And have the opportunity to interact with the rest of the team," I added, feeling like that was the right thing for a team player to say under the circumstances. "It would be so great if you could make that happen." I would get a checkmark for taking the course and get through the day with my body and dignity intact. My back might hurt a little, but my karma was doing just fine, thank you very much.

After she left, the nurse brought a woman over, her finger in a splint. "This is Denise," the nurse said. Denise was crying, not much, but enough to register her discomfort. In between sniffles, she managed a weak hello. "I'm going to leave her here while I talk with the instructors about the two of you."

Denise sat down beside me, sobbing softly and intermittently sniffing loudly like a vacuum inhaling a blob of dirt. After about a minute she gained control of herself and turned toward me. "I heard about what happened to you, are you okay?" She had the body of a gymnast, compact and rippling with muscles. I wouldn't have noticed, except she was wearing a form-fitted body suit.

"I'm in some pain, but I'll live. How about you? I heard that you caught your finger in webbing."

"Brigit tried to pull me down because I was so far ahead of her." Her tone made me glad not to be Brigit.

"I thought it wasn't a competition."

She gave me an indulgent smile. "Just like back in the office, no more or no less."

"I'm not sure what that means."

"Our manager is here. Impressing him might help when evaluation time comes around."

Of course. I should have known, but I'd been deluded by the day's stated purpose, as well as by my own personal fear of pain. "Sorry. Are you through for the day then?"

"I wanted to do it all," she said. "And I know crying about it is silly. The nurse says I can still do the rope walks and the zipline, if I'm careful. That's what she's talking to the instructors about. I may have to sign another waiver or something."

"That sounds good," I said, trying to sound sincere.

"But no rock climbing. I'd been looking forward to that."

"Me too," I said, still trying to sound sincere while my heart did a flip-flop. How could I have been so lucky as to hurt myself first thing?

The nurse returned. "Good news for both of you," she said. "Denise, you can participate in any activity you feel comfortable doing. And, ah, John, report to Winnie. She has some assignments for you."

My first assignment involved an on-ground obstacle course where participants hopped through tires, wiggled through the brush on their stomachs, and disappeared into giant pipes—popping out at the end, looking disheveled but triumphant. It reminded me of something I'd seen in a movie where they were training army recruits. Only there was no barbed wire or mud or anything like that. I thought I might have done okay on this one. I could hop and crawl, although I wouldn't have liked going through a pipe. I was much happier seated at the finish line in a comfy camp chair, holding a clipboard with everyone's names listed alphabetically. All I had to do was check each person off as they came over to let me know they had completed the activity. Everyone knew what had happened to me, and most offered a few "sorrys" or high fives.

My nemesis finished in the middle of the group and apologized to me again for letting me fall. "I'll never trust anyone again," I said. "Especially dogs," I added. When he didn't respond, I said, "Just kidding. Accidents happen." I could hardly thank him, even though that was what I wanted to do. Fortunately, the next finisher came along and our conversation was cut short.

After the hop and crawl activity ended, I managed a dramatic hobble to the next station, where people were flexing their muscles and testing their balance by standing first on one leg, then the other, in preparation for the rope walk. The rope was only about four feet off the ground, but it was a timed activity. The participant climbed up a short ladder, put one foot on the rope, and waited for the timer to yell "Go." Almost half lost their balance and either stepped or fell off before reaching the other end. I would definitely have ended up on the ground doing this one, probably landing on my face rather than my feet.

It was fun to watch everyone trying so hard to stay upright and keep going. Some scooted, some took tiny steps, some curled their toes around the rope, arms fluttering when they were about to fall. From the sidelines, colleagues cheered each other on, hooting and shouting encouragement. The camaraderie almost made me wish I was still in the game. Of course, it wasn't at all certain that I would have made it even this far. I would probably still be hanging from the net on the first wall exercise. It was far better being a cheerleader and record keeper…and definitely a lot safer.

At lunch, I sat at a table with Jack and several others I now recognized by name. In some ways I was learning more about people by observing rather than participating. Jack confessed that he was already feeling sore but was enjoying himself nonetheless. Then, after repeating how sorry he was about my accident, he lowered his voice and asked, "So what's with you and Carla?"

"Ah, you heard?"

"Everyone on the floor heard her last Friday, I'm afraid. I meant to ask you about it at the poker game, but I got a bit, involved, you know."

"By 'involved,' you mean focused on winning everyone's money," I said, trying not to sound judgmental.

"Well, I admit I like to win."

"No one can blame you for that." Well, maybe Bruno did, a little.

"So, what was Carla all hot and bothered about?"

"She and I had a little *misunderstanding*. She thought I didn't accept an appraisal she did on a couple of paintings, but she was wrong; I'd signed off on them. Then a family member had some questions and wouldn't let up until I did some research for her."

"I think I saw her—the client. Sexy, right?" Jack grinned, the leering grin of machismo.

"Desiree Defelice," I said slowly, like a verbal caress, giving Jack a macho grin back. It was something I'd learned to fake in high school when other boys were bragging about their conquests.

"I can understand why you agreed to help." The two of us sighed together.

"It was stupid, but I confess her, ah, request was hard to refuse."

"What did you find?"

"That Carla was right. Desiree didn't want to hear that, but she was going to talk to her family and tell them everything was fine. I'm hoping that's the end of it."

"Clients." Jack shook his head.

"Clients," I agreed.

The rest of the day passed quickly. With each new activity, I was even more thankful I was on the sidelines. My instincts had been right. I wouldn't have survived without injuring myself. And I would hate to take sick leave just when I was developing a new, cushy specialty. What if they gave the job to someone else while I was recovering?

At the end of the session, the instructors praised everyone for their hard work and called me out for fighting through my pain to cheer on other team members. I got a round of applause. The hardest thing I'd had to do during the afternoon was to remember to walk as though I was still hurting. But to be honest, after the pain pill kicked in, I didn't feel a thing. And the nurse gave me several more to "see me through the night and the next few days." I hesitated to ask if I could take them with alcohol.

As I drove home, I tried to remember the words to the catchy jingle I'd heard earlier during my drive to the park: "Whopper. Whopper. Whopper. Lettuce, mayo, pickle." I liked the ad—what I couldn't understand was why anyone would refer to it an *earworm* melody. It made *me* hungry.

"Whopper, Whopper, Whopper," I chanted. Life was good; I had survived Team Building!

Life got even better when there were no crows to welcome me to The Haven or chase me down the path to my floating home.

When I reached Valerie's houseboat, she came out to greet me. "Hi," she said in her bouncy, little girl voice. Then she took a long look at me and asked, "Why are you dressed funny?"

"I took an advanced ropes course today." I couldn't help but sound proud. After all, I'd made it through the day in one slightly damaged piece.

"Really? Did you climb over obstacles and walk on ropes thirty feet in the air?"

"Well, no, I mostly helped organize things."

"Then you didn't *take* the course."

"I almost did."

"You can't say you did something if you didn't."

"I got credit for taking the course. So, technically, I did take it." What was I doing defending myself to a kid?

"In my opinion…"

I interrupted before she could tell me her opinion. "Look, it's been a long day. If you want to think I didn't 'take' the course, that's fine with me. All I needed was the company's checkmark, and I got that. So, thanks for asking. Now I'm going to go fix myself something to eat."

"I'll come by later to visit," she said. I obviously needed to get a deadbolt so I could lock my houseboat from the inside against anyone who had a key, like Mother and Valerie. "Your mother is waiting for you," she yelled after me.

Valerie's warning didn't include the fact that Bruno was also in my living room. He and Mother were on the couch, sharing a plate of cheese and crackers.

"How was your team-building workshop?" she asked as I came inside.

"It was fine." I turned to Bruno, "What are you doing here?"

"Your mother stopped by the station to talk to me about Lonnie's death, and I offered to drop her off here." He added, "You spent the day in a team-building workshop?" Bruno looked like he was about to burst out laughing.

"Yes, it was a ropes course."

"YOU did a ropes course?" His amazement stretched across his entire face.

"Why is that so funny?"

"Well, you aren't exactly all that…" He hesitated, searching for just the right word to zing me.

"Athletic," Mother filled in for him. "But you look good in the outfit."

"It wasn't a physical competition," I said defensively. "It was about learning to support each other as team members." Except for the guy who'd failed to catch me.

Mother stood up. "Help me put the food out, and then you can tell us all about it."

"You brought dinner?" All I wanted was a long, hot bath and a stiff drink. Although now that she mentioned it, I could smell a familiar aroma wafting from my kitchen. "That isn't May's Mother's Tuna Casserole, is it?" It was a recipe she'd copied from a Donald Westlake book.

"I thought you might need something to cheer you up after your workshop."

Bruno smiled. "One of my favorites, too."

"Before we get dinner, there's something I need to tell you," I said. There was no way she would fail to inveigle the truth; I decided to get it over with so I could enjoy my meal. Speaking rapidly, I confessed: "My partner let me fall in a trust exercise and I hurt my back. They had me doing support stuff for the rest of the day so I could get credit for the course without injuring myself further. In the end, I got applause for working through my pain to help out."

"You're in pain?" Mother suddenly looked concerned.

"The nurse gave me a pain pill."

"Then you can't have any alcohol with dinner."

"They didn't tell me that."

"Everyone knows you shouldn't mix painkillers and alcohol."

I have never been successful arguing with her "everyone knows" statements, so I reluctantly gave in. Besides, maybe she was right.

Once we were seated and she'd served up healthy helpings of casserole, Bruno asked me about my day.

"Have you ever done one of those trust falls?"

"No way, I'm too big. I wouldn't trust anyone to catch me."

"Well, I did, and he didn't."

"And that's how you got hurt?"

"It wasn't that bad, but yes, that's how I got hurt."

"Bummer," mother said. "Did you get an x-ray?"

"No, I didn't think I needed one."

"You will have to get one if you're going to sue them."

"Why would I do that?"

"What if you're seriously hurt and start to rack up medical bills? And what about for pain and suffering?"

"Mother, I'm not going to rip off my insurance company. That wouldn't be ethical."

"You deserve some compensation for what they've put you through," she said, sounding sympathetic and reasonable. But greedy at the same time.

"That's what people who are in car accidents always argue when I interview them after an accident. Even if they're only hurt a little and it isn't permanent. I'm not going there."

"Okay, just saying. I think you've told me that sometimes a person doesn't know they're seriously injured until a day or two later. And that unscrupulous insurance companies try to get them to sign off right away."

"That was before I got a job at Universal. Besides, I already signed a waiver. I'm not suing anyone." I'd held off signing anything until the end of the day when guilt had overridden caution. But I was pretty sure I wasn't going to need further medical attention. On the other hand, I was harboring a teensy grudge against my supposed "catcher," who, during the afternoon, had excelled at every other activity. He'd better not get in any accident where I was the adjuster. And I was still a bit miffed about being signed up for an advanced course. What had Van Droop been thinking?

Chapter Sixteen: It's Gone!

I was surprised to get a call from Bruno about an hour after he left to take Mother home. "Weren't you just here?" I asked. Maybe the painkillers were playing tricks on me.

"We have unfinished business."

"Oh, oh."

"It's your mother."

I groaned. "What did she do?"

"Didn't it seem strange to you that she came down to the station?"

"I didn't think about it. It has been a long and complicated day."

"She grilled me on every little detail from the interviews. She knows we aren't telling her everything."

"You didn't mention Mrs. Gillmor, did you?"

"I came close. Fortunately, she got hung up on the teenage smokers. But she's going to try to get you to look for more evidence. Thought I should warn you."

"Thanks."

"It's the least I can do after you invited that card shark to our poker game."

"Jack?"

"I want a rematch. He took a lot of money off me."

"I can't afford another poker night. At least not for a while."

"You owe me."

"I'll think about it."

"I hate to say this, but I don't think Jack was drinking as much as the rest of us. I think he really wanted to win."

"You're not suggesting that he cheated, are you?"

"No, I don't think that. I'm just saying it wasn't about getting together for a friendly game and a little partying with him."

"Everyone likes to win. You can't blame him for that."

"Well, some of us like to eat and drink and talk bullshit almost as much as winning."

"By the way, I saw you shifting in your chair a lot. Next time, you ought to man up and bring your donut to sit on."

Bruno sighed. "I know. But just imagine the jokes."

"I know. Some jokes about hemorrhoids don't *sit* well with people."

"You've been saving that one, haven't you?"

"I've got more."

"Gotta run.... Oh, before I go, how was your date?"

"I had a good time. Laney is great. She's a paralegal. Started out in pre-law but changed her mind. Got certified as a PI but decided that wasn't for her either. Really interesting person. We have plans to get together again. To fly drones. And she likes to play poker."

"Hey, the guys did it as a joke, not to add another poker player to our group."

"It isn't nice to play jokes like that on people. Especially not on innocent strangers."

"You're right." Bruno sounded chastened. "They got a little carried away. Maybe we should collect cell phones if we're going to drink a lot."

"Well, I'm not happy about having to admit it was a joke to the women they set me up with."

"Does that mean you're going out with spider-lady too?"

"I feel like I owe her an explanation."

"You're a braver man than I thought," Bruno said. "She looked scary."

Within minutes of hanging up the phone, Mother called. It had been good of Bruno to warn me that she was still determined to prove Lonnie's death wasn't an accident, but I hadn't had time to think about it yet. In fact, I was finding it more and more difficult to think at all. I needed sleep.

"We have an appointment tomorrow at 5:00," Mother said. You may have to leave work a little early to pick me up so we can get there on time."

"Mother, you can't make appointments without consulting me." Well, obviously, she could, but I didn't have to like it.

"Just be at my place no later than 4:30. I'll be waiting out front."

"Wait," I yelled, sensing she was about to hang up.

"What?"

"Where are we going tomorrow?"

"To visit the Wellers."

"But why?" My question fell into a black hole. Mother had hung up.

Tuesday morning, I woke up and panicked when I couldn't move my feet. Then I realized I'd become cocooned in my sheet and managed to calm myself enough to unwind. I was a little sore but decided not to take anything to ease the pain so I could continue acting like I was in pain in front of Emma. Although if I was hurting, it wouldn't be an act. In any case, I would have to exaggerate a bit to justify how I'd ended up spending my day of team building.

When I arrived, I had the distinct impression that Emma had been waiting for me to show up. "Good morning," she said, sounding chipper, giving me a careful once-over. Maybe she was surprised not to see me on crutches or sporting a head bandage.

"Good morning." I tried to sound chipper in return, but my voice came out a bit scratchy.

"Wait," she said when I didn't stop. I paused and turned toward her. "How did it go yesterday?"

I couldn't decide whether I wanted to pretend like everything was fine or try to make her feel guilty for signing me up for something where I got injured. It was possible Jack or some other employee would tell her if I didn't, so I went for the latter.

"To tell the truth, not well. You see, my partner failed to catch me during a trust fall, and I was injured. I'm taking painkillers so I could come to work, but I may leave early." She didn't have to know the real reason I was leaving early.

"So…you didn't finish the session?"

"Actually, I did. They found things for me to do that didn't make my injury worse. So, you don't have to schedule me for a make-up session." I suspected that was what she was thinking. "In the end, I actually got to interact with almost everyone there. Mission accomplished." I smiled and left her there, stewing in disappointment. Eye of newt, toe of frog.

Mid-morning I went by to say hi to Jack, but he wasn't at his desk. It was nice to have someone at work I felt a connection to. Even if he was a superior poker player.

With manufactured resolve, I started in on the file folders in my in-box and managed to lower the level several inches. It was satisfying to complete a claim, but it made me feel a bit like Sisyphus; as soon I emptied my in-box, Emma would refill it, and the process would start all over again.

Emma poked her head in several times to see how I was doing. She even asked if I wanted her to bring me lunch. I wasn't sure if it was checking up on me to see if I was really hurting, or if she felt a teensy bit guilty for what she had done—at Van Droop's behest, of course. Still, she could have warned me that it was an advanced session. I thanked her but said the nurse told me I should try to get some moderate exercise, so I was going to the deli to get a sandwich.

When it was time for me to leave to pick up Mother, I made a show of being tired, limping conspicuously as I walked past Emma's desk on the way to the elevator. I hoped she noticed. It was a masterful performance that ended when the elevator doors closed. Like theater curtains coming together at the end of the play.

Mother was standing in front of her condo when I drove up. A half hour later, we were knocking on the Wellers' door. By then, Mother had explained our strategy, I had protested, she had explained again, I had protested again, and then we arrived, ready to carry out "our" strategy. Although, when she actually stated our reason for being there to Mrs. Weller, I got all of the *credit.*

"So sorry to bother you," my mother said when Mrs. Weller invited us in. "But John has been thinking about this, and he is convinced that your son saved pictures he had taken with his drones."

"But why would he have done that?"

"As a log of his drone activities."

"I'm not sure I understand…" She was starting to look concerned, but Mother was prepared.

"It's standard for hobbyists to keep records." When Mrs. Weller still looked dubious, she added, "Or perhaps he thought he might show them to neighbors. They'd all seen his drones around. Maybe he had some ideas about how to use them to make the neighborhood safer. Or maybe he had aerial shots of parties that he thought people might want as a keepsake—that sort of thing."

Unfortunately, Mrs. Weller's skepticism was building rather than dissipating—I could see it in her eyes.

"We aren't suggesting he was going to use them against anyone…" I began, hoping to ward off any unpleasantness. But Mrs. Weller wasn't buying our explanations and quickly interrupted with the question we were hoping to avoid.

"Are you suggesting my son kept copies so he could, ah, blackmail our neighbors?"

"No," I said, "Nothing like that." Mother was also murmuring reassurances.

She hadn't asked us to sit down, and, given the granite frown, I didn't think she was going to offer us tea and cookies either.

"We're not accusing him of anything," Mother said, taking a new tack. "But we think he may have seen something he shouldn't have. Maybe a kid buying drugs, or vandalizing someone's property. I mean, a parent needs to know if their child is doing something that could get them into serious trouble. He may have seen something and been trying to figure out what to do with the information. Or maybe he suspected someone was cheating on their spouse and felt sorry for whichever spouse was being cheated on. But sharing that kind of information isn't easy."

Mrs. Weller's frown softened around the edges. "Lonnie would find it difficult to approach someone with evidence of wrongdoing," she agreed.

"And, if he caught someone doing something they shouldn't be doing, he may have been worried that they would try to get the evidence from him."

Suddenly, Mrs. Weller's eyes widened in disbelief. "You aren't implying that someone may have pushed Lonnie over the edge of that cliff, are you?"

"The police have considered the possibility," my mother said before I could stop her. "But they don't have any proof. If we're right about the kind of thing Lonnie may have seen, John is certain Lonnie would have taken precautions to keep his proof safe. Aren't you, John?" Both Mother and Mrs. Weller turned toward me. What else could I say?

"Yes," I said. "Certain."

"What do you want?" Mrs. Weller asked. She didn't sound thoroughly convinced, but she apparently wasn't ready to dismiss us completely...yet.

"We want you to think very carefully about where Lonnie may have hidden something small, possibly a thumb drive." How did my mother know about thumb drives?

"How big is a thumb drive?" Mrs. Weller turned to me even though my mother was the one who had brought it up. I showed her the size with my fingers.

"If you have any suggestions...?" my mother said.

Mrs. Weller shook her head.

"Would you mind if John and I looked around?"

Mrs. Weller gave it some thought before responding. "My husband will be home by 6:30. You're welcome to look around as long as you're through by the time he gets here. I don't want to bother him with this."

"Can we start in Lonnie's room?" Mother asked. "Or did he work some other place?"

"He mainly stayed in his room. But the thieves took everything related to electronics, as you know."

"But they weren't necessarily looking for something he may have hidden," Mother said.

Mrs. Weller paused, staring Mother down longer than it takes to brush your teeth with an electric toothbrush before giving in and showing us to her son's room. "Please don't disturb things," she said, leaving us there on our own.

It felt to me like a hopeless task, but I knew Mother wouldn't give up until we did a thorough search. She immediately started looking for secret panels in the furniture, hollow sounds in the walls, and suspicious bulges in his mattress. "These are the places where they usually hide things," she said

"Who usually hides things in places like that?"

She rolled her eyes at me. "Don't you read the books I recommend?" She's always giving me books from her mystery book club. I put them next to the other books she's given me and only occasionally get sucked into actually reading one. I like capers and beach reads, not the heavy stuff or books where you're supposed to enjoy figuring out whodunit before the end. Entertainment to me shouldn't require too much strain on the little grey cells.

Lonnie's parents hadn't cleaned out his closet yet, so Mother ordered me to go through all of his shirt, pants and jacket pockets and to also check jacket linings. It felt like I was invading his privacy, but then, that's what a search of someone's possessions is all about.

"I'm going to the bathroom," I said after I finished with his closet. "Be right back." Mother was too busy tapping and squeezing to pay much attention to me. We had a deadline, and she was going to give it her all.

Being in the bathroom inspired me to start thinking in broader terms about where Lonnie might have hidden something small. Wasn't the bathroom where criminals often hid their stashes? Maybe I was thinking of drug dealers, but that didn't mean it wasn't a good place to look. Lonnie was a smart kid, why would he have left a valuable thumb drive in his own room? I immediately started checking out every nook and cranny. There were a lot of pill bottles in the medicine cabinet, mostly with Lonnie's parents' names on them. I shook each one, peeking behind taller bottles of this and that. I tapped walls like I had seen Mother do. I even looked in the toilet tank. Nothing. Zip. Zero.

On the way back to Lonnie's room, I stopped to admire a wooden sailor on a sideboard. Mrs. Weller saw me and came over. "Lonnie made that in shop," she said proudly. "He was never very good at that kind of thing, but this one turned out nicely."

I picked it up to take a closer look and felt something move inside. I shook it gently back and forth a few times. "You hear that?" I asked.

"He dropped it once and had to refasten the head. Maybe something has come unglued."

"No, there's something in there. Listen," I shook the sailor again, this time with more vigor, as we both leaned in to listen.

"I think you're right."

Instinctively, I twisted the head, and it lifted off. Then I tipped the body upside down, and a thumb drive fell out on the floor. "Oh, Mother was right." I hoped I didn't sound too surprised as I bent over to pick it up.

"That's a thumb drive?" Mrs. Weller asked.

"Yes. I'll go tell Mother."

Mother was still tapping and probing when I came in and said, "Ta-da," holding the thumb drive in the air. She didn't look up, so I said, "Mother, look what I found." That got her attention.

Instead of praising me, she said, "I told you so."

We promised Mrs. Weller we would let her know what we found on the thumb and either give it back to her or turn it over to the police if that seemed appropriate. It was getting late, and it was clear she wanted to make sure we left before her husband returned, probably still thinking about the possibility of her son as a blackmailer in spite of my mother bringing up more flattering reasons why he might have kept copies of his drone pictures. No matter what the outcome, as a good mother, Mrs. Weller obviously wanted to know the truth about her son's death. I wasn't sure if it would be harder or easier for Lonnie's parents if it was proven that his death wasn't accidental.

Mother had plans for dinner, but she made me promise I would ring her as soon as I'd had a chance to look at the drive. Maybe we'd discover he only kept pictures of half-nude neighbors or illicit bedroom scenes, perhaps for kinky reasons rather than for blackmail. If it turned out to be selfies of Lonnie's privates, we were definitely going to be disappointed.

The crows were apparently also dining out because they weren't there to greet me at my parking spot. Nor was Wild Thing around when I got home and went inside. Hopefully, he was napping in some secret corner and not out chasing the neighbor's dog. I took the thumb drive out of my pocket just as the phone rang in the other room. Although I seldom got an important call on my landline—mostly scammers and robocalls—like Pavlov's dogs, I was conditioned to respond and raced to answer it.

It was Bruno. He'd left his jacket in my entry closet and just remembered it. "Come on by to pick it up—I'll be here," I said. "And I may have another surprise for you."

"You do a lot of things that surprise me, John."

"I would like to think that I'm unpredictable, a man of mystery."

Bruno laughed. "That wasn't what I meant, but keep the faith."

I stood there for a moment after hanging up. If he didn't mean I had a flair for spontaneity, then what had he meant?

There was no thumb drive in my hand, so I concluded I must have set it down when I sprinted to answer the phone. But no matter how hard I stared at the hall table, there was no thumb drive there either. Where else would I have put it? I checked my pockets. Nothing. I looked on the floor. Nothing. I moved the table this way and that, thinking it might have fallen behind one of the legs. Nothing. Out of desperation, I checked my pockets again. Nothing. The thumb drive had vanished.

Had someone followed me home and seized the telephone call as an opportunity to make off with the thumb drive? I went over and tested the door. It was locked. Okay, John, I said to myself. Stay calm. THINK. There's an obvious explanation.

Then it hit me. "Wild Thing!" I screamed. "Where are you?" I went tearing around the place, searching for the black demon kitten. I found him standing next to his food bowl, looking like his usual angry self. "What did you do with it?" I asked. He growled at me. "Don't give me that," I said. "I know it was you. You took my thumb drive. And I want it back."

I ranted and yelled a little longer. But apparently, he wasn't about to confess to anything. Finally, I broke down and fed him. Then, I started another search. It had to be there somewhere.

By the time Bruno arrived, I couldn't decide if I was more frantic or exhausted from all of the crawling around and exploring hidden areas with my fingers. One thing I'd discovered was that I really needed to do a better job of cleaning the floors.

"You look like hell," Bruno told me.

"I'm definitely going to hell," I said. "And mother will never forgive me."

After I told him what had happened, Bruno took my side. "It's that damn cat. He did something with it."

"Where would he put it?"

"Does he have a bed? Or how about a litter box?"

"Yes to both."

We turned his bed upside down, squeezed the pad, and shook out the blanket. All we got for our efforts was cat hair up our noses and on our clothes. "You need to clean this stuff more often," Bruno said. "It's disgusting."

"Wait till you see the litter box," I promised. "It's the best reason for not having a cat."

"Why don't you get a cat door? Let him dig in the neighbor's flower pots."

"He's already dug in my landlord's garden. And terrified a neighbor's German Shepherd."

"Not bad for a little guy," Bruno said.

We poked around the litter box with a pen that I reluctantly contributed to the cause by disposing of it after we came up with nothing. Nothing. Absolutely nothing.

Then we tackled the job systematically, starting with the front door and working our way through the place. We found lots of dust bunnies, dead spiders, and mysterious stains and pieces of gunk. But no thumb drive.

"Sorry, John. I can't imagine what happened to it. But I know now where it isn't."

"What am I going to tell Mother?"

Chapter Seventeen: I Can Explain

I couldn't pretend to not be home, because eventually Mother would call a taxi or Uber and end up on my doorstep, let herself in, and there I would be. It was just a matter of time until I had to face the music. And it was definitely going to be a dirge.

When she called, I didn't say "Hello" but quickly muttered, "I can explain."

"Explain what?" Mother asked.

"No that's wrong, I *can't* explain. Because I don't understand. I've looked everywhere. Then Bruno came by and the two of us did a thorough search of the entire houseboat. And it's gone."

"What's gone, John? Don't worry, I'm sure everything will be okay."

"The thumb drive, Mother. It's disappeared."

There was a moment of silence, then a tightly controlled voice I barely recognized said, "Would you repeat that? I'm sure I misunderstood."

"No, you didn't, Mother. The thumb drive disappeared. It was there one minute, and then it wasn't."

"Disappeared? What do you mean it 'disappeared'?" Her last word had reached an operatic high note, just short of a screech.

"I think I set it down on the entry table when I went to answer the phone. Then, when I came back, it was gone."

Mother's deep breathing forced its way through the tiny speaker in my phone like an angry bellows. "I'm coming over there." I felt certain flames had issued forth from her mouth as she spoke.

"I told you, Bruno and I searched the entire place, everywhere. Unless Wild Thing ate it, it isn't here."

"Do you think that's a possibility?"

"Bruno and I discussed it. I could have him x-rayed." IF I could get him to a vet. Maybe Valerie would go with us.

"You look again. If you don't find it by tomorrow morning, take Wild Thing in to be x-rayed. You have to find that thumb drive."

I knew it was futile, but I kept looking for the drive in all of the places that Bruno and I had already searched. It was a clear example of the definition of insanity—doing the same thing over and over and expecting and praying for different results. Wild Thing glared at me from a blanket he'd dragged from his bed in the spare room. Maybe he just wanted to make sure no one touched any of his things again. I kept my eye on him, and he kept an eye on me, occasionally getting up and peering around the corner when I disappeared from sight.

For the umpteenth time, I asked myself if I was absolutely certain the door had been locked when the thumb went missing. I was so sure when I first checked, but doubt had crept in. And I was also starting to worry who Mrs. Weller might have already told or would tell in the future about the thumb. We should have warned her to stay mum. If someone had pushed Lonnie over the edge of the cliff, what else might they be willing to do to retrieve any pictures he had taken?

I kept hoping Wild Thing would show symptoms of digestive problems, but he seemed as healthy and cantankerous as ever. Even so, if I didn't find the thumb, I was going to have him checked out...as soon as I could arrange to have Valerie go with us to the vet. And if he'd swallowed the drive, he was going to have to cough it up, so to speak.

It occurred to me that once Wild Thing was in his carrier, I could put him on an airplane bound for some place, *any* place other than here, fail to attach a return address, and simply not retrieve him. He could start over with a new set of shelters in another city. Then I could honestly tell Valerie that I had not sent him to "the farm."

On my way to work Wednesday morning, I stopped off at Valerie's houseboat to ask her father whether he would allow Valerie to help me take Wild Thing to the vet. A dog growled when I knocked, sounding big for a Shepherd, more like a St. Bernard. Or a Great Dane. Maybe he'd got another dog to protect his Shepherd from Wild Thing.

When Glen opened the door, his Shepherd was right beside him. The dog looked ready to grab me by the jugular on command. Between him and the crows circling overhead, I felt like a dead man walking.

Glen was reluctant at first but finally agreed that Valerie could go with me to the vet. I thanked him profusely, as if he had agreed to give me a spare kidney. If the thumb turned out to have been devoured by Wild Thing, it could be "retrieved," and Mother would get off my back. I wasn't sure what "retrieval" would involve, but I anticipated it wouldn't be pleasant for Wild Thing, and I had no doubt he would take it out on me afterwards. But, once I had it back in hand, after sanitizing it, of course, I would finally get to see whether it contained incriminating evidence or porn. If the photos proved someone may have had reason for wanting Lonnie out of commission, I would turn the thumb over to Bruno. After that, no one would have any reason to come after me for the thumb. And if there wasn't anything legally relevant, well, Mother would be forced to move on. A win either way.

When I got to work and looked at my calendar, I remembered that I had a lunch date with Betty Noland, the thin woman with the large cat. It beat digging through the litter box for the thumb drive, but not by much.

I called several vets before finding one who had a late afternoon opening for an X-ray. It wasn't until tomorrow, though, and it was going to cost more than I thought it should. And, no, I didn't have pet insurance. And, no, there were no other pets in the household. And I didn't know whether the cat had his shots or a serious health issue or surgery in the past. Nor had I paid any attention to recent bathroom habits, couldn't remember the name of the cat food I'd been feeding him, and had no idea how much exercise he got daily. It all made me feel inadequate. I wanted to tell them about the catnip squirrel and climbing tree I'd purchased for Wild Thing instead of taking him to the farm, but I wasn't sure they would be impressed. Maybe they would take him away from me for being such an irresponsible pet owner. Preferably AFTER he gave up the thumb drive.

Before hanging up, I asked if she knew how long it took for a piece of plastic to work its way through a cat's digestive system.

"What size object are we talking about?"

"Something about the size of a thumb drive." I'm not sure why I didn't simply say I thought he might have consumed a valuable thumb drive, and I wanted it back. But that made it sound like I was more concerned with finding the thumb than with my cat's well-being.

"Hmmm. That could cause a problem."

"What kind of problem?"

"If your cat starts vomiting, has bloody diarrhea, or is straining to defecate, you should probably bring him in immediately."

"Otherwise?"

"Usually, something of that nature will work its way through the system in ten to twenty-five hours after ingestion, but it could take much longer. It all depends."

What it all depended on wasn't clear to me, but the one thing I knew for certain was that for the next day and a half, I'd better watch my step at home. And I should probably warn Valerie.

"Have a lunch date?" Emma asked as I left a little early for lunch.

"Yes, I do. But it won't be a long lunch." The only question was whether I should tell Betty about my bogus profile before or after we had something to eat.

Betty looked as undernourished in real life as she did in her photo. But she seemed energetic and had a pinkish bloom on her gaunt cheeks. I decided to let her have something to eat before giving her the bad news about our future, or our lack of a future. When the waitress came by, I was surprised at the quantity of Betty's order. When she noticed me gaping, she said,

"I'm a marathoner. I need a lot of calories to keep up my strength."

"You run?" I asked. Another reason we were a bad fit.

"Every day. At least ten miles. At first it was just a health thing. Now, I admit I'm addicted. Do you, ah, exercise?" She eyed me, assessing my BMI no doubt.

"Only mentally, most days."

"I see."

"And there's something else I should tell you." As long as we were sharing information about our lives, I decided to give her the bad news and blurted it all out at once: "My buddies did my bio as a joke. I don't have any drones, and I'm not a cat lover. Sorry."

"Oh, I was hoping you could follow me during a marathon and make a video."

"Drones aren't a hobby for you?"

"No, but I do have three cats."

"Ah, a cat lady."

She sat up straight, and her face turned bright red. "Don't call me that."

"I'm sorry, I…" I didn't know how to finish the sentence, but she didn't wait long before jumping in again.

"People use that term to speak disparagingly about single women. And I don't appreciate it. Not one bit."

Our waitress brought out the food, giving me time to think. But my mind was blank. "Sorry," I repeated. "I didn't intend it as an insult. Just that you are a single lady with cats."

"And you are a single man who lies on his dating app."

"I told you, my buddies did it, not me."

She waved at the waitress. "Could you bring me a box for this, please?" Then she turned to me. "I don't think we are a good fit."

"But you lied too," I said.

"I said I was *interested* in drones, not that I had any. That's not a lie."

"You wanted to *use* me." I don't know why I was arguing with her. I was actually relieved.

The waitress brought boxes for both of us. And the bill. I gave her a credit card and filled my box while Betty filled hers. "Better luck with the next woman you lie to," Betty said as she picked up her box of food and departed speedily on thin, muscular legs.

"Lovers spat?" the waitress said, handing me my receipt to sign.

"A mutual parting of the ways," I said.

"Sorry."

"Don't feel sorry, I'm not." I didn't mind Betty leaving in a huff, but I sincerely hoped Sherri wouldn't feel the same about the misrepresentations on my dating app. Maybe I should have updated my bio before asking her out.

Bruno and I met after work for a beer. He tried to cheer me up, but I couldn't get losing an important piece of evidence out of my mind.

"If I don't find it, Mother is never going to forgive me." The "never going to forgive me" was becoming my mantra. "And I keep worrying about Mrs. Weller. What if she blabs about me finding the thumb? And the killer thinks that I have it."

"First of all, we don't know that Lonnie was murdered. Second, I think there's a good chance Wild Thing swallowed it. And if so, we'll soon be able to see what's on the thumb."

"That cat is a finicky eater," I said. "And he doesn't seem to be experiencing any intestinal problems. He chowed down his breakfast this morning, like usual."

"Cats gulp their food, don't they?"

"That thumb would have been a big gulp for a kitten."

"Does that mean you aren't expecting the X-ray to show anything?"

"I'm not hopeful, but it's the only option at this point."

"Well, that drive didn't just vanish into thin air. Are you sure you didn't drop it outside somewhere? Like when you were being chased by crows?" Bruno gave me a big, mocking grin.

"I distinctly remember having it in my hand when the phone rang." I gave him the stink eye. "When YOU called."

"And you weren't drinking."

"I'd been with Mother."

"And the door was locked."

"I'm 95 percent sure. Well, make that 80 percent. Maybe 70."

"If no one from the outside stole it, it had to be Wild Thing."

"I agree; I just don't know how he did it."

"The answer is in the litter box. Or perhaps will be soon."

"Not funny."

"By the way, I got a call from a Desiree something. She wants to talk to me about art fraud. You didn't sic her on me, did you?"

"No. I thought that issue was settled. She went with me to meet Lars, the artist I talked to about how you tell whether a painting is a fake. But he wasn't there."

"Any idea why she called me?"

"None whatsoever. Maybe her niece still isn't satisfied, and Desiree is doing the legwork." A vision of Desiree's shapely legs flashed before me.

"Art fraud isn't my thing," Bruno said. "I should probably send her to someone else."

I sighed. "She lives up to her name. You may want to meet with her."

"That good, huh? Well, I suppose I could spare a few minutes."

That evening, when I fed Wild Thing his dinner, I got down on the floor and tried to check out his stomach. He turned away and mooned me.

"That wasn't nice," I said, pushing myself to my feet. "You'll be sorry if the vet finds a thumb drive in your stomach."

He paused long enough to hiss at me before retiring to the other room.

Chapter Eighteen: Cat Toys

Thursday morning, I donated another pen to the litter box search. Nothing. And I couldn't resist checking out this corner and that while Wild Thing watched, even though I knew there was nothing there except dust bunnies and spider webs. It was a relief to escape to work.

Bruno called me at two to thank me.

"What for?"

"Introducing me to Desiree."

"I didn't exactly introduce you. She called you, remember?"

"But if you had followed up on the second opinion…" he began.

I quickly interrupted. "I did follow up. With the painter."

"Well, she didn't actually meet him."

"But I did."

"Well, sorry, she just wants to be absolutely certain."

"So, how are you going to help her?"

"I'm going to recommend some appraisers."

"Why didn't she just get one on her own? Why go to you?"

"She wanted to know if there were any scams out there that she should be aware of."

"And you let her think that my company could be scamming her? How? We're giving her sister exactly what she asked for."

"She just wants to be sure." —

"You do realize it doesn't make sense, don't you?"

Bruno sighed into the phone. "I do. But you've met her. You've seen her…"

"Body," I finished for him. "Didn't notice."

"Come on. Besides, we hit it off. She likes big men."

"She told you that?"

"Like I said, we hit it off."

"You mean like in going on a date hitting it off?" I was mad. And jealous.

"That's why I called to thank you."

"You're welcome." I knew I sounded bitter.

"Anyway, I'll let you know who I recommend."

"Just spare me the details about your date."

After we disconnected, I knew I had to call Carla and tell her the news. She was bound to hear about it. And if she found out that Bruno had warned me and I hadn't told her—I had no choice. Getting backed into corners seemed to be happening to me a lot lately, and I didn't like it. The next thing I knew I would make the 10 Most Victimized list and they would post my picture with nine other patsies on the bulletin board at the post office.

She answered with an abrupt "What now?"

I got right to the point. "I'm afraid Desiree Defelice isn't giving up yet. I just wanted to let you know."

"I thought you said she was going to tell the family to back off."

"I did. That's what she told me. But I just learned that she went to the police."

There was the briefest of hesitations before Carla said, "Why on earth would she do that?"

"She wanted to ask about scams. Although I have no idea why since your appraisal was very generous. She also asked them for names of reputable appraisers for a second opinion."

"But I already authenticated it. What can she hope to gain?"

"It doesn't make sense, but for whatever reason, that's what's happening. I thought you should know."

"Thanks, John. I appreciate the heads-up."

Wow, that wasn't the response I was expecting. I was about to say something more, but she'd hung up.

The way my day was going, I knew I would never be able to sneak past Emma to leave early to go to the vet, so I decided to be honest. I stopped in

INSURANCE TO DIE FOR

front of her desk, looked her in the eye, and said that I was leaving early to take my cat to the vet.

"You have a cat?"

"Yes, a kitten, and he may have eaten something, ah, bad for him."

"What's your cat's name?"

"Wild Thing."

"That's nice. I didn't picture you as a cat person."

Ignoring the "cat person" remark, I asked, "Do you have a cat?"

"No, I'm allergic to cats. I have a dog, a Chihuahua named Pixie." She picked up a picture from her desk and turned it around so I could see it. The dog was wearing a plaid jacket and staring into the camera with eyes too large for its narrow head. At least, that's how it seemed to me.

"Ah, nice," I managed. "Sorry, I don't have a picture of Wild Thing."

"You should. Take one, and let me see it."

Did she require proof that I had a cat, or was that an olive branch between pet owners? "Will do," I said.

"Good luck."

I wondered if she would have wished me luck if she knew about the dysfunctional relationship I had with Wild Thing and that I couldn't even take him to the vet on my own.

The crows were nowhere in sight. I bravely left the umbrella next to my parking space, wondering if they would attack on my way back when I was with a child holding a small animal. Maybe Valerie could work her magic on them.

I stopped at Valerie's to tell her I was home, but no one answered. When I got to my houseboat, the door wasn't locked. I didn't know whether to go in search of a weapon, try to sneak in through the back door, or call the police. Then suddenly, the door swung open, and Valerie was standing there. "I thought I heard you," she said.

"Oh," was all I said. I was becoming so paranoid I'd spaced about her key.

"I thought you bought a cat carrier?" she said. "I can't find it anywhere."

What did she mean, she couldn't find it. Had she been searching my home?

"I put it on a top shelf at the back of the closet in the spare room; I didn't think I'd be needing it this soon."

"You should put a blanket in it," she said as I went to fetch the carrier.

"There's a blanket in the corner that he seems to like," I said.

"He should be getting regular checkups," Valerie called after me, sounding like she was the adult and I was the child. I had to remind myself that this was the deranged young thing who had tormented me since she was barely able to walk. I was still convinced that somewhere buried inside was her old diabolical self. But that didn't mean she wasn't right. And since I currently needed her assistance on a day-to-day basis, I had to be nice.

I fetched the carrier from the closet in the back room and grabbed Wild Thing's blanket on the way back. Valerie was on the floor playing with him. She and he were batting something back and forth. Something small, something that looked very much like..."

"The thumb drive," I yelled.

Valerie looked startled, and even Wild Thing seemed surprised. He backed up a few inches before snarling at me as I reached down to pick up the thumb. But Valerie was quicker; she beat me to it. "That's Wild Thing's toy," she said as she held the thumb tightly in her tiny fist.

"No, that's my thumb drive," I said. "It's why I was taking that damn cat to the vet. I thought he'd swallowed it."

"You shouldn't swear," she said, putting her hand with the thumb drive behind her back.

"That drive has business information on it. If you give it to me, I'll buy him any toy he wants."

She seemed to consider the possibilities. "He likes *this* toy," she said. Was she negotiating, or was that a firm "no"?

"What do you want?" I asked.

Wild Thing was sitting there, calmly watching the exchange. Valerie turned to him and said, "What do you think?"

I almost expected him to respond with the ransom price, then I reminded myself that he was a cat, and I was trying to reason with an eight-year-old. "If you want to continue playing with Wild Thing, you have to hand that over."

"I have a key," she said.

"And I can change the locks."

While she was thinking about that, I added, "And I can take Wild Thing to the farm, and you'll never see him again."

"You wouldn't…"

It took several minutes more of negotiating before we reached an agreement. When she finally handed it over, Wild Thing leapt up in the air, aiming for my outstretched hand. But I was even more determined than he was. He didn't know my mother like I did.

As soon as I had possession of the thumb, I called Mother to tell her.

"Did the vet, ah, retrieve it?" she asked.

"No, Valerie and Wild Thing had it all along." Suddenly I had a vision of Wild Thing while I was looking for the thumb drive and later when Bruno and I searched the place together. "You were sitting on it, weren't you?" I said to Wild Thing.

"What," Mother said into my ear.

If cats had more facial muscles, I was certain he would have been smirking.

"He was sitting on the drive while we were looking for it," I repeated, this time to Mother. "I'm sure of it."

"Well, the important thing is that you have it now. Just don't lose it again. And call me as soon as you've seen what's on it."

"I'm going to take a look as soon as I get back from the pet store. And don't ask—" I'd had to promise Valerie to buy some replacement toys for Wild Thing instead of the trip to the vet.

"Let's go," Valerie urged.

"Two more calls."

First, I called the vet and canceled what would have been a very expensive visit. The receptionist wasn't pleased, informing me that they required cancellations twenty-four hours in advance and that there would be a fee for a late cancellation. I haggled a few minutes before acquiescing. I had more important things to do.

Then I punched in Bruno's number. He didn't answer, so I left him a message.

Finally, I put the thumb drive into the zippered pocket on my jacket, and off we went, leaving a disgruntled cat at home. Valerie tried to talk me into taking Wild Thing with us so he could pick out his own toys, but that was where I drew the line. Admittedly, it was a pretty thin line, but a line nonetheless.

An hour later, I was back with a bag of chews and an assortment of toys and snacks for my undeserving pet. Valerie was going to share them with Wild Thing over time, although I was tempted to bestow at least a few tidbits tonight to get in his good favor. This hostility between us was taking its toll. I also promised Valerie that I would take him in for his shots…if she would go with me. The only question was whether I called the same vet back or tried a different one. Maybe if I made another appointment, they wouldn't charge me the late fee.

Just minutes after I got back, there was some insistent pounding on my front door. I'd already plugged the drive into my computer and hesitated to leave it for even a few minutes, but someone wanted in bad. I opened the door a crack to see who it was, and Bruno pushed me aside and burst into the room. "What's with those crows?" he asked. "One of them attacked me."

"I think they like human hair for their nests," I said. "And some of them are just mean."

"I thought you were kidding before."

"Until now, they haven't attacked anyone but me."

"Well, if they come after me again, they'll be sorry."

"You gonna arrest them?"

"Use them for target practice."

"I don't think that's legal."

"I'll use a water pistol."

"Water blaster—tried that."

"Noisemaker?"

"Neighbors complained."

"Jesus, John. This is absurd."

"Come on, we need to look at the drive." I led him over to my computer, and we started going through the files. Lonnie had them arranged by some sort of code; no names were used. But I'd visited the neighborhood enough that I could tell who he was targeting by looking at the house involved.

When we saw the drone peeking through the bedroom window at what could only be described as enthusiastic sex, Bruno said, "If we hadn't talked with her already, she would be at the top of my list."

"And which list is that?" I asked.

"Not funny."

"Wasn't trying to be." I was still miffed about Desiree.

We were almost at the end of the thumb before we saw anything new.

"There," Bruno said. "Pause."

"That's the Winslows' house. Their back yard."

"At dusk. And that looks like a man in a hoodie carrying a painting."

"But he's taking it in, not stealing it."

"If he's legitimate, why go in the back way?"

"I wonder if the Winslows were home when Lonnie took these?"

"There doesn't appear to be any lights on."

"Look. Now he's coming out...with what looks like the same painting. The same size, at least." The drone followed the man through the back gate and down the alley to a car. It focused on the license plate before the car took off.

"That's worth a follow-up," I said. "Do you think he exchanged one painting for another?"

"Not sure. But if that's the case and your company appraisal was accurate, then the current painting should be a phony."

"Look at the date. It's the day after we returned their painting, after I'd signed off on the appraisal." I paused the video again.

"So, it looks like the guy knew the appraisal was done, and he was stealing the real thing and replacing it with a phony."

"Unless...he was replacing a phony painting with the real thing."

"What makes you say that? You think your appraiser was covering up a crime? Because Desiree's niece said the painting smelled funny?"

"Carla doesn't seem like the type. But it makes some sense. Assuming there actually was a problem with the painting and she was somehow involved. Even before she learned about Desiree contacting me, she may have been worried because of Savannah's complaint about the smell. Although Lars said that the smell didn't mean anything."

"I don't think there's a special 'type' who commits fraud. Greed comes in all shapes and sizes."

"There were two paintings, though. Why replace just one?"

"Maybe they only faked one. In either case, that would be hard to prove at this point. Assuming both paintings in the Winslows' possession currently are authentic."

"Who are *they*?" I asked. "Who could have faked these pictures? And why? It isn't as if they were worth big money. Unless they are and Carla's appraisal was totally bogus."

"Well, Desiree has a second opinion scheduled for Friday. We'll know more then."

"Carla didn't seem all that upset when I called her about the new appraisals."

"Could be because she knows both paintings are the real thing."

"Because she authenticated them? Or because she replaced a fake with the real thing? That's kinda complicated. I mean, how would she have had a fake ready to give to them in the first place? And why take a risk like that for that amount of money?"

"Those are interesting questions, John. Maybe we'll learn more when we track this guy from the video."

The rest of the stuff on the thumb drive was pretty mundane. People in hot tubs, a neighbor dumping leaves over a fence, the kids smoking behind the garage, a couple of sunbathers, two kids in a car engaged in some heavy panting and petting, someone letting their dog poop in the neighbor's yard. All minor crimes and privacy violations.

"Nothing that exciting," Bruno concluded. "He could have kept the thumb hidden because of the guy exchanging the paintings or because of Mrs. Gillmor's late-night visitor, but it's also possible he just didn't want his parents to find out that he was spying on the neighbors."

"I don't think they were the type to search his room. He could have left it in his desk drawer if that's all it was about."

"I'll take the drive," Bruno said.

"Mother will want to see it."

"I know she'll think she's earned the right, but I can't share evidence with her. And we don't want her to see the part about Mrs. Gillmor. She may guess we lied to her or wonder why we don't have her on the suspect list."

"Maybe she'll understand if you convince her there is something the police will be looking into and that you will tell her everything as soon as it's appropriate for you to do so."

"Okay. But she'll question you."

"I may let her break me down and tell her about the painting thief, if she swears she won't tell you that I told her."

"I like that."

"And you'll let me know what you learn about the guy who either stole or returned a painting after you track the license plate?"

"That won't be public information."

"I'm not the public. And my company has an interest in what you find. Besides, I'm the one who found the drive. That must count for something."

Bruno rolled his eyes. "Okay, let me find out who he is and get back to you."

"The whole thing seems strange," I said.

"No stranger than a cat sitting on a thumb drive like he was hoping it would hatch." Bruno looked around as if concerned Wild Thing might hear him and attack. "Do they have cat therapists?"

Chapter Nineteen: Missing

"Mother, I'm sorry. But Bruno needs to hold onto the thumb drive, and he can't make copies for the public." Mother called only minutes after Bruno left. I knew what I had to do and prayed I could pull it off.

"I'm not the 'public,' I'm the one who insisted on looking for it in the first place."

"True, but it's not like he's trying to keep you in the dark. The police have rules about sharing evidence."

"But *you* can describe what was on the drive, right?"

"Mother, you're asking me to break a promise to Bruno."

"And…?"

"He's a friend as well as an officer of the law."

"And I'm your mother."

"Okay, you win. But you have to promise you won't tell Bruno what I'm about to tell you."

"You want a pinkie swear?"

"Not funny." I sighed loud enough for it to be audible on the phone. "Most of what's on the drive is petty spying stuff, but there is one thing on it that requires further investigation. It looks like someone exchanged one of the Winslow paintings for another painting. Lonnie not only caught it on video but tracked the thief to his car, so the police have the man's license plate."

"Well, that sounds like quite a good lead." Mother sounded pleased.

"Yes, Bruno is all over it."

"Maybe it's even a motive for murder."

"It could be. But it's kinda strange. If you had to guess, which do you think he was doing—stealing an original or removing a fake?"

"There's no guessing involved. He was replacing a fake. And Lonnie caught him in the act."

"I doubt Lonnie had the means to track him down."

"Not through the license plate. But if he suspected there was something illegal going on with the painting, maybe he talked to the wrong person about it. After all, it had to be an inside job. What if he got in touch with that appraiser of yours."

"She's not 'my' appraiser. And she's worked for the company for years. Has an outstanding record."

"Maybe someone's blackmailing her. Threatening to harm her family. Or maybe she wants to retire early." Before I could say anything, she added, "If I came by your office, could I meet her?"

"No, Mother. She is an independent contractor."

"Oh, so I could go to her office. That's even better."

"No, Mother. I don't know what you're thinking, but it's not a good idea."

"If you don't know what I'm thinking, then how do you know it isn't a good idea?"

"Whatever you're thinking, it's just going to make things worse. I like my job; I don't want to be fired." I knew I sounded whiny, but I couldn't help it. If Mother went to see Carla under some sort of ruse, and Carla found out she was related to me, Carla would make my life hell—of that, I was certain. I had barely gotten past her threat to never work with me again. I didn't want to risk backsliding just so my mother could satisfy her inner detective. Besides, I wasn't convinced that Carla was engaged in some sort of fraud scheme. She would know that given her role as appraiser, she would be the obvious suspect. So, doing something like that was a huge risk. She couldn't possibly think she could get away with it. There had to be another explanation.

"Don't worry, John, I won't do anything to get you into trouble." With that, Mother hung up.

I wasn't sure what I should do. Warn Bruno and see if he could dissuade her? If Carla was innocent, maybe I ought to warn her. It was like waiting for the anticipated big one, an earthquake followed by a crushing tsunami. Either my mother or the second opinion could be the earthquake that put me in the path of the tsunami. On the other hand, if I did nothing, maybe there wouldn't be an earthquake.

Before going to bed, I snapped a couple pictures of Wild Thing to show Emma. It wasn't easy. I used some of the treats I'd exchanged for the thumb to lure him into the open. Most of the pictures weren't that good, but I managed to take one that caught him with an innocent look of surprise in his greenish-gold eyes moments before he began snarling at me. The calm before the storm. Emma didn't need to see the storm. This wasn't about Wild Thing; this was all about getting Emma to see me in a different light, as the pet-loving male I wasn't.

Instead of nodding off instantly like I usually do when I go to bed, I tossed and turned. Actually, my body didn't, but my mind did. I kept worrying about what my mother was going to do. I could picture her trying to play an undercover art dealer, or pretending to own expensive art that she needed appraised, or even using her fake PI license to support some story about investigating art scams in the area—a few of her mystery book club members had put together fake IDs as a fun project. At least that's what she told me.

Not only could she get *me* in trouble, if someone killed Lonnie to protect some illegal activity, then my mother could put herself in danger by asking the wrong people questions.

Another thing that kept me awake was my mother's theory about it being an inside job. It could be almost anybody. What if the person pulling the strings was my boss, Mr. Van Droop? As unlikely as it seemed to me, I couldn't rule it out. After all, he tried to get me sidelined by sending me to an advanced ropes class. Unless he thought I could handle it...or did it as a test of some sort. Nor could I rule out Carla based on my gut feel about her.

On the other hand, it was also possible that someone from the outside was hacking into our system. Insider, outsider—there were so many possibilities. I didn't want to trip over vague accusations, and I knew what could happen to whistleblowers if they weren't careful. I needed more information. Maybe

I should talk to Lars again. Find out what he knew about scams in the art world.

One final thing was making me antsy. I hadn't heard from Sherri Sherman. I suggested we have dinner on Friday, and it was almost Friday. Maybe she'd taken a second look at my profile picture.

I was just about to finally fall asleep when the door to my bedroom creaked. My eyes snapped open. There was just enough moonlight slipping through the gaps around my blinds for me to see that my door was open a few inches. Not enough for a person to get through, but a kitten? Before I could take action, I sensed a presence next to me in the bed. I was too afraid to scream or move. Luckily, it wasn't necessary. Wild Thing snuggled up next to me and started softly purring. Now, I was really afraid to move for fear of startling him into aggression mode instead of sleep mode. Was he lonely? Cold? Did he do that every night, or did he sense my distress and come to comfort me? I dismissed two out of three possibilities and went with "cold." Then I fell asleep.

Friday morning, the sun followed the same path as the moonlight had at night, hitting me right in the eyes with an intense glare. I started to turn over when I remembered Wild Thing. But when I opened my eyes, there was no cat there. Had I imagined him sneaking into my bedroom in the middle of the night?

Over breakfast, I made my decision. I couldn't stop my mother from doing whatever she would do, and Bruno probably couldn't either. So, if possible, I needed to get out in front of the situation. Talking to Lars still made sense to me. He was part of a world that I knew virtually nothing about. Even if he hadn't heard about anything illegal happening in the local art scene, he might be able to tell me a little about possible types of scams. Or, he might know someone I should talk to.

I called and left a message for Emma so she would know where I was, kinda, that is. I could hardly tell her I was following up on a closed file, especially since I could be looking into possible fraud on the part of one of our trusted appraisers. I said something vague about needing to make multiple stops as part of an accident investigation—for a claims adjuster, there was always some accident to investigate. She could leave me a message if she needed to get in touch.

When I arrived at Lars' house and studio, it had the look of an abandoned place. I'm not exactly sure why, but it somehow seemed lifeless. Not after-the-apocalypse lifeless, but deserted, as if Lars had gone on walkabout on the spur of the moment.

His studio door was shut, and he didn't answer when I knocked. After glancing around, I turned the knob—it was still not locked, so I went inside. Everything looked exactly like it had when Desiree and I were there together. I walked to the back of the main room and checked out the storage area. It was still basically empty.

Next, I tried the house. No one answered. I considered trying to get inside, then thought better of it. Someone might see me. But now I was starting to worry about Lars. Why was his studio open when he didn't seem to be around?

I decided to talk to the neighbors. See if anyone knew what had happened to him.

The house to the east was a nicely kept rambler with a white fence and well-kept gardens. The elderly woman who answered the door said she, too, was worried about Lars. He usually came by for tea at least once a week and sometimes picked up items from the grocery for her. "It isn't like him to simply go away without a word."

No one responded at the house on the other side of his. But at the second house down, a young woman holding a baby answered the door.

"I've been wondering if he went on vacation," she said. "I haven't seen him for about a week now."

"You don't know how I could get in touch with him, do you?"

"Sorry, no."

Two down. I kept going.

Four houses later, I was none the wiser. At one, no one answered. At the other three, no one had a clue where he was or how to get in touch. But everyone agreed he hadn't been around of late.

Back at the office, I stopped to show Emma the picture I'd taken of Wild Thing. "Oh, he's so sweet," she oozed.

"Yes, although he can be feisty," I said, not wanting to nominate him for sainthood in anyone's eyes. "I may frame this," I added.

"It would look nice on your desk. You don't have anything personal in your office."

I hadn't thought about it, but she was right. Maybe I should get a cat calendar to go with the picture of Wild Thing. Add a little personality.

I spent the rest of the day catching up on the neatly piled files Emma had left in my inbox after removing the completed files I hadn't handed over yet. All but one represented small fender-benders, with page after page devoted to excuses for what happened. Minor injury claims, with everyone hoping to avoid rate hikes and to make a little money from their accident. For the most part, they didn't require a lot of work or emotional investment.

There was, however, one new file that made me very uneasy. Not because there were serious injuries and complicated issues involved, but because it required an appraisal of a painting. It wasn't that long ago that Carla had called me a back-stabbing little dweeb and made it abundantly clear that she would never do another appraisal for me again. Still, the last time I'd called to give her a heads-up about Desiree continuing to seek a second opinion, she hadn't bit my head off. In fact, she had thanked me for the information. Maybe she was having second thoughts about the public dressing down she'd given me. One way or the other, I would have to call her; even though she wasn't an employee, she was the company's preferred appraiser. We had an open contract with her, and all the fees and conditions were spelled out. Unless she proved to be guilty of something illegal, I needed to work with her.

Before making the call to Carla, I decided I needed a bathroom break. When I saw Jack at his desk, I made a detour to say hello.

"Looks like you're feeling better," Jack said.

I'd done away with the limp; it was too hard to keep it up consistently, and it seemed like enough time had lapsed for recovery. "Much better, thanks. How are you doing?"

"Good. And by the way, I want to thank you again for inviting me to your poker game. I hope I didn't offend anyone by winning."

"No one likes to lose, but maybe next time, we can get some of our money back."

"So, you'll invite me again?" He looked pleased.

"Yeah. Bruno wants a rematch."

"He's a good guy."

I nodded agreement. "By the way, you might be interested in knowing that I'm hopeful Carla is no longer boycotting me. I gave her a head's up about another matter, and she actually thanked me."

"Really? I didn't have her pegged as the forgiving type."

"I know. Me neither. That's why I'm a bit nervous about asking if she's willing to do an appraisal for me on a file that landed on my desk. As soon as I hit the restroom, I'm going to call her to see if she's willing to work with me on it."

"If she agrees to do an appraisal after that little dust-up between the two of you, I'd be on extra good behavior."

"You'd better believe I will. Although I really think what happened was a fluke. I still don't understand why the client wants a second opinion."

"Didn't you say it had something to do with smell?"

"Yes, but I assured them that was some sort of mistake." I was tempted to tell him about the exchange of paintings but I didn't want to prolong our conversation—I needed to take a whiz and go call Carla before I lost my nerve.

"Good luck," Jack said as I left.

When I got back and placed a call to Carla, I was pleased when she answered in person. That was a good sign. I assumed she had caller ID, so she must have known it was me.

"It's John Smith," I said, just to be sure.

"I know."

"I'm sorry we've had some, ah, misunderstandings recently…" I began.

"I don't consider you going behind my back a 'misunderstanding,'" she said abruptly.

153

"As I said before, I was confident your appraisal was good, and I was only getting a second opinion to placate the client. I hope you've forgiven me for that."

There was a long silence. "I need to know that you will talk to me in the future about any client issues instead of going rogue."

Going rogue? Is that what I'd done? "I didn't mean to offend you, and I certainly will come to you right away if anything like that happens again." Somehow it didn't feel like I was the representative for the company who engaged her services and she was the contractor, but then, she was the expert and I was the novice. And she had been working for the company a lot longer than I had.

"As long as we understand each other."

"Definitely."

There was another long silence before I felt confident enough to continue. "If we are in agreement, does that mean I can schedule an appraisal with you?"

"Sure." She didn't sound enthusiastic, but that didn't matter, as long as she agreed to do it. I needed to get the job done, and if I had to get a different appraiser, it might look like I'm not a team player. They could even send me to another ropes session to work on my people skills.

I told her the new client's name, and she said she would check out the painting and get back to me about scheduling. Then, in the name of transparency, I said, "There is one other thing I should give you a heads-up about." I hadn't consciously made the decision to share any of the thumb drive information with her, but it seemed like the right thing to do, given our professional relationship. And assuming, as I did, that she wasn't engaged in any illegal activities.

"Oh?" Her voice would have chilled a martini to perfection.

"It's possible someone switched one of the Winslow paintings."

"What does that mean, *switched*?"

"It means the police have reason to believe that someone may have substituted one of the Winslows' paintings with another painting."

"And how do you know this?" Now, she had reached the iceberg stage.

"The police contacted me about it. I assured them that the company was satisfied that the paintings we insured were authentic. I don't know yet what they found when they went to check on them."

"And if they discover that they aren't the originals?"

"We'll have to pay for their loss, of course. And the police will probably want to talk to us, but they can't expect us to know what happened after I signed off on the paintings."

Another silence. "But what do *you* think happened?"

"I have no idea," I said. "It's possible the picture that was switched wasn't one of the pictures we just insured. They'll know more when they get the guy who did it."

"Do they know who he is?"

"I don't think so. At least they didn't when they told me about it initially. But they may by now." I left out the part about the license plate and a few other details that I was sure Bruno wouldn't want me sharing with anyone. "Anyway, it's a police problem. Except for a possible payout, we're out of it. I just thought you should know."

As I hung up, I hoped I hadn't lied. Beginnings and endings are sometimes confusing.

Chapter Twenty: Framed!

That Friday evening, I was feeling pretty satisfied with my life. There was no crow escort to my houseboat, Wild Thing hadn't hissed at me when I asked how his day had been, Carla and I had a peace agreement in place, and Mother hadn't done anything outlandish to endanger my job…as far as I knew.

While making dinner, I turned up James Brown singing *I Got You* and managed to chime in now and then with a few words—*So good…so nice…sugar and spice…*" I was making chili from scratch, if you call adding some spices and a little hamburger to several cans of kidney beans starting from scratch. I planned on taking a bowl of chili and a sleeve of soda crackers into the living room while I binge-watched *Recipes for Love and Murder*.

When the phone started playing the theme song from Oklahoma—my latest ringtone—I almost didn't answer. But then I noticed it was Bruno. I turned the chili to simmer and tapped the phone icon on my cell.

"Have you seen your Facebook page today?" Bruno asked.

"I don't have a Facebook page."

"What about Twitter?"

"No, I'm not on Twitter."

"Like kiddie porn?"

"What? Say that again."

"I asked, are you into kiddie porn?"

"Why on earth would you ask that? I don't even like kids."

"Well, you've got a problem."

I was starting to feel itchy, like I was about to break out in hives. There was no doubt Bruno was leading up to something, and it didn't sound like something I was going to like. "Okay, you'd better be more specific."

"You really don't have a clue?"

"No, Bruno, not a clue. Now spill it."

When he got through telling me about what I'd supposedly posted on Facebook, Twitter and who knew what other social media sites, I at first felt numb, my brain as thick as the chili simmering on the stove. Then the anger started to simmer, threatening to come to a boiling point any moment.

"My name is John Smith, for heaven's sake; it must be some other John Smith."

"It's your email and your picture."

"They posted a picture of me with that...that..."

"I'm sorry, John. I knew it wasn't you. But it sure looks like you."

"Oh my god, you don't think Mother's seen it, do you?"

There was a blip on my phone; another caller. No ID. And my computer was making strange noises. I hoped that didn't mean what I feared it meant. "Can't you help me?" I asked. "You're the police."

"You should report it, but I don't know who you report it to. I haven't a clue how you go about getting things like that removed if you didn't post it in the first place. It might be complicated."

My phone bleeped again. "I gotta go." I hung up and stared at my phone. Did I want to answer? *Oklahoma* echoed off the walls of the kitchen. It was Laney.

"Hello?" I said, sounding like the victim I was.

"John, have you seen..."

"Laney, Bruno just told me. I want you to know that I didn't put that horrible stuff out there. I don't do Facebook or Twitter or whatever. You've gotta believe me."

"Of course, I believe you. That's why I called. You need to remove these posts as soon as you can."

"But they aren't my accounts. How do I stop them if I didn't start them?"

"I was afraid of that. It would be fairly easy to eliminate something from a hacked account, but you don't have control over someone else's posts. Not even when they're using your identity. Fortunately, I know someone who will probably be able to help. But it may cost you."

"I don't care what it costs. I need to make this horrible stuff disappear."

She gave me a name and a number, and I called immediately. When I got his voicemail, I almost hung up. But I was desperate, so I left a rather incoherent message: "Someone is using my name to promote kiddie porn, and it isn't me, and I don't know what to do, and Laney said you might be able to help, and I definitely need help." Then I hung up. After a minute or so, I called back to leave a number, although as soon as I did, I realized that hadn't been necessary. But a name would have been nice. Before I could call a third time, *Oklahoma* started playing, and the number I was about to redial flashed on the screen.

"Hello?" My voice sounded timid even to me. Timid and upset at the same time.

"Stay calm," a raspy male voice said. He sounded like a smoker. Maybe he had a cold. "If someone is catfishing you on social media, I can help. Just give me the details."

"Catfishing?"

"Impersonating. Setting up a phony account using your identity."

"Oh." I didn't care what it was called as long as he could get it offline. I told him what I knew and begged him to do something as soon as he could.

"It depends on how sophisticated the setup is," he said. "I'm on it." He hung up without explaining more or telling me what he was going to charge. But if I had to sell a kidney and the rights to my first child, it would be worth it.

The phone kept playing bits of *Oklahoma* over and over. Once I could think more clearly, I was going to change that ringtone—it was too perky for words. I broke down and answered once, then dropped the phone like it was burning my hands as well as my ears. It seemed that a lot of people objected to what had been posted under my name. How did they get my number? I couldn't bring myself to pull up the sites to see what profile information was there, but I feared the worst. I locked my door and pulled down the blinds.

When I got the text from Sherri Sherman saying she'd been out of town and was looking forward to arranging dinner with me, it was my one moment of joy in an otherwise joyless day. I immediately texted her back and suggested the following Friday at the restaurant of her choice. When I didn't hear back from her, I worried that she had seen the phony social media sites. My suspicions were confirmed when she texted me, "Please do not contact me again." I didn't have to ask why. Should I tell her it was a frame? Could I offer references as to my good character? What if she was my one chance at love? I felt helpless against the gods of technology. My dreams of living happily ever after with the lovely Sherri were shattered.

Instead of spending the rest of the evening eating chili while watching someone cook gourmet food and solve crimes, I paced back and forth, my stomach in knots, complicated knots like bowlines and timber hitches. Not a granny that could easily be undone. Why would someone do something so vile to me? Was I a random target and they had done it simply because they could? Or was someone trying to destroy my reputation? Though I wracked my brain for answers, I had no idea about either the who or the why. Nor did I have any ideas about whether there was something else I should be doing to protect my heretofore-neutral name and nondescript face.

I'd switched my phone to vibrate, and it continued to quiver like an animal in its death throes. I'm not entirely sure when it stopped quivering because I fell into a fitful sleep on the couch while watching reruns of *Night Court*.

Suddenly, I leapt up, unable to decide what had awakened me. Was my houseboat being attacked by angry parents? Was someone noisily writing graffiti on my front door? No, the sound was coming from a much closer source. Looking down, I saw that Wild Thing was playing whack-a-mole with my phone. Somehow it must have vibrated its way to the edge of the end table, falling off when still another call shook it into action.

I hesitated to try to retrieve it. Fortunately, Wild Thing lost interest when it quit vibrating, honored me with a pink-tongued yawn, and returned to whatever he'd been doing before all the excitement.

When I checked the last number, I realized it was from my hacker. Heart racing, I listened to his message: "I took down the catfished postings and reached out to the guy who put them up. He agreed not to do it again in exchange for us not turning him in. That doesn't mean someone else won't try something. I'll touch base tomorrow."

That was it? It was over? What about all the people who had already seen the pictures? How did I let them know that I wasn't responsible for those disgusting posts?

I emailed Laney to thank her, and she called back. "I was just turning off my computer when I saw your email. Glad my friend could help. You must be relieved."

"What about all the people who already saw it and think it was me?"

"You can complain to the social media sites who allowed it to happen, but I realize that doesn't address your concern. And, more importantly, do you know who did this to you?"

"No, I don't. Your hacker friend didn't mention getting a name from the guy who set it up."

"You need to see if he can find that out. If not, you'll have to hope it all blows over and whoever did it doesn't try something else."

"Unless it was random, why me? That's what I can't figure out."

"You don't seem like the kind of person who has enemies," Laney said.

"Not until lately."

"You've made enemies recently?"

"Well, not exactly. A woman at work is mad at me because I did something that she thought questioned her professionalism. But I think we've worked that out. And my admin thinks I spend too much time out of the office. And a client wasn't satisfied that I'd done everything I could to help her. And..." And my cat and the local crows hate me, I said to myself. "And my cat got out and terrorized a neighbor's dog. But I can't think of anything I've done to make someone angry enough to smear my name and reputation on social media."

"If it isn't to punish you for something, maybe someone is trying to distract you."

"From what?"

"From whatever you're working on."

"I'm not a PI or homicide cop," I said. "And I don't get involved in high-roller cases. I handle small claims and low-profile stuff."

"Then maybe they simply want to discredit you, make you seem like an unreliable source. Think about it. And if you want to bounce any ideas off me, we could get together for dinner tomorrow."

"I owe you more than a dinner. But that sounds good."

When I got off the phone, I realized I was exhausted. Being accused publicly of something you didn't do was more tiring than spending a day team building in a ropes course. Or more tiring than I imagined it was to actually do a day of ropes course activities. Something I would hopefully never have to know for sure.

I started through my evening routine: hanging up my clothes, putting on my PJs, going to the bathroom, brushing my teeth…. It was while I was brushing my teeth that I started considering the likelihood of recently acquired enemies.

Had the person responsible for the painting switch found out I was the one who turned in his license number to the police? On the one hand, that seemed unlikely—the police didn't give out that kind of information. Still, I couldn't totally discount it. Another possibility was one I had considered before, that Mrs. Weller had told someone about me finding Lonnie's thumb drive. Maybe one of their neighbors had heard the rumor and was afraid I was ready to point the finger at them. Although none of what we saw on the thumb seemed like that big a deal, except for the picture thing. Of course, we didn't know for sure that we had all of the videos Lonnie took. Someone could think I'd found something I hadn't.

One other thought flitted across the corner of my mind—what if it had to do with me trying to find Lars? Then again, how could it? I didn't actually know him, and only a couple of people even knew I'd talked with him. But I had asked neighbors if they had seen him recently.

I'm familiar with the recency bias with cause-and-effect arguments, but my past was pretty bland. It seemed to me it *had* to be related to more recent activities. Laney's suggestion that someone was either trying to distract or discredit me made as much sense as anything. Unless it truly had been a random act.

As I stood there contemplating, one thing was clear: I should have turned off my electric toothbrush when I took it out of my mouth!

Chapter Twenty-One: Guilty Until Proven Innocent

I was just about to make a pot of coffee when Emma called. I couldn't remember her ever calling me on a Saturday before. I was pretty sure it wasn't to tell me I'd been chosen employee of the month.

"It's been suggested that you work from home on Monday," she said.

"What do you mean?"

"The bottom line? Mr. Van Droop would like you to not come to the office until further notice."

"Why?"

"Really, John? Do you have to ask?"

"Is it about those social media posts?"

"Of course."

"But I didn't do it. Someone catfished me."

"I can't speak to that. All I know is that I was asked to inform you not to come in on Monday."

"What should I do? I mean, I had the posts and the sites removed."

"I can't say." After the briefest of pauses, she added, "But you might want to contact a lawyer." Then she hung up.

Contact a lawyer? Was this really happening? I thought it was over.

I went back into the kitchen and made myself a cup of tea. That had always been my mother's answer to stress. OMG, my mother. I needed to get in touch with her.

As if on cue, there was a knock on my door.

"Mother." She was standing there, shoulders back, chin thrust forward. "What are you doing here?" I asked, although it was all too obvious why she had come to visit her son.

"We need to talk."

"I didn't do it," I said. I sounded like I used to when she accused me of sneaking a cookie. Although back then, I was usually, well almost always, guilty.

"I know you didn't. But we need to get this straightened out."

She stepped around me, went into the kitchen, and started making herself a cup of tea. "I see you already have some. You didn't put sugar in it, did you?"

"No, Mother," I lied.

"Of course you did," she said. "Given the circumstances, I guess it's okay."

We sat down at the kitchen table, dipping our tea bags up and down in sync. "I had someone take the sites down," I said.

"You've never been on Facebook or Twitter before."

"No, someone set up phony accounts in my name. The hacker I hired left me a message after he took them down, but he didn't say if he knows who was behind it. I'm hoping today to find out."

"It's too bad they used your picture. And one of the posts mentioned where you worked."

"Oh no!" No wonder Emma had called. "I didn't know. I couldn't face looking at the posts."

"This is not good," was her concise and firm conclusion.

"That explains why I got a call from work about not coming in on Monday. I need to figure out how to explain that I'm a victim, not a—"

Mother reached across the table and put her hand on mine. "It's going to be okay," she said in a tone that transported me back in time. She was putting a bandage on a boo-boo and telling me not to cry.

"I don't even like kids," I said, feeling desperate to make sure she knew I was innocent.

"Of course you do, or you will when they're your own."

In the midst of my trauma, she was still thinking about grandchildren.

"Emma suggested I get a lawyer."

"You probably need to, but for now, here's what you do." She was always good at reducing complicated situations to manageable pieces, like eating an elephant one bite at a time. "First, get in touch with your hacker buddy and see what proof he can provide that someone else set up those accounts. Second, you ask him to find out who was behind this. And, then, after we have that information, we'll get you a lawyer and decide next steps."

It seemed to me like a lot was resting on what the hacker could or would do for me. I just hoped he was willing and able. And I hated to think what all this was going to cost. Especially the lawyer. I could already picture the meter as it started running up the tab. Ka-ching, ka-ching, ka-ching.

"Where's Wild Thing?" Mother asked, glancing around.

"I don't know; he doesn't always keep me informed. But he's been here." I pointed. "He ate his breakfast."

"Most cats spend a good part of the day on their cat tree. Maybe he doesn't like the color."

"It's not a color, it's gray. Besides, he isn't most cats."

For the second time this morning, there was a knock on the door. It was Valerie. She slipped inside and quickly closed the door behind her. She looked upset.

"My father won't let me come here anymore. He took away my key."

Mother quickly jumped to my defense: "I'm so sorry, dear. But don't worry. We're going to take care of this. As soon as we can prove John hasn't done nothing wrong—which he hasn't—I'm sure your father will give you the key back."

"Yes," I said. "I'm working on it."

"Thank you." She stood there motionless, staring at me. "I told him you didn't like kids." Then she turned toward the door and motioned for my mother to come closer. "Would you check to make sure my dad isn't out there watching?"

Mother obliged, gave Valerie the "all clear" sign, and Valerie ran off. Wild Thing came out just in time to see her leave and skidded into the door as Mother closed it. He swatted at her before hastily retreating.

"Feisty," I said as she checked out a scratch on her ankle.

"Don't be sarcastic, Johnnie."

"Wild Thing isn't going to like not seeing Valerie."

"All the more reason to take care of things quickly."

"What do you think she meant by me not liking kids?"

"They sense these things, you know."

"You don't think she knows about the kiddie porn, do you?"

"Kids know about everything online these days. Don't worry about it. She as much as said she believes you're innocent."

"I'll call the hacker," I said, mortified and feeling totally out of control.

"Well, I'll leave you to it. If I hurry, I can catch a bus downtown. I have some shopping to do."

"Okay." I was actually sad to see her go. It was nice to have someone accept you unconditionally. Well, almost.

"I'll check back in a few hours."

My hacker didn't answer, so I left a message: "I'm grateful to you for shutting down the posts, but I need to prove it wasn't me to my boss and others. I also need to find out who did it so I can keep it from happening again. Can we talk?"

Alone with my thoughts and only Wild Thing for company, I wasn't sure what to do with myself. When the phone started playing *Oklahoma*, I eagerly answered it, even though it was Emma again.

"Mr. Van Droop wants to see you in his office first thing Monday morning."

"I thought he wanted me to stay home on Monday?" Before she could comment, I came to my senses and said, "No problem, Emma, I'll be there. But I need you to know that I didn't do this; someone set me up. And I can prove it."

"You might want to bring that proof with you to the meeting."

"I will." At least I prayed I would be able to.

I thought she was going to hang up abruptly again, instead she said, "Good luck, John." I felt overwhelmed with gratitude for those two words of encouragement.

Desperate to talk to someone friendly, I called Bruno.

"John, what's up?"

"Is that all you have to say?"

"What should I say? How are the kids?"

"Not funny."

"Okay, but I saw you've managed to shut down the kiddie porn stuff. You must feel good about that."

"Except it apparently isn't innocent until proven guilty, but guilty until proven innocent. I'm just hoping I can get sufficient proof to do that."

"How did you get the stuff taken down?"

"A hacker friend of a friend."

"So, can't he or she help you with the proof?"

"I hope so, but I'm going crazy waiting around for his call."

"So, you called me to pass the time."

"I thought you might have some suggestions about what I need to do to get my reputation back."

"You had a reputation?"

"This is serious."

Bruno sighed. "I know, John. Sorry. Let me ask around and see if anyone here has any thoughts on what you should do. I'll get back to you."

I ended up pacing and fretting most of the day. I left two more messages for the hacker, anxiously awaiting his verdict.

At one point, I decided to see if I could get a few more pictures of Wild Thing for my office, assuming I still had an office. But Wild Thing apparently didn't want anything to do with me either. I finally managed to get a quick snap while he was eating the tuna fish I'd used to lure him out of hiding. Wanting him to hang out with me to pass the time, I also offered up some kitty treats and a whiff of catnip. He downed the treats, sniffed the catnip, and disappeared again. At least he hadn't assaulted me.

Mother hadn't called, so I tried calling her but got her voicemail. By late afternoon, I'd accomplished nothing except eating an entire box of stale Wheat Thins left over from my poker party. It was a good thing they'd drunk all of the beer.

It was starting to feel like I was in solitary confinement when Bruno finally called back. I was ecstatic to hear a human voice. Instead of saying "hello," I asked: "Do you have some advice for me?"

"No, sorry. No one I've talked to so far has any suggestions; they all say to give it time. But that's not why I called. I got the report from the appraiser on those two paintings you were concerned about. They are both authentic. Not terribly valuable, but authentic. And while our appraiser was there, we had him take a look at their other paintings of about the same size. All good."

I wasn't sure whether to feel relieved or not. "That means either the guy was exchanging a real painting for a fake. Or he was carrying the same picture both coming and going."

"Well, I can narrow that down a bit. Here's the other news—we caught the guy from the video. He confessed that he swapped out one of the paintings, a picture of a cow next to a stream or a cow under a tree, whatever. Unfortunately, he doesn't know much more than that. It was a one-off job for him. Someone told him when the Winslows were going to be away, warned him not to make a mess breaking in, instructed him on the location of the painting and paid him well for making the exchange. He says he has no idea who hired him or what the deal was with the painting."

"And you believe him?"

"His story is odd, but credible. He's a petty thief, not in any way connected to the art world as far as we can tell."

"What's he being charged with?"

"We're working on that. The problem is that he no longer has the painting he removed. He'd been told to destroy it, and he did. Without the painting, we can't prove it was a fake."

"But there can't be *two* originals."

"I'm aware of that. We need to figure out who paid him to make the switch. And how a fake became involved in the first place."

After our conversation ended, I sat there speculating. OMG. The painting exchange had to have something to do with Carla, didn't it? Or, like me, was she a victim? Given what I was going through, I didn't like labeling her guilty until proven innocent. It seemed like I owed it to her to give her the benefit of the doubt or to at least remain open to other options.

I was still trying to decide whether Carla was perpetrator or victim when the hacker called. "Good news," he said. Those two words instantly relieved some of the tension in my neck, like a magician snapping his fingers and ordering the subject to wake up. "I got in touch with one of your tech guys at work and showed him what I found. He's going to send it to your boss, someone named Droop?"

"*Van* Droop. That IS good news. So, there isn't any question that it came from somewhere other than me?"

"You got it."

"Do you have a name?"

"Unfortunately, no. My friend was contacted and paid anonymously."

"A friend of yours did this?"

"Buddy, friend, fellow hacker. Not a bro."

"Did he say why he did it?"

"The pay was good."

"He didn't care about what he was doing to me, to my life and reputation?"

"He doesn't know you."

"That's not…nice."

"Bad form, yeah. He's sorry he did it."

"But not sorry enough to find out the source or to give the money back."

"Not that sorry, no."

There was nothing else to say. "How do I pay you?"

"PayPal. I'll invoice you."

I'd almost expected him to ask for cash in a brown paper bag. PayPal was easier.

Chapter Twenty-Two: Trapped

I met Laney at a small Italian restaurant that smelled like garlic, but in a good way. It felt a little like a celebration dinner, even though I feared my job was still hanging in the balance. Normal people don't get accused of hosting kiddie porn sites on social media. And if I wasn't able to identify a motive, I wasn't sure what I was defending myself against. Nor could I guarantee it wouldn't happen again.

We ordered wine and toasted her hacker friend for bringing down the kiddie porn posts.

"You must have some idea who might have been behind this," Laney insisted. "Someone's toes you've stepped on recently. Someone who wants you at least temporarily out of the picture." When she got serious, her dimples went into hiding.

"It seems to me that it has to be related in some way to the picture exchange I told you about. There's obviously something illegal going on there, but I don't know that much about it, so why target me?"

"You were investigating it, right?"

"Kind of."

"What does that mean?"

"Well, the police are officially investigating it, not me. But I was also trying to get in touch with a painter to see what he knew about local art fraud, and now he's disappeared. That seemed strange to me, so I asked some of his neighbors if they knew where he went. I don't see how that would make anyone mad at me, though."

"Maybe there's a connection between his disappearance and what happened with the picture switch."

"I don't see how there could be. I got his name from my predecessor, Cornell Sutton. Cornell handled all of the art appraisals and claims for years, and Emma says he's networked with the local art community. An expert in his own right. And a collector. He said he has several of Lars's paintings."

"So, Emma lined you up with Cornell, who in turn introduced you to Lars. And now Lars is missing."

"You think Emma is somehow involved in what's happened to me?"

"Well, she doesn't seem to be your biggest fan."

"That's true enough."

"Maybe your predecessor is behind this, whatever 'this' is."

"Cornell? I've only talked to him that one time."

"He could be involved with someone still working for Universal."

"I'm getting so paranoid; I've even suspected my boss of targeting me."

"I'm not ruling anyone out...except you, that is."

I shook my head to clear it of the accusations swirling in my brain. There were too many possibilities and not enough facts.

"Putting possible bad guys aside, let's consider our options," Laney said. I was touched by her reference to "our" options. "The police are all over the painting switch. My friend won't or can't give you the name of the person who created phony sites in your name. And Lars may or may not be a lead. Anything to add?"

"No."

"Okay, rather than sitting around waiting for the police to come up with something, I say we take a look around inside your painter's house. See if we can figure out where he went."

"*Inside* his house?"

"Unless he left a note on his front door." I knew she was being sarcastic, but I still wasn't sure I'd heard her correctly.

"We?"

"You and me. The two of us."

"But that's illegal."

"We could do it, though. Unless you have a better idea."

I didn't. "But why would we do that?"

"Because if we find him, he might know something about art fraud in the area. Like you originally hoped. Also, because he mysteriously disappeared, and the timing is suspicious."

"His disappearance has nothing to do with me."

"You asked around about him for a reason, didn't you?"

"It was a vague, gut feeling."

"That's good enough for me."

"But how do we get in? And what do we do if we get caught?"

"I mentioned taking some PI courses, right? Well, I also did a brief, what you might call an internship, with a somewhat shady PI. I learned a lot from him. If we do it right, we won't get caught."

"You sound like you enjoy this kind of thing."

Laney smiled. "Loved all of the clandestine stuff. But being a PI is ninety percent boring and less than ten percent exciting. And it doesn't pay very well. As a paralegal in a large firm, I get to do interesting research as well as occasionally some challenging investigative work. It's a better fit than any other job I considered."

I was impressed. Laney was smart, supportive, not afraid to take a risk, and...very persuasive. So, after dinner I didn't resist when she said she'd drive. I even gave her directions to his house. Still, somehow it didn't seem real. Especially when we arrived and Laney started putting a few "tools" in her backpack. Real or not, I was getting very cold feet.

"Remind me what happens if we're caught?"

"We say he's been missing, and you were worried about him. That's true, right?"

"Then why didn't I call the police?"

"Hmmm. How about we had a little too much to drink at dinner and decided we couldn't wait any longer."

I *was* feeling a little lightheaded, and the way she put it made sense. Or maybe I just wanted it to. In truth, there was something about Lars' disappearance that made me uneasy, even if I couldn't connect it to the painting switch, Carla's art appraisals, or Lonnie's death.

The next thing I knew, Laney had picked the lock on his back door, and we were inside. "Your eyes will get used to the dark," she said. "Just stand here a moment and look around."

"You've done this sort of thing before, haven't you?"

"It was part of my supposed internship. And I read heist novels."

We stood there in the dark, and like she promised, I slowly started to make out vague shapes and shadowy objects. There was a table and chairs to the left leading to what looked like the kitchen. A little further down the hall, I could make out what I thought was a door. Laney got out a flashlight and said, "I'll keep the light pointed down; don't look directly at it. Let's go."

She started down the hall, and I followed. The first closed door was a junk room. There were boxes piled everywhere along with extra chairs and a couple of upright vacuums. Why did he need two? I was still thinking about that when we got to the second door. It looked like he was using the room for an office.

"Let's start here," Laney said. She went over to the window and shut the blinds. Then she switched on a light. "We're better off if someone thinks he came home than if they see a flashlight bobbing up and down." She looked around. "You take the desk; I'll do a random search."

"What am I looking for?"

"You won't know until you see it."

"How do I know I'll know it if I see it?"

Laney smiled. "John, you underestimate yourself."

In spite of her optimism and thoroughness, neither of us found anything to suggest where Lars may have gone. Nor did we find anything linking him to any names I recognized. We did note the lack of a computer. "He probably took that with him," I said.

"Let's hope so."

"What do you mean?"

"Well, we are assuming he left by choice, right?"

It hadn't occurred to me that he may have been forced to leave…or…. "You don't think—" I couldn't finish the thought.

"Don't panic, John. Chances are he left of his own volition for reasons that we don't yet know. Maybe he's run away from paying child support. Or maybe he did decide on a spontaneous trip somewhere, a vacation. Forgot to lock his studio door. He could be on a sunny beach, drinking a margarita. A missing computer doesn't mean that much out of context."

We left the office, turning out the light, and went to what was obviously his bedroom. Again, Laney shut the blinds and switched on the light. This time, the search was shorter. "It looks like some of his underwear is missing," Laney said. "There are some spaces in the drawer. Same is true for the drawer with his jeans."

"They could be in the laundry."

"We can check."

"Otherwise, you think it suggests that he went on a trip?" The bad feeling I had about his disappearance might be way off base.

"Maybe."

We didn't turn the light on in the living room; there were too many windows facing the street. Fortunately, the streetlight on the corner allowed us to see enough to get a feel for the room and its contents. "Everything looks normal," Laney said. "I doubt he was dragged away after a fight. Unless they cleaned up afterwards."

Before I could ask Laney what she thought the worst-case scenario was, a car turned into the driveway, its lights sliding along the side of the house before it stopped, and everything went dark again. I froze, my feet incapable of flight. Not Laney, though; she didn't miss a beat. "Stay calm," she said. "Let's see who it is and what they're up to."

I managed to follow her to the window, tiptoeing, as if we could be heard by the car's passenger. We watched as a man got out and headed toward the back yard.

"Is that Lars?" Laney asked.

"I can't tell for sure, but I don't think so."

"Come on," Laney hurried down the hall and into the kitchen. Peering out of a small window over the sink, we saw the man enter Lars' shop. In just a few minutes, he came out carrying several canvasses. As soon as he disappeared down the driveway, Laney said, "Quick, we need to follow him."

Once again, I blindly obeyed. She seemed so sure of herself. We barely managed to get to her car and catch up with the mysterious stranger as his car was turning toward the main road.

"You're sure that we're following the right car?" I hadn't paid much attention to the make and color; I'd been too afraid we were about to be caught.

"Yes, a dark sedan with AB the first two letters of the license plate."

"You saw all that in the dark?"

"You need to learn to be more observant."

"You mean, if I'm going to become a successful B & E guy."

Laney laughed. "Something like that."

We followed the car out of the city to where there were one and two acre lots with houses set back from the road, hidden by foliage, some protected by tall gates. The car we were following turned into a driveway. Moments later an ornate iron gate opened to let him through, closing immediately afterwards.

"Do you think Lars is hiding out here?" I asked.

"An automatic gate in a fancy neighborhood," Laney said. "You sure he is on the up-and-up?"

"He didn't seem like a crook."

"Well, let's give it a few minutes, then check things out."

"You mean trespass?"

"I don't see any signs."

"But people have gates for a reason."

Laney smiled again. "To make it more challenging to see what's inside?" She grabbed her backpack from the back seat and set it on the floor beside her. "Okay, while we're waiting, tell me something I don't know about you yet."

"I usually lose at poker."

She laughed. "Why doesn't that surprise me? You need to work on your poker face."

"Okay, tell me something about you."

Laney hesitated. "Have you guessed that I'm gay?"

"To be honest, I hadn't thought about it."

"Well, I am. I hope you aren't disappointed."

"I don't see how that changes our relationship."

She reached over and squeezed my left hand. "Good. Now, all I have to do is get you to invite me to one of your poker games."

A few more revelations later, Laney suggested it was time to trespass. It occurred to me that no light came on when we opened our doors. Maybe I was already becoming more observant.

We followed the fence until we reached an area that was totally hidden by trees. "Let's go over here," Laney whispered. I eyed the six-foot wood barrier. Before I could ask, "How?" Laney pulled some spiky things out of her pack and began screwing them into a wood post. "Want me to go first?" she asked.

I nodded.

She used the tiny spikes to climb part-way up the fence. Then, she swung one leg over, straddling the fence, before swinging the other leg over. I heard her drop to the ground on the other side with a soft whump. When no alarms went off, and no dogs started barking, I had no choice. It was a mini ropes course obstacle, but surprisingly easy to climb. Until I got to the top. I got the first leg over, but had trouble getting the second leg across and fell backwards, landing on my butt. Not exactly graceful, and somewhat painful and humiliating, but it did the job.

We were lucky we hadn't waited any longer because we were barely in time to get a glimpse of Lars through the door that was closing in a small building behind the main house. "That's Lars," I whispered.

When the man leaving the building not only shut the door behind himself but secured it with a padlock, Laney turned toward me and raised her hands in question. I shook my head. It didn't look as though Lars was there willingly. Not if he was locked up.

We waited until the man entered the house. "Well?" Laney whispered. "We going to free Lars?"

"We could call the police." People who locked other people up didn't seem like ones I wanted to cross.

"Let's get him out of there first and then call the police after we hear his story, okay? Once the police get involved, we might not get a chance to talk with him."

Before I could come up with a convincing argument in favor of calling the police first, Laney was on the move. Looking over my shoulder when I should have been paying attention to where I was stepping, I stumbled along after her. When we reached the building where Lars was locked up without any spotlights coming on, land mines exploding underfoot, or any salivating great Danes charging us, I was able to breathe again. Laney took out an odd-looking metal thingy and fondled the padlock. "With this and a shim, I can force open most padlocks," she whispered. "If that doesn't work, I have some cutters with me."

I stood there, again holding my breath, while she worked her illegal magic. It felt like hours, but it couldn't have been since I couldn't hold my breath that long. Leaving the padlock hanging, we slipped inside. Lars was sitting in a chair, turned slightly away from us.

"Lars," I said. "Don't panic. It's me, John Smith—remember?"

Lars didn't look panicked when he saw us, just deeply puzzled. "What are you doing here? Are you with *them?*"

"I don't know who 'them' is, but no, we're here because we have some questions for you."

Laney interrupted. "Are you a prisoner? Because it sure looks like it."

"You shouldn't be here. They are dangerous people."

"Why did they bring you here? And why are you locked up?" I asked.

"They need my services, but I never know from one day to the next when they will decide I'm dispensable."

"Dispensable?"

"A liability to be eliminated," Lars said, sounding almost resigned to the proposition.

"We'd better get going then," Laney interrupted. Just then, a dog started barking.

We stood very still and listened. When it sounded like the barking was headed in our direction, Lars motioned for us to duck under the cluttered desk off to the side of the room. He didn't have to ask twice. Laney and I pressed together, arms and legs entangled as Lars covered the end with a drop cloth.

We barely managed to get out of sight before I heard a voice say, "Lucky for you, you're still here."

"Where else would I be?"

There was a brief silence.

"Is something wrong?" Lars asked.

"No. I just forgot to give you these paints you asked for."

"Good. I'll need them tomorrow when I start on the abstract."

There was another silence.

"Anything else you need?" the voice asked.

"My freedom."

The man sighed. "Hey, I don't like babysitting you, but that's what they're paying me for."

"Well, as a good babysitter, I could use better snacks."

"Put in your order tomorrow."

"Will do."

"Goodnight."

I heard the door close and either heard or imagined I heard the padlock clicking shut. Unless Laney knew some Houdini escape trick, we'd become prisoners along with Lars.

When Lars pulled back the drop cloth, Laney and I literally rolled out of hiding. Once on our feet, I asked, "I don't suppose there's a back door?"

Lars almost laughed. "No, I think we are cellmates."

Laney was checking out our accommodations and not looking pleased. "Looks pretty secure," she said.

"Believe me, I've given escape a lot of thought," Lars said.

"What do we do?" I asked, although I wasn't sure I wanted to hear the answer.

"We wait," Laney said. She looked at Lars. "I assume this last guy wasn't the same one who brought you the canvasses."

"No, he's probably being chewed out at this very moment."

"Hopefully, they'll continue to think that he forgot to close the padlock."

"Otherwise?" I asked, again not wanting to hear the answer.

"We'll officially become prisoners, making escape highly unlikely." Laney stated her conclusion in a matter-of-fact tone rather than the panicky voice screaming in my head.

"How do we know he didn't just go for backup?" I asked. I pictured a swarm of men surrounding the building with assault rifles.

"We'll know soon enough," Laney said. "John, get ready to dial your police friend if things go sideways."

"Shouldn't I do it now?"

"No, hold off for now." Turning to Lars, she asked, "What's the routine?"

"If they don't come back with guns blazing…the day starts with breakfast at about 9:00. Brought by one of the two gun-toting tough guys. Neither of them has told me their names. I think of them as 'mustache guy' and 'tattoo guy.' Not very original, I know. There may be more, but those are the only ones I've had contact with.

"Anyway, the guy bringing breakfast knocks, pushes open the door with his foot, and keeps his gun ready until he assures himself that I'm far enough away not to be a threat. I've been instructed to stand back from the door, and he asks me to step back further if he thinks I'm too close. Then he leans in with the tray and sets it on the floor. Sometimes, he asks if I need anything. Then he leaves."

"Okay, we can work with that."

"Can we?" I asked.

"Who are you?" Lars stared at Laney as if seeing her for the first time.

"A paralegal trying to help out a friend." She smiled at me.

"A paralegal with some interesting skill sets," Lars said with a touch of admiration. He turned to me. "And you're here because you have questions for me. Since it doesn't sound like the stormtroopers are coming, have at it. It's going to be a long night."

"Your name was given to me by Cornell Sutton as an art expert; I didn't have any idea you might be connected to a forgery scheme involving a painting my company insured. But you are, aren't you?"

Lars smiled. "You don't believe in fate?"

"*You* faked that painting?"

"I like to think I *reproduced* it."

"Why just the one and not both?"

"Lack of time. There were several other appraisals right before you came on board as the adjuster."

"You mean you've done more than one?" I looked around and noticed Laney examining a couple of paintings leaning against the wall.

"Nice," she said. "I don't know what the originals look like, but these are good. Do you work from photos or the real thing?"

"Photos. They're usually excellent photos. It's challenging, but so far, it's gone smoothly." He nodded in my direction. "Until *he* came along."

"Is Cornell, my predecessor, involved?" Was that why he'd given me Lars' name?

"I don't know. My only connection is with Carla."

"Does that mean Carla's mixed up in this?" I was having a hard time wrapping my mind around the combination of coincidences.

"She's my contact," Lars said.

"Is she running the scam?" Laney asked.

"I have no idea. I'm one link in the chain. I only know what they think I need to know to get my part of the job done, painting the pictures."

"Why are you here?" I asked.

"Because you started nosing around, and I decided it was time to get out."

"And they—whoever *they* are—didn't take kindly to you leaving Dodge," Laney said.

"You got it. I was naïve enough to think I could just quit."

"So, it's a big enough operation to make it worth their while to keep you from rocking the boat."

"Yeah, initially I was under the impression it was a small-time, local con. A way for me to make a few bucks with little risk and no one really hurt by it. But now, I'm thinking it's a question of volume, and whoever they are, they don't want to take 'no' for an answer."

"I think they do jewelry too," I said. "That would explain why there was a loose gem in a piece Carla appraised the other day."

"It sounds like this Carla is a busy little criminal," Laney said.

"She has a partner too. Farley." I turned to Lars. "Is he involved?"

He shrugged. "Since they've gone to all this trouble to keep me here, I'm thinking it's a lot bigger than Carla, but like I said, she's the only one I've had contact with…before now."

"There could be multiple companies involved, and a cadre of artists," Laney said. "That's the only way it makes financial sense. Smart, actually. Who's going to question appraisals of moderately-priced paintings or jewelry?"

"Seems to me it has to be someone with a few coins pulling the strings," Lars said. "Someone who can organize things on a large enough scale to make it worth the effort. Someone who will go to great lengths to keep their cover from being blown."

"All the more reason for us to break out of here," Laney said. "If we bring in the police too soon, we might never find out who's behind this."

"But isn't that their job?" I asked.

Laney turned to Lars. "Tell me why you got involved."

"Confession time, huh?"

"At this point, why not?"

"Well, I didn't set out to become a criminal. Then, I lost everything but a mortgaged house during my divorce. And I haven't been selling many paintings of late. Some people might say I should find a 'real' job, but I love to paint. It wasn't as if I was trying to pass off my work as a Picasso or a Rembrandt. Although I know that's no excuse. But that's the 'why.' Sounds like a bad 'made-for-TV' movie script, huh?"

"You will do better if we break out of here and you turn yourself in than if we call in the police to rescue us," Laney said. Turning to me, she asked, "You okay with that, John?"

"You really think we can escape on our own?"

"I do. Let's go over what happens at breakfast again."

Lars described the guard's delivery process again, and Laney said, "We will have to be fast and efficient. We can't risk anyone becoming suspicious when the guard doesn't return to the house right away. Especially since we have no idea how many people are in the house."

"Where are you parked?" Lars asked.

"Ten minutes away tops," Laney said. "If we hustle. But since I wasn't planning on needing a fast getaway, I didn't put any spikes on this side of the fence. We'll have to punt."

Punting didn't sound all that good to me. "So, what's the plan leading up to the punt?" I asked.

"We'll assume the guy delivering breakfast won't be expecting an ambush. I'll stand behind the door and step out when he bends down with the tray. Then I'll cover him while you take his gun, John."

"You have a gun with you?" I asked. She was full of surprises.

"Wouldn't go anywhere without it."

"You could have used that earlier," Lars said.

"We didn't know what your situation was or whether the person outside was armed. Or if there was more than one. Things could have gotten messy."

"You're right," Lars said. "This is a better plan. So, what do we do with him once he's inside and disarmed?"

"Tie him up and gag him. Then make a run for it."

Lars smiled. "Free at last."

"Okay, we need to figure out what we're going to tie him with and decide how we are getting from here to the car in daylight without being seen. Lars, tell us what you know about the layout."

We talked and planned for about an hour. Then Laney said we needed to get some rest to prepare for our great escape. I wasn't sure I could sleep, especially lying on a hard floor with my clothes on, a single blanket for cover, and no pillow. But the next thing I knew, Laney was shaking me and telling me it was "time."

Chapter Twenty-Three: The Great Escape

Laney sat down on the floor next to the door while I silently practiced my Clint Eastwood lines: "Go ahead. Make my day." Of course, I wasn't going to have a gun. All I had to do was take his away after he put it down. Once Laney had a gun to his head, that should be fairly straightforward. OMG, who was this woman? What had she gotten me into? No, wait, I was the one who originally got "into" this mess. She was trying to help me get out of it.

Lars' role was to stand off to the side and draw the guard's eyes away from the door. The one thing left hanging, assuming we got away, was what Lars was going to do after that. Laney had advised him to go to the police and confess his role in the scheme. "I'll bring you painting supplies if you go to prison," she'd said. "It could even be a career-enhancing move. You never know. You just need a good story about the whole affair, something that appeals to people who are intrigued by an artist's ability to get away with a forgery and want to buy art with an interesting story behind it."

"You can make a deal," I said. "That should reduce your sentence." Then I asked, "Did you mention my name to them?" That would explain the kiddie porn "warning."

"No, but Carla also knew that you and your cop friend were spooking around."

Spooking around? "But only because a client got suspicious. That wasn't my fault." I thought it best to leave my mother out of it.

"These guys don't care about whose 'fault' it is; they intend to protect their scam. Whatever it takes."

"It would help if we knew who 'these guys' are," Laney said. "And who they work for."

"Once we tell them what we know, the police can probably figure it out," I said.

"*Probably* doesn't make me feel all that safe," Lars said.

Laney looked at me. "You agree that what he does after we bust out of here is up to him?"

I nodded. Bruno might think otherwise, but I was a claims adjuster. There was nothing in our code of conduct about turning in criminals if we happened upon them. But staying alive was definitely in my own personal code. Once I told Bruno everything I knew, I would wash my hands of the entire mess. And stay away from dark alleys.

The knock on the door came right on schedule, and we quickly took our positions. I had the urge to sneeze and had to squeeze my nose to keep from letting forth an earth-shattering achoo. Lars also looked a bit nervous, but Laney appeared totally calm.

After that, everything happened quickly.

Instead of focusing on Lars, "tattoo guy" stepped inside and glanced in my direction. Happenstance? My bad karma? He held onto the tray with one hand and pointed a gun at me. I noted the snake tattoo on his arm but didn't have time to read what was written intertwined with the snake's body before Laney leaped out and pressed her gun to his head. It was the perfect opportunity to say, "Make my day." Instead, she ordered him to drop his gun and kick it toward me. Then she nodded for me to pick it up. It was my big moment. I bent down and picked up the gun by its barrel. It felt cold and hard. Like a weapon should feel.

"Now step inside slowly," she ordered. "John, get the tray."

I obeyed, placing the gun on the tray and shutting the door behind me. The food smelled good. I was tempted to at least take a sip of coffee. But Lars and Laney were busy tying up our delivery guy with strips of sheet. "What should I do?" I asked.

"Keep an eye out."

I peeked out the window and was relieved not to see anyone headed in our direction.

"Want to tell us who's in charge before we gag you?" Laney asked.

The man shook his head.

"Didn't think so. You're lucky we don't have time to try to persuade you to share information with us."

I grimaced at the phrase "persuade you," but the man didn't look worried. I guess he figured if we were tying him up, at least we didn't intend to shoot him.

Minutes later we were ready to depart, Laney in the lead, Lars in the middle, and me bringing up the rear. It crossed my mind that I would be the first one picked off if we were caught. Not a reassuring thought.

One thing I learned as we made our escape: it's surprising how easy it is to scale a fence when you're worried about being shot. I don't know how I managed; I didn't even think about it. I just scurried up and over behind Lars, praying no one shot me before I got to the other side.

We made it to Laney's car in record time. Lars got in front with Laney, and I jumped in the back. Still panting from the race to the car, I didn't start breathing normally until we were several blocks away. "Made it," I said.

Laney gave me a thumbs up and glanced at Lars. "Where do you want to be let off?"

"I'm not sure. I need some time to think this through."

"Well, John and I are headed to the police station, but we can take you wherever you want."

"The Bahamas?"

"You want a ride to the airport?"

"No, I think I need to go to the police station with you. I don't want to, but that's probably what I should do. I never intended to become a career criminal."

"That's wise," Laney said. "They'll come after you, you know. Once they know you've escaped."

"And you too. They will have your descriptions."

"No one usually remembers me," I said.

"I don't think you can count on that," Laney said over her shoulder.

"The sooner we tell the police everything we know, the better off we'll be. Although I think we should avoid going home for a few days."

"I need to feed my cat," I said. Maybe her father would let Valerie feed him if he knew I wouldn't be around. Then again, he probably wouldn't care if Wild Thing starved. And I couldn't send Valerie to my place if there might be bad guys waiting there.

"Okay, I'll go with you to get your cat. After we talk to the police." I didn't say "no," but until she faced off with Wild Thing, she had no idea what she had agreed to do.

I called Bruno at home because I knew it was his day off. I was hoping for a friendly reception, although I wasn't sure how he was going to feel about what Laney and I had done.

"John, I'm kinda busy at the moment," Bruno said when he answered the phone. I could hear the television in the background blaring out plays in some game and pictured him with a beer in one hand, even though it was early.

"Sorry, this isn't a personal call. I have information about a forgery ring and a kidnapping."

"You what?" I imagined him putting down his beer and sitting up straight.

"It's a long story, Bruno. I'm with two other people, Lars and Laney. Lars was kidnapped because he wanted to stop forging paintings for some pretty nasty people, and they wanted him to keep doing it for them. He's a good guy and wants to help you catch the rest of those involved. And Laney is the woman I met through the dating app, and she, ah, well, *we* rescued Lars and are kinda, like, on the run. I mean, on the run from them. We're headed to the police station."

Bruno didn't hesitate, but he did sigh rather loudly before responding: "I'll meet you at the station. We need to sort this out."

"You might want to send someone over to see who's in the house where Lars was being held captive. Also, we left one of the bad guys tied up in the workshop in the back yard."

"You what?" That was the second time he'd asked that, but this time, his voice was louder.

"Ah, we had to tie someone up to escape. Because—"

"Don't explain. Just give me the address."

When we finally arrived at Bruno's office, he was already there. Everything was a bit confused at first. Bruno seemed to have a difficult time understanding how the three of us ended up together. Still trying to make sense of everything that had happened in my own mind, I tried to start from the beginning, but Bruno said, "Get to the point." So, I jumped ahead to our conclusions about the scheme and who was involved. This time he shook his head and ordered me to "Start from the beginning."

It took him a while to digest the key points. Then, he looked at each of us in turn and asked: "You really don't know who is behind this?"

Laney, Lars, and I simultaneously shook our heads. "We're hoping that you'll be able to figure it out," I said.

The phone rang. "Yes," Bruno said. "Okay. Keep looking." Then he made a call and asked someone to find out who owned the house we had escaped from. He hung up and turned to us: "It was empty. No one there."

"They got away?" Laney, Lars, and I said in unison, sounding equally disappointed. They must have found "tattoo guy" sooner than we'd hoped.

"Not good," Lars said.

"I'll send you a photo I snapped of the guy we left behind," Laney said. I hadn't noticed she had done that. What a smart move. "Meanwhile, Lars will need protection."

"What about us?" I asked. Then, before Laney could say, "I'll protect you"—which would have been embarrassing—I added, "You're right, it's Lars they will probably go after first." I hoped I was right. But going after him "first" wasn't very comforting. Maybe I'd have time to give Wild Thing a meal before going into hiding. But where was I going to hide? And what would I do about my job? And what about Mother? If I had to stay out of sight, who would drive her where she needed to go? Who would she boss around?

"The only way we can all be safe is to catch whoever is in charge." Laney's pronouncement rang true to me, and I could tell Bruno agreed.

Bruno said, "If I understand correctly, John, the only other person you

187

know of who might have information about this is Carla, the appraiser your company uses. Is that right?"

I nodded.

"My guess is that she won't know much more than I do about the larger operation," Lars said. "Whoever is at the top of the food chain keeps his or her distance from the rest of us."

"Then we need a plan to smoke them out," Laney said.

"No," Bruno interrupted. "All of you need to stay out of this. I'll take it from here."

"Can I stay in custody?" Lars asked.

"I don't have anything to charge you with yet."

"But I've confessed to a crime," he said.

"I don't have any proof that a crime has been committed. You can hang out here if you want, but I can't arrest you, unless you have something specific to give me."

"Do you know the names of the clients you did paintings for?" I asked Lars.

"No. Carla never shared any information, just pictures of the art she wanted copied."

"So, you don't know where your forgeries ended up," Laney said.

"No. I have no idea. I didn't keep any records; it seemed safer that way. And Carla always asked for the photos back after I'd finished an assignment. Although, I can describe most of the paintings from memory. Maybe you can cross-reference descriptions with the claims."

"That's possible," I said. "But it would be faster to get the list from Carla."

"She will probably lawyer up," Lars said.

"Maybe Cornell can help." I turned to Bruno and explained that Cornell was my predecessor. "We don't know if he was involved or not."

Bruno started to say something, then clamped his mouth shut. Changed his mind again and said, "I appreciate what you've done so far. But I'll take it from here. You need to stay away from anyone directly or indirectly involved. Got that?"

"There's a fine line between letting the police handle this and pulling together evidence for Lars to use to negotiate a deal," Laney said to Bruno.

"My advice is to keep a low profile until we track down the people who kidnapped Lars," Bruno said firmly. It seemed to me that he had chosen his words carefully.

"When you find out who owns the house, will you let us know?" I asked.

"You're no longer part of this investigation; do I make myself clear?"

"That's a 'no' then?"

"I'll let you know when we catch up with them so you can stop looking over your shoulders, but that's the best I can do."

As we left, Bruno admonished us to be careful and to get back to him if we thought of anything that might be helpful.

While standing in front of the elevator, Laney asked me, "Want me to see if my friend will help? He could probably get Carla's list."

I was horrified. "No, that would not only be illegal, it's a violation of the company's privacy policy." Did I sound like an uptight jerk or what? "Maybe there's an easier way." Before I could change my mind, I said: "I'm an employee; I can probably get the list off the claims department site. But I'd need to go to the office to access my computer."

"We'll go with you," Laney said, looking at Lars for confirmation. He nodded. He obviously wasn't ready to be on his own.

"Since it's Sunday, will anyone be at your office?" Lars asked as we stepped into the elevator.

"Claims never cease. We work seven days a week."

"You do?"

"Well, I personally don't. We have different shifts." Thankfully, that meant Emma wouldn't be there. She didn't work weekends. In fact, a lot of the weekend work was outsourced, but there would still be a few people around.

On the way there, Laney said: "I think the police are going to have a hard time finding out who's in charge, unless it's Carla and we're underestimating her. But it has to be someone inside the company, right?"

"Why do you say that? I mean, it's a good company."

"It may be a good company and a great place to work, but there are always a few unscrupulous people willing to take advantage of any weak spots in

189

processes and bookkeeping to make a few bucks."

"But couldn't it be a hacker, like your friend? Well, not your friend, but someone like him?"

"It has to be someone who understands how the appraisal process works."

For a moment, I tried to picture Van Droop as a criminal mastermind. "I haven't met a lot of the people at the top," I admitted.

"We will go where the trail leads," Laney said, sounding a bit like a junior Sherlock. "Maybe you'll meet the CEO along the way." She smiled. "Kidding."

"The CEO makes several million dollars a year," I said. "Why would he be involved in something like this?"

"Okay. Maybe you'll meet a low-level executive wanna-be. But there could be more money involved than we're thinking."

"Maybe a janitor is running the whole thing out of the boiler room," Lars said.

"There is no boiler room. It's electric heat."

"Hey, if I still have a sense of humor with a target on my back, you should be able to take a joke."

As things turned out, I wished it had been the janitor from the boiler room.

The skeleton crew of employees made the place seem like it was a business on the verge of collapse instead of the booming enterprise that it was. Our footsteps echoed on the fake wood floor as we made our way to my office.

"Nice," Laney said as the three of us crammed ourselves into the tiny space.

"At least you have a door," Lars said. "How does anyone get any work done in those cubicles out there? It would drive me crazy."

"I do enjoy my privacy." Even without being able to lock my door. I started up my computer and tried to prepare myself mentally to violate company rules. Although it could be argued that I had a right as an employee to research art appraisals since that was almost my specialty, I still felt guilty. Especially since I'd been ordered not to come to work on Monday before I'd been ordered to meet with Van Droop first thing Monday morning. It wasn't clear if being summoned before Van Droop was good news or more bad news. At least I hadn't been locked out of the building or my office in advance of my meeting with Van Droop. And my computer was still capable of accessing company business records.

It took me a while to locate the right files. Lars had wandered off to look around and had just returned. "How far back should I go?" I asked.

"I bet I've done at least one a month for the last two years," Lars offered. "It's been a nice sideline for me."

"Go back two years," Laney said.

"Carla may not be the only appraiser involved," Lars said, "but that would be a place to start. As we discussed earlier, this is most likely happening in other locations with other painters and appraisers. And you mentioned jewelry, didn't you, John? Maybe we should follow up on that, too."

"Okay."

Forty-five minutes later, we had two lists. One was all the appraisals Carla had done in the last two years. The other was of some miscellaneous appraisals done by other appraisers.

"It might be interesting to know why Carla wasn't chosen for these other jobs," I said.

"It could have been a question of availability," Laney said. "Let's see if there are any patterns."

We spread the lists out on my desk and studied them.

"Well, there is one thing of note," Lars said. "I mean, I obviously wasn't involved in any of the jewelry stuff, but I recognize all of these paintings Carla handled. I was apparently her main 'go-to' artist. But if any of the paintings in these other appraisals are phony, then there are more people, including other painters, involved."

"No rumors about this in the artist community?" I asked, not for the first time. Lars might have had reason to sidestep the question before, but not now. His only chance to reduce his sentence was to be as helpful as possible.

"No. But it isn't something one admits to."

"How did *you* hook up with Carla?" Laney asked.

"She approached me opening night at a show I had at a small gallery in Pioneer Square. We talked about how hard it was to make a living as a painter, especially these days with so many amateur artists out there. She told me she liked my work and asked if she could drop by my studio. We also commiserated about our respective divorces. Like me, she ended up on the short end of the stick. Told her ex all she wanted was the dog, and he claimed the dog was his. Things apparently got really nasty after that. And she was pregnant. No child support once the kid came. You get the picture.

"When she finally got around to telling me what she wanted me to do, I confess I didn't express moral indignation. Like her, I was pleased to make a few bucks. And I didn't think I would get caught. I guess criminals never do.

"Also, I admit it was satisfying to be creating something I knew people were going to proudly display in their homes. Even if the inspiration was from someone else, it was still 'original' in a sense."

"Choices have consequences," Laney said. "But sometimes in the moment, it's hard to look ahead." She turned to me. "Your friend Bruno will undoubtedly get around to asking for this information. If not before, then when he interviews Carla. The question is what we want to do with the lists now."

My mind was swirling with concern about what this might mean for the company. And for my small part in approving some of the appraisals. "This sounds like one of those choices you were referring to," I said. "This is a ticking time bomb for Universal. But I don't see any other option—Bruno needs to have these lists as soon as possible."

She nodded. "That's what I was hoping you would say."

"He'll be mad that we ignored his instructions, but he'll get over it." I sat down at my computer and emailed him a copy with a two-sentence cover: "I got this online from company files; thought you would want a copy. Lars Lane has verified that the paintings Carla handled are forged."

"It's too bad we don't know more. Unless Carla is the mastermind, the list could be a dead-end."

"And *we* are still *loose* ends," Lars said.

Until whoever was orchestrating the scam was caught and put in jail, Lars was right—we were loose ends. And that did not sound like a healthy thing to be.

Laney's face suddenly lit up. "Let's bait a trap," she said. "That's something

192

the police can't do, but we can."

Chapter Twenty-Four: Baiting The Trap

"What kind of trap?" I asked. I'd executed a sting not so long ago that caught an innocent person and damaged my front door in the process before landing on the guilty party. That made me leery of setting traps for criminals.

"Well, let's think this through. *They*—whoever *they* are—know that you and Lars have a connection," Laney said, looking at me. "And, they know that the police caught the anti-burglar returning the real painting to its owner. They also have to be worried about Carla, unless she's the boss." She paused. Then she made a palms-up hand gesture obviously intended to encourage Lars and me to add something.

"That's a summary of the facts," I said. "But what's the plan?" My mind was blank.

"You two have to help me on this." She motioned with her hands again as if she could coax ideas out of us with the right gesture.

"Well, they need to think they can still salvage the operation," Lars said. "Otherwise, they will fold up shop and move on."

"That has its advantages," I said.

"But how would we know for sure?" Lars said.

Laney dropped her hands and turned her head to one side. "Maybe we should warn Carla about what's happening."

"She got me into this," Lars complained.

"But we don't know the extent of her involvement," Laney said. "She could be in danger too. Another loose end."

"Bruno won't like us talking to Carla," I said, wavering.

"I think we should call her," Laney said firmly. She turned to Lars. *"You* should do it. Tell her you need to talk. Right away."

"And then?" I asked. "What happens then?"

"First things first. We'll talk with her. Then we'll flesh out the plan. Okay?" Lars and I nodded. Laney is persuasive. "Why don't you call from the front desk—that ought to get her attention. But don't say anything incriminating. You don't know who might be listening."

"You don't think Universal taps our phones, do you?" I was surprised and discomfited by the thought. Although if they had cameras, why not recording devices?

Laney raised her eyebrows and shrugged.

Fortunately, there was no one around; we had the area to ourselves. Lars made the call, and Carla answered. She must have wondered about who was calling from Emma's phone on a Saturday. Lars had her on speaker, so we could all hear the surprise in her voice when he said who was calling. She didn't ask any questions about why he wanted to meet her at a nearby coffee shop. Maybe she, too, was afraid of being recorded. Or maybe she was so surprised by getting a call from Lars on a Universal phone that she was speechless. Or…maybe she knew all about Lars being held against his will and planned on calling his captors so they could abduct him again.

We walked to the coffee shop, strategizing on the way about the best way to play the hand we'd dealt.

"There are two issues," Laney said. "Will she come alone? And what's her role in the scheme?"

"What if she doesn't come alone?" I asked.

"We're meeting in a public place, and we'll be able to call the police if we have any concerns." Laney made it sound so simple.

"They could shoot us," Lars said. "Make it look like some sort of random thing."

"We should sit near an exit," Laney said. "Near the back."

Lars and I looked at each other.

"And if she's the boss lady?" I asked.

"She'll want to know how much we know and what we've told the police."

"And if she isn't?"

"Then it all depends on how she communicates with whoever gives her the assignments," Laney said. "Once we know that, we can figure out what to do next. If she's simply a link in a chain, we need to find that next link, and the one after that, until we reach the person running the show."

"It doesn't sound like much of a plan," I said, wishing I hadn't agreed to come along.

"I'm in," Lars said suddenly. "What do I have to lose?"

I wanted to scream "your life," but I didn't have anything better to suggest.

We stationed Lars at a table by himself at the back of the coffee shop with Laney and me, a kangaroo's giant hop away. He was facing the door, and we were facing a bank of windows that looked out onto the street with a clear view of the door. There was a restroom off a hall behind us. Laney had checked to see if we could get out that way and decided we could by breaking a window and squeezing through. But we were hoping we'd have time to call in reinforcements if needed before doing anything that desperate.

Even if Carla came alone, she might spot me when she arrived and decide not to stay. Our hope was that she would see Lars first and focus on him, not noticing me until we chose to make our presence known.

We were barely settled in when we saw her pass by the windows on the way to the entrance. I kept my head down as planned. Fortunately, she didn't know Laney, so Laney was able to casually glance around as Carla entered the coffee shop.

"I think she's alone," Laney said, loud enough for Lars to hear. She moved her body in time with some music playing softly in the background, looking like someone enjoying herself rather than someone prepared for a shoot-out.

As soon as Carla sat down across from Lars, Laney took one last look around before she and I pulled our chairs over to their table. "Hi, Carla," I said.

Carla blinked, staring at me, her mouth frozen half open. I could see her back molars. She had good teeth. Then she closed her mouth and turned to Laney. "Who are you?"

"A friend of John's. He and I are here to help you and Lars, although I admit it will probably be impossible to get you off the hook completely. As they say in the comics, 'The jig's up.' No matter what you do next, you will be facing some serious legal consequences."

Carla turned toward me with venom in her eyes. "I knew you were trouble."

"I'm not the one trying to defraud clients."

"Until you got involved, there were never any complaints."

"Take a step back, you two," Laney said. "We all have a common interest in resolving this. Lars, tell her about what happened to you. In case she doesn't know."

When he started explaining how he'd been kidnapped, Carla's face said it all. She wasn't surprised. Lars stopped mid-sentence and said, "You knew they kidnapped me, didn't you?" When she didn't protest, he said, "How could you let them do that to me?"

"It was better than the alternative," Carla said.

"We could say the same to you now," Laney said. "Now *you* are a loose end, too. Unless you're running the operation...?"

"Me? No. How could you think that?"

"Do you know who is?"

It was easy to see the full impact of her situation becoming clear to her. "Do the police know about this?"

"Yes. They are looking for the men who kidnapped Lars as well as for sufficient proof to put you and Lars away. If you aren't in charge, we will have to act fast to find sufficient leverage for the two of you to use when you're picked up."

I could tell Carla's mind was in overdrive. She looked alternately frightened, angry, and confused.

"Did you tell anyone you were meeting Lars?" Laney asked.

"No, I wanted to hear what he had to say first."

"But you knew he escaped."

"Yes."

"And did they tell you how or with whom?"

"They asked me if I knew who helped him get out, but I didn't know."

"And they believed you?"

"Why wouldn't they?"

"And do you know who 'they' are?" Laney asked.

Carla looked around as if trying to decide whether to make a run for it. Then she turned to Laney and asked, "Why should I help you?"

"If you want to try to get out of the country, go for it. Otherwise, if you help us catch the person running this scam, maybe you will earn enough points with the police that they will make a deal with you."

"That's what *I'm* hoping for," Lars said. "I went with John and Laney to talk to John's police friend. My feeling is that this is the best chance we have to make a deal. Otherwise, we will be left holding the entire bag."

Carla looked as if she was about to cry. "My daughter," she said. "I can't go to jail."

I wanted to scream that she should have thought of that before involving Lars and me in her little game, but I had a scant ounce of pity for her rattling around inside of me that made me keep my mouth shut.

"Carla, we know what you've been doing, but we don't know how long this has been going on," Laney said. "Can you tell us that?"

The three of us sat there silently, waiting for her to make up her mind. When she finally caved, I didn't know if fear or reason had won out. Maybe a bit of both. The important thing was that she'd decided to throw her hat in the ring with us. Figuratively speaking. My recollection was that the phrase originated when men wore toppers, or top hats. It was an era of elegance rather than knit caps and floppy-billed rain hats.

"I've been involved for about two years, the same as Lars."

"But you've been the recommended appraiser for longer than that," I said. "Do you think you two were in at the beginning?"

"That's the impression I got," Carla said. "But I can't say for sure."

"Did Cornell know what was going on?" I asked. "Could he be the head guy?

"I never got the sense that he had any idea about what was going on." She turned to Lars. "What do you think?"

"I have no idea. But he's an art lover. Well-known in the community. He came to one of my gallery openings last year. I remember because he bought a painting, and we had a long talk about current trends and how art is valued. That's probably why he gave you my name, John."

"What about your partner, Farley?" I asked. "Is he in on this?"

"No, I've kept him out of it. I have someone else that makes the fake gems for me. A lot of people want cheap copies. And as long as I pay him, he doesn't ask any questions."

"So," Laney interrupted, "let's assume that this whole scheme to defraud Universal's clients started two years ago. That still doesn't help us figure out whose idea it was in the first place. Who's pulling the strings." She bit her lower lip in concentration. "If I had to guess, I think it will take some time for the police to track down the owner of the house where you were being held, Lars. You don't kidnap someone and keep him in a place where your name is on the tax rolls. They might, however, get lucky with the picture of the guy we tied up, if he's a convicted criminal. Although as hired muscle, he may not know much."

I could practically see the gears meshing and whirling in Laney's brain before her eyes lit up. "Carla, we need to know how you get in touch with your contact. That might help us work our way up the chain."

Carla hesitated.

"You're either in, or you're out," Laney said.

"Okay. I'm in. They contact me with a message via the mail. The regular mail. In a PO Box."

"Do you have any of their messages?"

"Yes, but if you're thinking of fingerprints, I'd be surprised."

"How do you get paid?"

"Off-shore account. Then I pay Lars in cash."

"How many of the forged paintings have you replaced with the real ones to cover your tracks?" I asked.

"I couldn't believe the police found out about that."

"The police arrested your thief, the one who returned the original to the Winslows. He was caught on camera."

"Cameras are everywhere these days." She shook her head. "After you first mentioned knowing about the switch to me, I was afraid of something like that."

"So, how many?"

"Just the one. I happened to still have the original. The others are long gone."

"What do you do with the originals?" Laney asked.

"A messenger service picks them up. I don't know who they deliver them to or what happens to them after that."

"The police can follow up on that," Laney said to me. "They obviously go to some dealer for resale. Think about it, they could sell, insure, steal and resell the same paintings over and over. That's something they couldn't do if the artwork was famous."

I was listening, but my mind was still back on the fact that there were two years' worth of forged paintings out there with Universal clients. "Think of what this is going to cost Universal when this comes out. To say nothing of the hit to our reputation."

Carla blinked several times. I could see it slowly sinking in that she had drawn the "go directly to jail" card. "I didn't expect it to end like this."

"No criminal ever does," Laney said.

"Why did you do it?" I asked. I really wanted to know.

"For the money. What else?"

"But you must have known you'd get caught eventually. All those paintings. At any point, some owner could try to sell one. Then another appraiser might get involved."

"I didn't intend to do it indefinitely. Just long enough to accumulate enough for a down-payment on a house. I'm a single mom. With a deadbeat ex. It's hard to make ends meet. Kids are expensive these days."

"That's no excuse," I said.

"You asked *why*."

"Sorry, I did. And I do understand. In a way. But the risk—"

"At first, I really did think I could stop any time I wanted. I was naïve. Then Lars wanted to quit, and I realized what would happen if I crossed them. I mean, they didn't need me the way they needed Lars—and look what they did to him."

"Well, it's over now," Laney said. "The only question is what happens next." She looked at Lars and me. "Should we keep trying to figure out who the boss is? I could see if my hacker friend can track the offshore account."

"No," Lars and I both said at the same time.

I let him explain first. "It's too dangerous. For your friend and for us if they catch us poking around." He turned to me. "Carla can use that as leverage, and the police are better equipped to track such things."

Carla had the look of someone caught in a maze but still determined to find her way out.

"One way or the other, you're going to lose your money," Laney warned.

Carla looked at Lars, then reached out and touched his hand with her fingers. "Sorry. About the kidnapping that is. I was too scared to speak up."

"You didn't consider an anonymous call to the police?" I asked.

"The people holding him would have guessed it was me. There was no one else who knew about it. I was hoping they would resolve any, ah, differences, and Lars would continue as usual."

"What about when they killed Lonnie?" I said. "Didn't that suggest what they might be capable of?" If she thought she was going to get much sympathy from me, she was wrong. She'd put us all in danger and perhaps ruined my career path.

Carla's face turned ashen. "What?"

"You didn't know about that?" Lars said.

"They killed someone?"

"Why did you think I wanted out?"

"I thought you were just tired of painting under someone else's name."

"I started piecing things together when John came around asking questions. You worked with him, so I thought you would know more than I did."

"I wish I'd known. But I didn't." She looked at me. "Honestly."

Laney suddenly became animated. "I have an idea. There is one more thing we can do. Carla, are you still getting requests for appraisals on paintings and jewelry?"

"I have one pending, but now that Lars isn't, ah, available, I'm not sure what they will expect from me."

"Is there any way to find out about the need for an appraisal except through your company claims department?"

"No, they need an inside person to start the process. I thought Cornell was feeding them the info, but when he left, I wasn't sure." She turned toward me. "And you didn't seem like the right person to carry on. I figured you were going to torpedo the whole thing."

"So, even if Cornell was identifying the possibilities for them, when he left, they needed an inside source," Laney said.

"Or someone to hack the system," I said, still hoping an outsider was responsible.

"It's possible," Laney said. "But my money is on an inside person running the whole operation. But not necessarily someone at or near the top of the food chain. Think about it. If this scam was presented as a business proposition to the Shark Tank, I doubt they would be offered a deal—it's probably a nice enough business on a small scale, but not one that could make millions."

"But it could be someone running multiple operations based on the same model. Almost like a franchise," I said.

"Even if they were, the potential profit margins still aren't that great," Lars said. "Although those with money are always greedy for more. And if someone has operations going in other companies, it could add up."

Laney turned back to Carla. "Okay, give me the name of the new claimant involved, and I'll see if my friend can track who has accessed that information. If, John, you will permit that minor invasion of privacy into your company's data system."

"No trap?" I asked, feeling almost cheated.

"We need to know who we are setting the trap for first."

Chapter Twenty-Five: Aha!

We decided to return to the office while Laney's hacker friend performed his hacking magic. He seemed to think that taking a look at employee transactions within Universal's system would be a piece of cake. I didn't understand how it worked, but the idea of sanctioning someone to invade our technology made me uncomfortable. I could get fired for being part of this. Maybe even convicted of a criminal act. But no one else seemed concerned. And it wasn't as if we were flooded with other ideas.

Time always slows down when you are waiting for something to happen, like boiling water for tea, or praying for the dentist to quit drilling, or killing time while a hacker's searching your company's files.

Carla called her sister to make arrangements for her to take care of her daughter for a while. I heard her say that it was a last-minute trip she had to make for work. When she clicked off, she looked deflated.

"Your daughter will be fine," I told her.

"You can't know that. What if I go to jail for a long time?"

"Get a good lawyer and cooperate with the police," Laney said. "I can recommend a lawyer who I think you would like."

"Thanks."

"We'll get through this," Lars said. "They will want a strong case against whoever put this together. It will help if we can give them details about the process."

We all fell silent. Laney wandered around, checking her phone from time to time, her mind probably considering what to do "if" this or that. Thinking about next steps. Always thinking ahead. Whereas I was wallowing in fear about my job, wondering if this, on top of the catfished social media sites, would be one thing too many for a conservative company to overlook. Lars was doing some sketching on a pad of paper he'd nicked from someone's desk. And Carla was moping.

Lars stopped drawing, looked up, and announced: "I'm starving." My stomach rumbled in agreement, and everyone laughed.

"Let's get something to go and bring it back here," Laney suggested. "This is more private than a restaurant, and my friend should be calling back soon."

"There's a Thai take-out on the corner," I said. "Why don't you go get it? I want to check out a couple things on my computer." Actually, I was tired and wanted a chance to rest before tackling whatever came next. So, when they left to get food, I returned to my office and collapsed. The back of my chair wasn't high enough to allow resting my head for a snooze, so I leaned forward and folded my arms to cradle my head on my desk. "Just a few minutes," I told myself.

My thoughts started drifting, like they do before sleep descends. But just as I was about to doze, my mind started chewing on an idea that my mother and the others kept bringing up—the person running the scam didn't have to be someone at or even near the top of the food chain. Sure, people at the top always want more, no matter how much they already have, but someone at a lower level, an employee who thinks he deserves more and wants to get back at his boss, for instance, they too might be motivated to construct a profit-making illegal venture. And they would know how things worked at the operational level.

Poor Carla. She was a pawn in someone else's game. As was Lars. The king had yet to be checked. Whether from the top echelons or somewhere further down. And what if the king was simply a disgruntled employee rather than a criminal mastermind? Someone who knew enough about the way things were done to build a money-making scheme with far-reaching tentacles. If so, there were probably lots of candidates in a company as large as Universal. I didn't know that many employees, but I did vaguely remember a conversation at my poker party in which there was complaining about this and that. Not that I remembered it clearly; the words were hazy, heard through the din of alcohol and merriment. Still, sometimes, it doesn't take much for everything to fall into place.

If my memory was accurate, I knew someone with the smarts and expertise to pull off the scam who was also extremely frustrated with Universal Heartland Liability and Casualty Assurance Company of America, Incorporated. He'd griped about employees being treated unfairly and how executives did very little but were paid tons more than those who actually did the work. My recollection was that I'd defended the company against his bitter accusation that it was actually a *heartless* company when it came to its employees, not the company with the heart as it claimed.

Unfortunately, Jack was also someone I liked. Not that my feelings toward him mattered. You can't let someone off the hook because you like them. Especially if he was doing damage to the company's reputation, to say nothing of ruining careers, kidnapping Lars and possibly killing Lonnie.

On the other hand, just because Jack was the only employee I'd personally heard complaining about Universal didn't make him guilty. There were lots of other lowly employees who might resent the company enough to try to get even by ripping it off. Still, Jack *was* the only one *I* personally knew with possible motive, and his desk was just a stone's throw away. It might be a good idea to take a look around his cubicle before making what could be a baseless accusation that I would later regret. If he was the person behind the fraud scheme, and I found evidence to prove it in his workspace, I would impress everyone by solving the puzzle all on my own. At the very least, if Laney's friend found a link to Jack at the same time I proved him guilty, I could claim part of the credit.

Although I was irritated with myself for interrupting my own nap, I was eager to see what I could find. Pulling myself upright, I forced my reluctant body to walk to Jack's cubicle. Laney was fond of saying you'd know it if you found "it," whatever "it" was. At the same time, now that I was fully awake, I was starting to think this was a foolish move. If whoever was responsible for the scheme was careful enough to use an offshore account and remain anonymous to those working for him, hiring thugs to do the dirty work, there was no way they would leave anything incriminating in a cubicle anyone could access.

Oh, what the heck—as long as I was awake and there was no one around, I might as well have a look.

Unlike some of the other desks in the area, Jack's was tidy and uncluttered. There wasn't much on top—an empty in-basket, a square plastic container of pens and pencils, a red stapler, and his computer. I fired up his computer but gave up as soon as I was asked for a password. The top drawer of his desk contained the usual items neatly arranged in a wire mesh organizer made for the purpose: rubber bands, paper clips, a ruler, some magic markers, a few pens, a pair of scissors, Post-it notes, scotch tape, and, off to the side, tucked partly under the organizer, a package of condoms. Hmmm. Well, maybe not "the usual" for me.

Next, I went through the two side drawers. One held hanging files, all the folders precisely labeled. I glanced through them, but nothing leapt out at me. The other also contained hanging files, one labeled "Miscellaneous" and another "Warranties and Directions." I glanced at the miscellaneous file and was about to throw in the towel when, on impulse, I opened the file marked as "Warranties and Directions." In the front was a manual on how to use a Corvette key fob. As I thumbed through the rest, I was amazed at some of the things he'd kept, like directions on how to load his stapler and how to replace the tape in his dispenser. Then there were the kinds of things I always wished I could lay my hands on—warranties and troubleshooting guides to his cell phone and computer.

I was about to close the drawer when it hit me: what would someone making his salary as a claims adjuster who complained about being hard-pressed to send his kids to private schools be doing with a Corvette key fob?

When I looked more closely, I noted that the manual had a stamp from a local dealer. I stood there staring at it. There were all sorts of explanations. First, having a manual didn't mean he actually had a Corvette. Second, going into debt to buy a Corvette wasn't totally out of character for a divorced man wanting a little fun in life. A Corvette and condoms. They seemed to go together. Besides, I only had his whining to suggest he was having financial problems. Maybe he wasn't that pressed for money. Or, maybe he'd won the car in some sort of contest. Or at a high-stakes poker game. Or on a game show. The possibilities were endless.

I was still fantasizing about all the ways one could acquire a Corvette when I heard Jack's voice say, "What are you doing, John?" I dropped the manual and twirled around to find myself nose-to-nose with Jack.

My brain leapt to the first excuse I could come up with. "Ah, I was looking for a, ah, a pen. My pen ran out of ink."

"And you chose to look for a pen in my bottom desk drawer?" He pointed to the container full of pens and pencils on the top of his desk. "What about simply using one of those?"

"Sorry, I didn't see those." I started to reach for one, but he put out his hand and stopped me.

"What are you really doing here?"

"What are YOU doing here?"

"Okay, let's stop playing games. I know you were looking at appraisal files."

I was truly puzzled. How did he know that? "What makes you think that?" A bluff seemed like the appropriate response, but there's a reason I'm lousy at poker.

"Quit lying to me. I set up an alert on my home computer in case anyone got nosy. And you just got nosy."

"I didn't think that was possible," I said. "The alert, I mean."

"You need to bone up on computer security. Now, let's go." He motioned for me to move out ahead of him.

"Ah, I'm waiting for some friends." I should perhaps have asked 'go where' or 'why,' but my mind was once again in stall mode.

"Then we'd better get out of here quickly." With that, he pulled an evil-looking beast of a pistol out of his jacket pocket and waved it to let me know that I should proceed him.

"When you put it that way." I realized too late that I should have shown surprise or outrage or done something, anything to stall for time. How long had it been since the gang went to get our take-out dinner? Was it too soon for them to return with our food?

"Let's take the stairs," he said. The entrance to the stairs was in the corner of the room, about thirty feet past the elevator. Seldom used by employees, the cement stairway, with its bare walls and metal handrails, was not a place I wanted to be alone with a criminal and his gun. A gunshot might echo, but there probably wouldn't be anyone to hear it.

I was walking as slowly as I could, taking tiny steps. Until he nudged me with this gun, that is. Then I gave in and walked normally toward the stairs, still trying for shorter steps than I usually take. "Why not the elevator?" I asked. If we waited for the elevator, maybe the door would open, and we would be faced with three surprised but hopefully quick-acting colleagues.

"The stairs," he repeated.

"I can't prove anything," I said, sounding pathetic even to myself.

"But you would talk, and then there would be an investigation, and…well, I don't think I have to spell it out. You're an inconvenience."

"Like Lonnie?"

"That was unfortunate."

"You call killing someone 'unfortunate'?"

"I was just trying to make enough money to escape from this hellhole. And he had to go and poke his nose in with that damn drone of his."

"If you don't like your job, why not quit?"

Jack made a noise halfway between a cough and a guffaw. "You've got to be kidding me. I've given twenty years to this company, and for what? A tiny desk in an old building, a bitchy admin, a skimpy paycheck, and little time off."

"You think Emma is bitchy?"

"You don't?"

"Well, yes, but I wouldn't label her like that." I almost added, "That isn't nice," but bit my tongue. Jack obviously didn't have "nice" in his wheelhouse of virtues.

We'd reached the door to the stairs. What was he going to do? Shoot me and leave me in the stairway? Force me to go with him and shoot me somewhere else? It was undoubtedly one or the other. After all, he'd called me an "inconvenience." Like Lonnie. By comparison, being loathed by your cat and dive-bombed by crows seemed pretty tame.

Distracted by thoughts of death, we were at the first landing when I stumbled. My body twisted sideways, and my hands automatically jerked outward in anticipation of falling. My right arm collided with the gun Jack was holding, knocking it out of his hands. I heard it clatter as it bumped down a few stairs. He lurched forward to grab it at the same time I partially regained my balance and fell to my knees instead of crashing downward.

The next thing I knew, Jack tripped over me and was tumbling out of control, ass over teakettle, as my mother would have said. I didn't wait to see what happened next but made record time hot-footing it back up the stairs. No shots rang out as I reached the top and burst into the main room.

"Help!" I yelled to an empty room.

Should I try to hide? Was there anywhere safe in an open-concept office space? He'd look for me in my office; I couldn't go there. Why hadn't I grabbed his gun before running away?

The elevator. Once I got on the elevator, he wouldn't be able to catch me. I ran to the elevator and punched the down button with all the force I had in my index finger. Like magic, the door opened, and I was enveloped in Thai food smells.

The three of them stood there looking startled. When the doors started to close, I leaped forward, half in and half out of the elevator, with the doors massaging my hips as they bounced back and forth. "Help," I screamed.

"Hey, no big deal," Lars said, laughing.

Laney pushed the open button.

"Jack has a gun," I managed to say.

"Jack?" Carla said. "Who's Jack?"

"Where is he?" Laney asked, reaching into her handbag with one hand while balancing a take-out container with the other. She was truly agile.

"In the stairway," I said. "He tried to kill me. We need to get out of here." I started to step into the elevator, but Laney elbowed me back as she pulled out her handgun.

"Show me," she said, handing Lars the take-out container.

"If he tried to kill you, shouldn't we be calling the cops?" Lars said.

"They prefer 'police officers,'" I said automatically. Bruno had told me that enough times that I had it embedded in my brain.

"I'll call them," Carla offered, pulling out her cell. She seemed to grasp what I hadn't spelled out, that Jack was the head guy.

"Show me," Laney repeated, looking around. She saw the door to the stairs before I could say anything else and started toward it. I couldn't let her go alone, so I reluctantly followed. Laney glanced back at Carla and Lars. "You two stay here. Keep the elevator open. If we don't come back, go down and let the police know what's going on."

If we don't come back? I could feel myself starting to hyperventilate.

"What happened?" Laney asked.

"Jack, one of my colleagues, is the mastermind," I said, my voice weak and breathy.

Laney stopped and turned toward me. "Take a deep breath and hold it," she said. I obeyed. "Now let it out slowly." It worked—I instantly felt calmer. Not relaxed or confident; but not about to pass out. Laney swung around and headed for the door again. When we were only a few feet away, she asked, "Is he trying to escape?"

"I don't know. I'm pretty sure he intended to shoot me. Then he fell, and I ran."

She motioned me to stand to one side as she opened the door. When no one shot at us, she stepped inside and waved me in behind her. Jack was still spread out on the landing, face down. "Stay," Laney said as she slowly descended the stairs. When she reached him, she put her fingers on his neck, like I'd seen detectives do on television. "He's alive," she yelled. "Call 911."

Chapter Twenty-Six: Hero

To say that Bruno wasn't pleased when he answered his phone was definitely an understatement. "John," he'd said. "It's Sunday evening. I'm busy."

"I think you'll want to hear this," I said, my voice flat and slow. Instead of the adrenaline rush I'd experienced when escaping from Jack, all I felt now was lethargy, as if I was being weighed down by invisible forces that were making it difficult to move and to think. And I couldn't get the vision of Jack lying face down on the landing out of my mind. Even though he'd been trying to kill me, I felt guilty about causing him to fall down the stairs.

Both the ambulance and the police were on their way. But I knew Bruno would want to hear first-hand from me about what had happened. After I gave him the highlights of the incident and what we'd done to precipitate events, he groaned and said he'd be there as soon as he could. Before he switched off, I thought I heard him say "Desiree." If she was there with him, I was both sorry and glad I'd interrupted his busy evening.

Soon after talking with Bruno, the ambulance arrived. Jack was rushed away on a stretcher, surrounded by EMTs and people shouting orders. As far as I could tell, he was alive but unconscious.

The police came next, invading our quiet office by storming in, crouched over, guns drawn, as if they were expecting a confrontation with a gang of armed criminals. When they realized we were the only ones there, huddled together around Emma's desk, they put their guns away. Even though we had placed the call to them, initially they treated us more like suspects than victims. And they seemed disappointed that there was no body to look at. I had to repeat several times that the injured party, the one with the gun, had fallen down cement stairs and was already on his way to a hospital. But the gun was still there. Two officers were sent to check out the "crime scene" and to retrieve the gun.

The fact that Laney had a handgun caused them pause, but I quickly explained that she hadn't even been in the building when I'd had my altercation with Jack, and besides, no shots had been fired. Nevertheless, an officer very carefully checked out her gun.

The officer who seemed to be in charge started grilling me about what had happened. Lars interrupted to hand me a bottle of water. "You look like you need this." Then he looked at the officer and said, "He thought he was going to be shot. You might give him a little slack." The officer looked unimpressed, but he waited while I took a couple of swigs before continuing.

"You say he had a gun and was planning on shooting you, correct?"

"Yes, to the best of my knowledge. That was his intent."

"And you knocked the gun out of his hand, and then he just fell down the stairs without any help from you."

"Well, I didn't push him, if that's what you're implying."

"What caused him to fall then?"

"He was reaching for the gun. And, well, I may have tripped him."

"You tripped him?"

"I didn't want him to get his gun back." Did I need to admit that I tripped him by accident? Was that better or worse from a police perspective? Did tripping him make me a criminal? And what would Jack claim when he came to?

Bruno showed up just in time to keep me from digging myself into an even deeper hole of guilt and recrimination. He asked me to repeat the highlights, starting from the beginning, shaking his head from time to time as if to say, "Please tell me you didn't do that, did you?"

When I got to the part about Jack forcing me into the stairway ahead of him, the first officer interrupted. "Tell him what you told me about how you disarmed your alleged attacker."

Bruno jumped in. "Under the circumstances, I think you can drop the 'alleged.'"

"We need to verify this man's version of what happened."

"John's version *is* the truth," Laney said from the sidelines. "Sergeant McGinty is familiar with the case. Tell him, Sergeant. Tell him how the police have been trying to identify the head of a local art fraud ring, and how tonight John not only discovered who is responsible, he solved a murder as well. And captured the murderer. You should be treating him like a hero instead of a suspect." She sounded really angry. I made a note not to get on her wrong side.

"She's right," Bruno said to the officer. "There's been a team working on the fraud case."

A hero, huh? Mother was going to be so proud.

"What about Lonnie's murder?" Laney said.

Yeah, what about that? I'd caught a murderer. It was even hard for me to believe.

"You should have notified me as soon as you figured it out," Bruno said to me. To him, I wasn't a hero but an interfering civilian.

"If I'd had a few more minutes before Jack arrived, I would have."

The other officer took a step forward. "Does anyone object to, ah…" The officer glanced at his notes. "…John Smith making an official statement for the record?"

"I'm staying with him," Laney said. "It's been a long day, and he's been through a lot."

The officer and Bruno exchanged looks. Neither challenged Laney's right to stay.

Laney and I sat down while the officer and Bruno remained standing. Even a hero needs to rest. For what seemed like the umpteenth time I explained what had happened from the point when I figured out Jack was probably the head of the fraud gang until he forced me into the stairway and fell down the stairs.

"You knocked the gun out of his hand?" the officer asked one more time, emphasizing his doubt about my ability to manage such a maneuver.

"It happened pretty fast," I said. I'd gone over it too many times to suddenly admit it had been by accident. "I was convinced he was going to kill me."

"Then you threw yourself in front of him, and he fell over you?"

"That's not what I said." Was he trying to trip me up? "I was off balance and dropped to my knees. He fell over me when he tried to catch his gun. I was in front of him; I didn't push him."

"Even if you had, it's okay to push someone who is trying to kill you," Laney said before the officer could stop her. "That's a legitimate self-defense move."

Laney's phone started playing what sounded like whales grunting, and she stepped away to take the call.

"If that's how it happened, you were lucky," the officer concluded.

"I know," I said. "I thought I was going to die."

"When faced with death, you have to take risks," Bruno said, defending me like he had when we were kids. I flashed him a thank you with my eyes.

Laney rejoined us, all smiles. I raised my eyebrows in question, but she shook her head. I got the message; she didn't want to say anything in front of the officers.

The officer who was interviewing me finally realized he'd squeezed as much out of me as he was going to get. He warned me that he might have more questions later, and he and Bruno went off to look at the "crime scene" together.

As soon as they were out of earshot, Laney explained that her friend had verified what I had discovered—Jack had been accessing company appraisal requests and had an "alert" code set up to let him know when anyone else accessed one or more of the files. "That's why he showed up. He knew you were onto him." She glanced around before continuing. "Let's keep this to ourselves, okay? At this point, the police can track the same information, and it's better if my friend stays out of it." Grinning, she added, "Besides, this way, *you* get all the credit."

We found Carla and Lars at a desk in one of the cubicles, probably planning their defense strategies, and left them alone to continue. My guess was that Lars had a better chance of getting a reduced sentence since he had been trying to quit when he was kidnapped. But given Carla's family situation, a good lawyer might be able to position her as a victim, someone who made one tiny mistake and then couldn't escape from the clutches of an evil schemer. And if she was able to provide evidence to help convict Jack and the kidnappers, that should also work in her favor. Especially if she could prove she hadn't known about Lonnie's death.

Laney handed me a box of Pad Thai and some chopsticks. "Might as well eat while we wait." She started chowing down.

"No forks?" I asked.

She rolled her eyes. "Hold them like this." She demonstrated, oohing and aahing over the food to encourage me. But I was hopeless with chopsticks. I stabbed some noodles and tried to get the tantalizing glop into my mouth. And I almost made it. It landed with a tiny "plop" on the floor. Laney reached down with a napkin and grabbed the glop. "Just hold up the box and shovel it in," she said, demonstrating.

I was almost getting the hang of it when Bruno came over. "I have a few more questions," he said.

"Sure." I had already decided to stick to the edited version with him. I might tell Laney the truth, but not right away. And I definitely didn't want the truth to get back to Mother. I wanted her to think her son was a hero.

"How did you disarm him?" Bruno asked, getting right to the point.

"As we turned onto the landing, I swung around and knocked the gun out of his hand, just like I said. He fell trying to retrieve it."

Laney was scrutinizing me with a questioning yet admiring look on her face. Maybe I shouldn't admit what had actually happened even to her.

"You just knocked the gun out of his hand?" Bruno looked and sounded surprised.

"Like you said, I had to do something; he was going to shoot me."

"I'm proud of you. That took guts," Bruno said.

"It was an act of desperation." I hated lying to my good friend, but I hated even more having to admit I saved my life by being clumsy.

He asked a few more questions before telling Laney and me that we were free to go.

"What about Lars and Carla?" I asked.

"We're taking them to headquarters. They have quite a bit to answer for."

"Don't forget, Lars was kidnapped and forced to cooperate. And he could have run off after we rescued him. Instead, he went to the police and then stayed around to help us."

"Carla was also trying to be helpful," Laney said. "She regretted ever getting involved in the first place, but given what happened to Lars, she was afraid to drop out."

"I sense that most of her regrets came after her part in the operation was exposed," Bruno said.

I wanted to say that she wasn't a bad person, but then, I'd also liked Jack. Before he decided to shoot me, that is.

Once we were back in her car, Laney turned to me and said, "What really happened? You can tell me."

"I'd rather not."

"It will be our secret."

"Promise?"

"Of course."

"I really did figure out that he was the one we were looking for."

"And that was brilliant. If it hadn't been for the alert, that would have been enough to turn over to the authorities."

"I realize you don't see me as the macho type who knows how to handle himself in a showdown with a bad guy."

"Sorry, John. I don't. But that's not a bad thing. You are kind and smart and…a bit klutzy at times. In a lovable way."

"So, you won't think less of me when I admit that I stumbled and knocked the gun out of his hand by accident? And that I fell down, and he flipped over me?"

Laney started to laugh, a sound rumbling up from her stomach and out of her mouth, a robust, tinkling sound of mirth. The dimples on her cheeks got deeper and deeper as her giggles grew louder. She bent forward, gasping for breath.

"It's not *that* funny…is it?"

She struggled to get herself under control, and I started to see the humor in it. Then I began to laugh. We continued laughing together, chuckles and hoots and snorts…until we slowly wore down.

'You have good karma," Laney said approvingly. "I'm glad to be your friend."

"I didn't start out trying to lie, but the way it happened was embarrassing. What I don't know is whether Jack saw me stumble."

"If he did, you could claim it was a ploy. But I bet it doesn't come up. He has nothing to gain by calling you out, and he will have other more important things to deal with."

"You won't tell anyone, will you?"

"Friends keep their promises, and I promised I wouldn't. But you need to be prepared."

"Prepared for what?"

"Everyone loves a hero."

"I'm definitely not a hero."

"To the public, you will be. Mark my words."

The choices Laney laid out weren't that appealing—pretend to be a hero or confess to being a klutz. They say that confession is good for the soul, but being praised as a hero sounded more appealing.

She dropped me off at The Haven. As I made my way down the dock, looking out over the calm water, it felt good to be alive. The lights of the city danced across the water, shimmery and soft. A kayaker slipped by, oars dipping silently, startling the flat surface. I imagined fish and other sea life doing their thing in the dark depths. It was all so idyllic. So soothing.

Feeling mellow and thankful to be in one piece, I opened the door and immediately left peace and tranquility behind. Wild Thing was angry. He yowled and ran to the kitchen, glancing back to make sure I was coming. He didn't care if he was served by a hero or by a klutz. He wanted his dinner, and he wanted it NOW.

Chapter Twenty-Seven: The Day After

The next morning, I was awakened by the phone. It was a reporter wanting a comment. I mumbled something about being asleep and hung up. The phone rang again moments later. I had rolled over to catch a few more zee's and was tempted not to answer. But it was Emma.

"Why are you calling so early?" I asked.

"It's 9:00," she said.

"But it's…MONDAY." OMG, I was supposed to be at a meeting with Van Droop.

"I heard about what happened on the local news. And the police are here asking questions."

"I forgot to set my alarm," I said. "If I get there in forty-five minutes, can I still meet with Mr. Van Droop?"

"Given what you did yesterday—"

"I'm so sorry," I interrupted. "I know how much trouble this makes for Universal."

"John, you are a hero. We unfortunately had a bad apple in our midst, but you, a valued employee, saved the day. At risk to your own life."

I was stunned by her response. "Seriously?" I asked. Morning brain fog was at work, fortunately in sync with my streak of good karma. Instead of adding something even more stupid, I said something Emma interpreted as humble. "I don't think I'm a hero—"

"Well, that's what everyone is saying."

"So, I'm not fired?"

"Fired?"

"Because of the, ah, other thing."

"If you're referring to the social media posts, it's clear someone was trying to discredit you. Most likely, it was Jack. And you've proved your innocence. Now this. Congratulations, John."

Even given everything that had happened, it hadn't occurred to me that Jack was most likely the one responsible for hiring someone to create the phony social media accounts. If that had worked and I'd been fired, maybe he wouldn't have felt it necessary to kill me. Indirectly, he'd been trying to spare my life.

"Are you saying that I can reschedule my meeting with Mr. Van Droop?"

"He's going to be holding a press conference today at 1:00. He's meeting with our lawyers now and would like you to join him for lunch at noon in the conference room. Can you make it?"

If this was the new Emma, it was going to take some getting used to. "Yes. Thank you."

As soon as the call with Emma ended, the theme song to *Oklahoma* sounded again. It was Mother.

"Can I call you back?" I asked. "I just woke up and haven't had a chance to make coffee or feed Wild Thing yet." Or take a leak. I badly needed to go to the bathroom.

"Of course. I know you had a late night. I saw it on the early news and read about it in the Times." There was a touch of reproach in her voice.

"I was going to call you this morning."

"My son, the hero," she said with a hint of pride that more than made up for the mild criticism. "Call me as soon as you make some coffee."

Laney had apparently called it right. I needed to accept the mantle of hero and work on keeping my story straight. *He was going to kill me, so I had to do* **something**. *As we turned the corner on the stairs, I took my shot, so to speak. I knocked the gun out of his hand, dropped down to one knee, and he cascaded over me and down the stairs.* As a script, it wasn't bad. Except I think I'd told the police that I'd dropped down to both knees. I'd have to check on that. If I was convincing enough, even Jack wouldn't know that it wasn't the truth.

Wild Thing was waiting by his dish, not making a fuss. Not even one

219

small hiss of impatience. Maybe he had seen me on TV and had gained some respect for my ability to handle myself. Sure.

After feeding Wild Thing and making myself coffee, I called Mother back.

"They say you dismantled a fraud ring and caught the head of it single-handed." She sounded a bit surprised but also very pleased. It would be a great story to tell her book club.

"Well, kinda. But not really. I had help."

"They didn't mention any 'help.'"

"There were four of us working on it," I said truthfully.

"Bruno credited you with catching the criminal."

"Bruno did?" That was good of him. I hadn't impressed Bruno with anything for as long as I could remember. He was the athlete with the square jaw and confidence to spare, the one all the women went for. Like Desiree. I needed to ask him about that.

"It's on all the local TV channels and made the front page of the newspaper," Mother said.

"Well, I didn't really do that much." I hated lying to her. Well, actually I didn't mind lying, but it did make me feel guilty.

"You disarmed someone who was going to shoot you. That's impressive."

"It was more luck than skill," I admitted. She'd raised me to feel guilty when I told even the tiniest white lie.

"That doesn't matter. You did it. That's what everyone will know."

I was fixing myself some toast when Valerie popped in a few minutes later. Literally "popped in." I must have left the door unlocked.

"My dad says you did something really good. And it was on the news." Wild Thing was purring as she cuddled him and tickled his stomach.

"I was in the right place at the right time." I did kinda hate lying to a young girl. On the other hand, she might as well get used to it—she would run into liars her entire life.

"Did you have a gun?"

"No. I don't like guns."

"But the bad guy had one."

"Yes, bad guys often have guns."

"Was he going to shoot you?"

That seemed like a topic I shouldn't be discussing with an eight-year-old girl, but she'd asked. "I think so, but he didn't get a chance. So, we'll never know."

"Can you show me what you did?"

"No, and if someone points a gun at you, you shouldn't try to get it away from them."

"But you did."

"I was really lucky. But you can't count on being lucky."

When I left for work, the crows were lined up on the fence, but they didn't attack. Did all the animals watch TV, or did they have some sort of hotline?

My landlord came out to congratulate me, looking a bit dubious, but clearly impressed by the media coverage I was getting.

The day turned into one big celebration of my amazing feat. Reporters, friends, colleagues—everyone wanted to hear the story first-hand. I got so good at telling it, I almost believed it myself.

The lunch with Van Droop would have been uncomfortable if I'd had to make small talk with him, especially since I'd had him high on our suspect list. But he'd invited two company lawyers as well, and they all chatted about the upcoming press conference, so I was able to focus on eating. Jack would have complained that too much had been spent on the food, but I enjoyed it. There were prawns with some kind of tasty dipping sauce, croissant sandwiches with a salmon filling, several different salads, and mini cupcakes with fantastic frosting. I managed to sneak three cupcakes without anyone seeming to notice. I twisted the foil liners into tiny logs and tucked them under my plate.

At one point, one of the lawyers said that he wanted to make sure I understood my role at the press conference. My heart started racing...until he explained. Then, I was able to relax again. "You don't have to say anything," he said. "Stand next to Mr. Van Droop and smile when he thanks you for what you've done for the company by exposing a scam. And that's it. Our advice is that for the time being, the company should provide as few details as possible. Until we know more about the extent of the fraud."

"Yes," Van Droop agreed. "Your role is to play the hero; mine is to reassure our clients that we will pay for all of the stolen artwork. That we are indeed 'the company with a heart.'"

"It's too bad Jack has been with the company for such a long time," I said. "That may make some of his earlier clients nervous."

"As soon as we have the complete list of art and jewelry impacted by this, we will contact everyone with a loss and begin the process of reimbursement."

"Will it involve more than the appraised value of the art?" Was there pain and suffering associated with enjoying a fake painting?

"There's a team working on the payment process. We won't know the total amount of damage for a few weeks. But we're anticipating this will be a costly learning experience for us. Even if we sue for compensation and win, we may not recover much. We are, however, determined to get out in front of it as quickly as possible. We don't want to lose the confidence of our clients."

The plan was clear: minimize losses and concentrate on reputation rebuilding. I was just a prop, but that wasn't necessarily a bad thing. They referred to me as a "valued and loyal employee" and suggested that my investigative prowess and courage would somehow outweigh Jack's criminal act in the eyes of our clients. I hoped they were right, since it looked like my job was secure as long as the company survived.

The one niggling thing that I wanted to ask Mr. Van Droop was why he had recommended me for a Level 3 Ropes training session. If it wasn't to get me out of the way so he could appoint another adjuster to handle appraisals, then why? Did he mistakenly think I was athletic? Or had he suggested it because it was time for me to go through team building, and it was the only thing available? Maybe I should be satisfied thinking there was at least a possibility that he saw me as Level 3 material and leave it at that.

The press conference went exactly as planned. Except for my face almost breaking under the strain of maintaining a smile in front of the cameras. To make things worse, all the carbohydrates I'd had for lunch were conspiring to make me sleepy. Not only did I have a difficult time keeping a smile on my face, it was all I could do to keep my eyes open.

When I returned to the office, everyone stood and clapped before gathering around Emma's desk. There was a cake with a tiny plastic Superman on it—probably a kids' birthday cake ornament, but I didn't care; I liked it. Colleagues took turns telling me how great I was and what a fantastic employee I was for "saving" the company.

The cake was good, with lots of sweet frosting over a moist interior layered with cream filling. When the celebration petered out, I took a huge piece of cake back to my office for later. I also took the Superman as a memento. It was about time I personalized my office space.

Sugar and carbs battled for dominance in my system, and after a brief sugar spike, the carbs won out. I put my head on my desk and promptly fell asleep. Until Bruno called and woke me up.

"You sound groggy," he said.

"It's been a long day."

"I saw you at the press conference."

"I'm glad I didn't have to say anything. It was hard enough just standing there smiling."

"So, did you enjoy your fifteen minutes of fame?"

"Well, I think it was about twenty minutes' worth, but the reporters have already stopped calling. I guess it's officially over."

"Seriously, John, even though I don't approve of what you and the others did, it was remarkable."

When I went home, I was pleased to find that the crows were still giving me a pass, and Wild Thing held back his usual displays of hostility. To top it all off, Laney came over with a pizza to hear about my day. As the only person to know the truth about the incident, I admitted that it had been hard as well as enjoyable. I liked being a hero, but the pretense wasn't easy. It would be good to move on and go back to my nondescript existence. "More than anything, I'm just happy to be alive."

"I shouldn't have left you alone yesterday."

"I know you have skills that I don't, but you shouldn't have to protect me."

"Hey, we have different talents. We make a good team. Don't you think?"

I couldn't help but smile. "Yes, I think we do." My poker buddies had chosen well.

"Good. And now we have time to play with my drones. You're going to love it."

Later, I watched some TV and went to bed early. Being a hero is exhausting.

Chapter Twenty-Eight: Back to Normal

Tuesday morning, Wild Thing was grumpy, the crows were back to attack mode, and there was no applause when I got to the office. In fact, except for Emma, no one seemed aware of my existence. I knew for sure that things were back to normal when Emma glanced at the clock as I approached. Then, she informed me that Mr. Van Droop wanted to see me in his office. Right away. Like Yogi Berra once said, it was "déjà vu all over again."

As I made my way to Van Droop's office, I couldn't help but worry. What if he had changed his mind about my continued employment with the company? Maybe the press conference was the lawyers' idea, a strategy for appeasing clients. Van Droop, on the other hand, might think that I should have figured things out about Carla and Jack sooner. It was also possible I'd been tainted by the entire fiasco. I had, after all, signed off on Carla's appraisals and failed to get a second opinion when a client asked for one. The company didn't need a hero; they needed a savvy employee.

There was also the kiddie porn stuff. Clients could have complained. The fact that the sites had been catfished wouldn't necessarily filter down to everyone who had seen them or heard about it via social media. Salacious news and gossip spread quickly; people seemed to enjoy the titillation. Proof of innocence wasn't as inherently interesting.

By the time I arrived at Van Droop's office, I was starting to sweat. I ran my hand across my damp forehead, patted my hair down, and straightened my shoulders before tapping lightly on his door. I'd been in the limelight for a day, enjoyed my moment of fame; but I'd known it couldn't last. Still, I had hoped to ride the hero coattails for a little longer.

Van Droop was seated behind his massive desk, the chair in front of it turned slightly as if inviting me to sit. "John," he said. He waved me to the chair. He wasn't smiling, but he wasn't frowning either. And he'd remembered my name. That could be either good or bad.

I nodded and sat. The sun shimmering between the buildings was aiming straight for me, creating a blurry halo around Van Droop's head, causing me to squint to avoid the piercing glare. Was the chair positioned to emphasize his glorified position within the company? Or was it like an interrogator's spotlight intended to intimidate the interviewee into telling the truth? If so, what was my "truth"?

"I'll get right to the point," Mr. Van Droop said. In my experience *getting right to the point* was seldom followed by good news. I braced myself for what he was about to say.

"Given what has happened, there will be quite a few clients clamoring for reimbursement and claiming damages." I nodded. He was absolutely right, and it wasn't good for the company. And I was about to pay for my part in the company's current woes; I was sure of it.

"Our legal team is working with Carla Bridges on the list of clients who had their originals replaced with fakes. Getting some background so we know what to expect going forward. We want to contact each one as quickly as possible. Fortunately, Ms. Bridges is being quite cooperative." He paused. "Of course, she could have said *no* to Jack when he first approached her. And if she had reported his scheme to us at the start, we could have avoided this, ah, messy and costly situation. So, I don't have a lot of sympathy for her." Knowing her situation, I felt a tad sorry for her; still, I wouldn't say I had "a lot of sympathy" either. And if I lost my job, what little sympathy I had for her would vanish as quickly as a chocolate chip cookie left on a table in a room full of children.

Van Droop tented his fingers in what I assumed was a contemplative gesture. But what he was contemplating still wasn't clear.

"That said, I suspect our clients won't take our word for who is and who isn't on the list. A lot of them will demand second opinions on the authenticity of their art, whether it was appraised during the critical time period or before the fraud began. It's going to be a long process and cost us a lot of money."

I wanted to argue that firing me wouldn't help much to reduce the financial loss. Still, Mother always insists that every penny counts.

"That's why I've asked you to come in this morning." He paused again, his halo quivering in the sunlight. One part of me wanted to get up and leave before he could fire me, but I felt anchored to the spot, caught in the sun's headlights, like a raccoon on the road facing down a car at night. Although in the end, the raccoon always ran off. But I couldn't move; I could barely breathe.

"John, I want you to put together a team to develop strategies for handling any and all complaints that arise as a result of what's happened. Do you think you can do that?"

I was so surprised by the request it took me a moment to mumble the required "yes." No need to run, after all. Unless this was a ploy to get me to leave of my own volition. This sounded like an ambitious and challenging assignment.

"In addition, the team you assemble will be responsible for creating guidelines to ensure we avoid this kind of debacle in the future. I intend to demonstrate to our board that we are getting out in front of this. And that it will never happen again. Your team will provide the ammunition I need to do that."

If I took Van Droop's offer at face value, that meant my karma hadn't deserted me after all. I wasn't getting fired; I was being given a prime assignment, one most of my colleagues would kill for. Only this was so far out of my comfort zone and expertise that it sounded like a foreign language to me, *advanced corporate speak* when I needed *Strategic Planning for Dummies*. I had absolutely no idea how to tackle this kind of project. My mind was as empty as my wallet after a poker game. I had never sought out challenging assignments or aspired to work my way up the ladder of success. I was happy as an amoeba in the company hierarchy, as long as I stayed employed. For me, this assignment wasn't a reward; it was a high-profile opportunity to royally screw up.

"Once they find out the extent to which Jack's scheme included other companies, you may want to coordinate with them. Find out how they are handling things; piggyback on whatever seems to work."

Even though I lacked corporate savvy, I had enough street smarts to realize it wasn't possible to decline what Mr. Van Droop was offering. Putting on my hero hat, I bravely said, "What a great idea, Mr. Van Droop. I'm sure the board will be impressed. Thank you for giving me this opportunity." If I sounded like an AI spouting an appropriate response, Van Droop didn't seem to notice. He gave me a quick smile before waving me off. His job was done; mine was just beginning.

As I walked away, I wondered how long I had to complete my new mission. He hadn't given me a deadline. Assuming I could come up with something initially, a place to start. Not on my own, of course, but maybe Emma would have some suggestions. Surely, Mother and Laney would. With a little luck and a small chunk of karma, maybe I could muddle through. He had, after all, referred to this as being a team effort. And I had successfully survived team building.

The one positive takeaway was that I had job security, at least temporarily.

Bruno called late that afternoon to give me an update on Jack. "He's conscious," Bruno said. "But as soon as he could speak, he lawyered up."

"That doesn't surprise me. He's a smart guy."

"The evidence against him for the fraud case is pretty solid and getting stronger by the minute. The only question is how many companies are involved."

"And the owner of the estate where Lars was being held?"

"A rental. Still working on that. Haven't caught your thugs either. But we'll get them eventually."

"How about Lonnie's supposed accident? Any updates on that? Doesn't having the video of the guy replacing the picture suggest that the case should be re-evaluated?"

"Even with the video, it's not easy to link Lonnie's death to Jack. First of all, there's still nothing concrete to suggest Lonnie's death was anything but an accident. They may take a run at trying to establish that Jack was at the park when Lonnie went over the cliff, but I wouldn't count on them being able to place him there. And I don't think there's a chance in hell that he is going to voluntarily confess. Why would he? So— no suspicious circumstances, no witnesses, and no confession. If I were to place a bet, I'd say the odds are good that he won't be charged with Lonnie's death."

"But he killed Lonnie. We both know it."

"There's 'knowing' and there's 'proving.' For instance, based on other evidence, we think we *know* he hired the guy to switch out the Winslow painting, but we can't prove it. And even if we link him to that, it won't be enough to charge him with homicide."

"But it speaks to motive."

"Yes, I agree. But that isn't enough."

"How frustrating."

"I come up against a lot of unsolved cases. Sometimes, they haunt me. Just keep in mind that even if he isn't convicted of all of the crimes he's committed, Jack will be going away for a long time. And don't forget, in addition to art fraud, he also ordered a kidnapping. I'm pretty certain we can eventually make a strong case for that. And kidnapping adds quite a few years to any sentence. Even your mother should be more than satisfied with that outcome."

"Maybe. But she was counting on getting Lonnie's death resolved. She will be disappointed."

Bruno emitted a large sigh that said it all. Oscar Wilde may be right in saying that "Life imitates Art far more than Art imitates Life." Perhaps my mother "should" be more than satisfied by the fact that Jack would probably go to prison for a long time, but we both knew that for her, Lonnie's unresolved murder was like tearing out the last twenty-five pages of one of her mystery books.

In my experience, nothing good ever lasts for long. It's like eating an ice cream cone in the sun—you need to savor what you can before the ice cream melts and runs down the side of your cone and drips on your pant leg. By Tuesday evening, my ice cream cone was melting. The crows were tormenting me again, there was a dead garter snake in my mailbox, and Wild Thing was in a bad mood. He didn't know that Valerie had her key back and would be visiting him regularly again. And I couldn't prove that she was the one who had put the snake in my mailbox. Nor could I understand *why* she would have done it. Maybe it was the work of a gang of crows.

Then, Mother called to say that she wanted me to invite Laney to dinner at her condo. I knew she was thinking about grandchildren and wanted to see if Laney was a candidate for daughter-in-law. I would have to warn Laney so she could slip into the conversation that she was a lesbian before Mother had us engaged and was lining up bridesmaids and ordering the wedding cake.

As I started to nod off while watching a rerun of the Friends episode in which Rachel switches identities with Monica so she can use her health insurance, my thoughts drifted to my own recent experiences with insurance. First, there was the window repair that I still blamed on Valerie. My car insurance deductible was two dollars more than the cost of the repair to my window, so I was close to being totally out of pocket on that. The two-dollar check I would eventually get from the insurance company wouldn't even buy one Venti Caramel Ribbon Crunch Crème Frappuccino.

Even worse was the fact that in a moment of high spirits, I'd offered to pay for the German Shepherd's vet bill, never dreaming Valerie's dad would actually take me up on it. I assumed he had pet insurance and would therefore refuse my offer, but he didn't have insurance. Nor did he recognize that my offer was simply an attempt to improve our relationship. Instead, he quickly handed over the bill before I could change my mind.

Finally, in addition to those two setbacks, there were all of the anticipated headaches associated with the insurance problems my new team would be facing. I feared that Van Droop expected me to perform some team magic and thereby minimize what the company ended up paying while at the same time coming up with a strategy to salvage the company's heretofore good reputation. Although I didn't have a clue how I would make either one happen, I kinda liked the sound of saying "my" team.

As a claims adjuster, I was well aware that having insurance was no guarantee of a payoff. Still, I'm always impressed by the creative ways in which people try to make money off of insurance. Sometimes legitimately. Like in the case of Lonnie's parents. They successfully got reimbursed for the loss of their son's drones by using pictures instead of receipts, as I had suggested. More often, people tried to rip off the insurance company by lying, claiming something was worth more than it was, or insisting they had come to a full stop or the light was still yellow when they started into the intersection, that sort of thing.

And, sometimes, people like Jack came up with complicated schemes that involved blatantly illegal activities. I had to hand it to Jack, though. His approach had been clever. And if not for Lonnie and his drone, it may have been the retirement plan he'd intended. Instead, it ended up being "in$urance to die for."

A Note from the Author

I enjoyed writing *In$urance to Die For* and hope you enjoyed reading it. I would appreciate your feedback in the form of a rating and/or review—a sentence or two is all it takes to satisfy Amazon's voracious algorithm. I know how valuable your time is, so I thank you in advance!

Acknowledgements

People often ask where authors get their ideas. In addition to still vividly remembering the Hitchcock movie, I know two people who have been attacked by birds. The first, a former colleague, was unlucky enough to come close to a nesting bird who decided he or she needed a lock of his hair. After his involuntary donation, Gary quickly left the area. The second person was my husband. His impulsive clapping to scare a murder of crows resulted in never being able to go out into our back yard without causing a noisy barrage of complaints.

Wild Thing, a cat belonging to Dina Guttmann, was the model—in name only—for John Smith's Wild Thing. His personality was based on a friend's experience with a demon kitten who was also an unwanted gift.

Although the animals in my book have their origins in real life, all of the other characters are fictional. The Seattle setting is part real but mostly fanciful. Seattle is a constantly changing city, so my goal is to capture tone and not reality.

Finally, I want to thank supportive friends and colleagues in the Puget Sound Sisters in Crime, the 15th Avenue Marketing Group, the Ladies of Mystery Book Club, the Third Sunday Book Club, and the Fabulous Four.

With special thanks to Shawn Reilly Simmons my editor and cover designer for her hard work and support, not only for me, but for the other authors at Level Best.

About the Author

Charlotte Stuart PhD is an award-winning mystery writer who enjoys walking in the woods, black licorice and making people laugh. Before she started writing full time, she left a tenured faculty position to go commercial fishing in Alaska, spent a year sailing "around the world" in the Washington and Canadian San Juans, became a partner in a management consulting group and later a VP of HR and Training.

Her current passion is for writing character-driven mysteries with twisty plots. Most include at least a dollop of humor, but she describes her "In$urance" series as "Murder with a Laugh Track." *In$ured to the Hilt*, the first in this series, was a semi-finalist in the Chanticleer International Mystery and Mayhem Awards and was a Reader Views Silver winner. Her *Discount Detective Mysteries* took a 1st place series award in the Chanticleer International Mystery and Mayhem competition. She's won or placed in a number of other competitions, including a Global Ebook Gold, A Global Book Award Bronze, and was a finalist in Foreword Indies, Killer Nashville's Silver Falchion and Eric Hoffer Awards.

Charlotte lives on Vashon Island in the Pacific Northwest and is the past president of the Puget Sound Sisters in Crime and a member of the Mystery Writers of America and the International Thriller Writers.

SOCIAL MEDIA HANDLES:

Twitter: https://twitter.com/quirkymysteries

Facebook: https://www.facebook.com/charlotte.stuart.mysterywriter

Instagram: https://www.instagram.com/cstuartauthor/

Goodreads: https://www.goodreads.com/author/show/19305587.Charlotte_Stuart

AUTHOR WEBSITE:

https://www.charlottestuart.com

Also by Charlotte Stuart

In$ured to the Hilt (A John Smith Mystery) - 2023

Raven's Grave - 2023

Moonlight Can Be Deadly (A Discount Detective Mystery) - 2023

Shopping Can Be Deadly (A Discount Detective Mystery) - 2021

Campaigning Can Be Deadly (A Discount Detective Mystery) - 2020

Survival Can Be Deadly (A Discount Detective Mystery) - 2019

Not Me! Speluncaphobia, Secrets and Hidden Treasure (A Macavity & Me Mystery) - 2022

Who, Me? Fog Bows, Fraud and Aphrodite (A Macavity & Me Mystery) - 2021

Why Me? Chimeras, Conundrums and Dead Goldfish (A Macavity & Me Mystery) - 2019

Bogged Down (A Vashon Island Mystery) - 2020

Disastrous Interviews: The Comic, Tragic and Just Plain Ugly - 2013